HERETIC

Also by Sarah Singleton

CENTURY

HERETIC

Sarah Singleton

SIMON AND SCHUSTER

For Fuchsia

SIMON AND SCHUSTER
First published in Great Britain in 2006 by Simon & Schuster UK Ltd
A Viacom company

1 3 5 7 9 10 8 6 4 2

Simon & Schuster UK Ltd
Africa House
64–78 Kingsway
London WC2B 6AH

A CIP catalogue record for this book is available from the British Library

ISBN 1-416-90403-4

Set in 12/15 pt Adobe Garamond by
Rowland Phototypesetting Ltd, Bury St Edmunds, Suffolk

Printed and bound in Great Britain by Cox & Wyman, Reading, Berkshire

www.simonsays.co.uk

Author's Note

In 1527 King Henry VIII asked the Pope, the leader of the Roman Catholic Church, to grant him a divorce because his wife Catherine of Aragon had not borne him a male heir. The Pope would not agree, so Henry broke with the Church and in 1534, through the Act of Supremacy, made himself the Head of the Church of England. In the 1530s he closed down some eight hundred monasteries across the country, taking over their land and property.

His daughter Mary became Queen after Henry's death and she tried to restore the Roman Catholic faith in England. When she died in 1558, her younger sister Elizabeth was crowned Queen, and England became Protestant once again. In 1570 Elizabeth was excommunicated by Pope Pius V who called upon loyal Catholics to remove her from the throne.

English exile William Allen set up a seminary in Douai in France to train missionary priests, ardent young men prepared to risk their lives to serve the Catholics in England. By 1580 over a hundred priests came to England, but a number of plots by Catholic conspirators and the Northern Rebellion made the Queen suspicious of all Catholics – and this led to the execution of around two hundred priests and ordinary Catholics by 1603. In 1584 Parliament agreed it was treason to be a Catholic priest in England.

Heretic: A person who holds an opinion at odds with the official or orthodox position; having a religious belief contrary to the views of the established Church – from the Greek *hairesis*, meaning 'to choose to depart from the truth'.

Awakening

Pale November light gleamed through wet, black branches. Fallen leaves lay in a sodden cloak on the floor of the forest. Among the dark stripes of tree trunks, the last autumn leaves were glimmers of gold. The rain had passed, but the forest dripped.

Curled in the empty stomach of an elderly oak, the child was half awake, half asleep.

The tree was like a long, hollow cup, open at the top, the child lying like the dregs of a drink, at the bottom.

The forest poked cold fingers into the child's dreams – the sound of birds in the treetops, the perfume of damp wood and rotting leaves.

At last the child turned in its sleep. It hadn't moved for a very long time – so long that strands of ivy had grown down into the long cup of the hollow trunk and right over the child's body. Now the child tugged at the tough cords with its hands, but the ivy was tight, leaving thin red marks on its skin.

The child was still dreaming of the other place – the shadow land with its circles of stones and bright fires, and the crowds of tall people dressed in green and gold and black. They spoke in deep, cold voices and wore thick bracelets above long, white hands. Jewels burned on necklaces and rings. The child didn't belong to them, the crow people, but didn't want them to leave either. They had taken something that didn't properly belong to them and the child wanted it back. They weren't always kind, the other people. Now they drew away, taking the shadow land with them, like a sea tide sinking away, leaving the child high and dry – stranded in the forest.

If someone had peered into the tree trunk, while the child was in the shadow land, what would they have seen? A heap of dried leaves, perhaps shaped like a figure, and underneath, a dry bone or two – the link holding the child to the ordinary world. Now the child had left the shadow land behind, and its body had emerged and formed itself again around the bones and dust of its earthly remains.

The child turned, scratching at the ivy. A crow landed on the oak tree. The wind ruffled its feathers. Spotting the creature inside the trunk, perhaps the bird was surprised. It hopped from one lip of the tree cup to the other. The bird considered, head tipped to one side. Then it flapped silk black wings and gave one rough call. The sound echoed in the hollow of the tree and the child opened its eyes.

Nothing made any sense at first. The round of light above was broken up by the shape of the bird. The child struggled out of the ivy ropes and sat up. It straightened its fingers, and then rubbed its hands over its face. It was hard to gather fragments of self together, after so long in the shadow land. The body moved of its own accord, but memories were

2

scattered. Who am I? Where? How? It was frightening not to know these things, like standing at the edge of a cliff with nothing to hold on to.

Don't be afraid, the child reassured itself. Wait a while. You'll remember.

There was nobody else to lend a hand. The child tugged away the last strands of ivy and stood up. A litter of leaves fell away, strays that had fallen into the tree. The bird, alarmed by developments, flew off.

Although the child could not remember who it was, the method of climbing out of the tree was not a problem. The inside of the oak was rough and woody knobs provided convenient steps. The child's feet were bare and excellently flexible. It reached the top and climbed out, to see the forest from a viewpoint some twelve feet up. Trees spread away, in every direction. The sky, through a gauze of bare twigs, was dull grey. A huge fungus, like a toad, clung to the broken bark by the child's right hand.

What to do now? The child clambered down the tree to the ground and sniffed the air. At first the child found it difficult to walk upright. Perhaps the muscles and ligaments of its legs had shortened. With a stoop it half walked, half ran, using hands to help itself along.

The forest hadn't changed, except in the detail. The generality of trees and undergrowth, the familiar outfit of the autumn season, were just as before. But many of the individual trees had altered. New grown, or gone, or split in storms.

Not far from the oak tree, the child halted and tried to stand up straight. Then it hurried on, clambering over fallen

3

branches, ignoring the scratches of brambles. Ahead stood a tumbled hermitage – its soft brown walls standing among the trees. The child remembered this. It was a holy place, a spring and a tiny stone hut where an old man had lived. How inviting and welcoming it looked. The child hurried, out of breath now, loping like an animal on all fours.

Then it skidded to a halt. The hut was a ruin. The door on the hermit's cell was ripped away. The child hesitated, afraid to look any further. A picture rose in its mind – an archway where a statue stood, above a pool of water and the bubbling spring. Now the statue was gone and the arch was broken up. Chunks of stone lay half buried by leaves, all around the little clearing.

The child began to shiver. Panic rose, like a flock of dark birds flapping about in its head.

Who am I?

The child scurried into the ruined cell, a bare room with one window. Not a scrap of furniture remained. No ash in the fireplace. The child ran around the room, like a trapped animal. Then it stopped and banged its head on the wall, once, twice, trying to force a memory, wanting to remember. But it hurt very much. The pain stopped the birds flapping in the child's head, but blood trickled down its forehead. In a daze it stumbled out of the hermit's cell to the spring. It dipped fingers into the chilly pool and dabbed the water onto the wound. The sun broke through the cloud and spilled light into the clearing. The child leaned over the pool, startled by the reflection in the pool.

What did it see? Long, long hair fell over its shoulders. Skin was stained green and brown, from the long years of

4

fallen leaves, ivy, moss. A child? Not really like a child any more. Something else.

It searched its face, looking for clues. Who was it? Where did it belong? It strained to remember, gritting its teeth. The child beat at its head with the palms of its hands. It threw itself on the ground and thrashed its arms and legs in a desperate blind panic. The inside of its head seemed to burn up in a storm of black and red, and the outside world disappeared altogether.

Then – the sound of a snap.

Someone had trodden on a twig, close by. The child froze. It lay still on the ground, in a sudden terror. Who was coming? Often the child had to hide. The hermit had been the only one to be trusted. So the child lay still, listening intently. A minute passed, and another. Perhaps it was safe. The child's heart beat fast. It waited another minute, in the cold bed of leaves. All was quiet. Like an animal, the child lifted its head, looking for the intruder. It crept to its feet, snuffed the air. It turned back to the spring in the broken shrine, and looked directly into the eyes of another human being.

A girl. Yes, a girl. The child held its breath.

They stared at each other, wide-eyed, hypnotised – face to face, just a few feet apart. The girl's mouth dropped open.

The wind rose in the trees. The moments passed. Feelings churned. The impulse to run wrestled with the desire to ask for help. What to do? The child ground its teeth.

How long would they stay like this, just looking at each other, neither knowing what to do?

The child moved first. Fear was winning out. It shrank back, preparing to flee, bunching fists. But the girl dropped her basket and held out her hand.

'No, wait,' she said. 'Don't go. Wait. I won't hurt you.'

The child turned again, considering the girl. It knew it should run away and hide but the sound of the girl's voice was sweet. It was so long since the child had heard a truly human voice.

'Wait,' the girl repeated.

The child trembled, torn between hunger for companionship and a fear for its life. It hopped from one foot to another, in an agony of indecision.

The girl reached into her basket and took out a loaf of brown bread wrapped in a piece of cloth, and an apple. She took a step forward.

'Are you hungry?' she said, stretching out her hand.

The child could smell the bread, and its mouth watered. Still it was suspicious. Was this a trick? There had been tricks before. No-one could be trusted, except for the hermit. The girl sank to her knees, making herself less threatening. She waggled the bread in her outstretched hand. The child took a small step forward.

'Take it,' the girl said. Her voice lured as much as the perfume of the fresh bread. The child's keen nose also registered the scent of the girl herself, a mixture of wood and tallow smoke and baking. The child took another step forward. It could see the girl's pale, clean skin, her blue eyes and a few stray strands of blonde hair escaping from the rim of her white cap. The girl's hands were pink from the cold and her knuckles were raw, from work. The child snatched

6

the bread and darted away again. The girl didn't move. She just nodded and smiled reassuringly.

'That's it,' she said. 'Eat it. I've got some more.'

Keeping its eyes fixed on the girl, the child tore into the bread. How hungry it was. Perhaps its belly was packed with bark and moss and acorns. The bread tasted good. The small loaf disappeared in a minute or two. Then the child regretted its greed, for right away its stomach began to ache. After so long in the shadow land, perhaps it should have eaten more cautiously.

The girl held out the apple next and the child took that too, though it didn't eat it.

'Are you living here?' the girl asked. 'My mother sent me out to the shrine, to tidy it up. We're not supposed to, of course. I haven't been here for ages. And I don't know what I can do, because they took the statue of the Virgin away and broke it up. But I'll do what I can.'

She stood up and walked to the spring beneath the broken arch. The child followed her, hanging back. The girl picked up half a dozen birch twigs from the ground to make a simple brush and she swept away the fallen leaves from the low wall around the pool and the ledge beneath the arch where the statue used to stand.

Then she turned to the hermit's cell, sweeping out the leaves. She poked around in the empty fireplace, clearing the dust. The child slunk in behind her, to watch. The girl talked a lot. She chatted away as she worked, explaining what she was doing. Although she seemed relaxed, the child was aware the girl was still wary, keeping a watch. Then something else caught her attention.

7

'Oh!' she said, squatting in front of the hearth. 'Oh! Look what I've found.'

She tugged at a loose brick at the back of the fireplace. Her efforts dislodged a fat lump of soot, which fell into the hearth in a puff of fine black dust which settled on the girl's face and apron.

'Oh!' she exclaimed again, wiping the soot from her eyes. She pulled out the brick and thrust her hand into the hole behind. She took out a small pewter cup on a piece of broken chain and showed it to the child.

'This is for the spring,' she said. 'It used to be fastened in the wall, so people could drink. There's something else though, further in.'

She put the cup on the hearth and again reached into the hole at the back. She drew out a large bundle of very ancient parchment, haphazardly folded and rolled. The papers cracked as she pulled them open. The parchment was damp and mouldy, brown-stained. Still the black ink marks were clear to see. The girl glanced at the words of the pages, turning from one to another.

'Latin,' she said. 'Prayers.'

The child hopped from one foot to the other, peering over the girl's shoulder. The parchment smelled unpleasant, except for the faintest familiar aroma of the hermit, once the child's friend. The girl, however, did not seem impressed. She stuffed the parchment back into the fireplace and replaced the brick.

'It'll be safer here,' she said. 'There are papers everywhere. We have to be careful.'

The child didn't understand what she was talking about

but it squatted beside the girl. They were very close to each other now and the girl wrinkled her nose. The child realised its own smell must be very strong.

'Where are you from?' the girl asked. 'Have you lived here a long time? Are you an orphan?'

The child stared into the girl's small, oval face, studying her features. She had very fair lashes and shapely, pale pink lips. Her teeth were clean and white. The girl stared back with equal curiosity.

'Can you speak?' she said softly. 'Do you understand me?'

They stared at each other. The child frowned. Then it nodded. Yes, it understood perfectly. Could it speak? Once, before this last long, long sojourn in the shadow land, yes it could. The child was beginning to remember. Memories of the ordinary world were coming back. But it had to be patient, not to grab, not to want it all at once.

It opened its mouth.

'Yes,' it said. The sound was like a croak. It was hard to speak after so long. Its voice sounded very odd.

'Yes,' it repeated. 'I can speak.'

The words came out slowly, as though the child had to find each word.

Wide-eyed, the girl smiled. Her eyes were shining.

'My name's Elizabeth,' she said. 'What's yours?'

This was the question the child dreaded. A name. It wrinkled its face, knowing not to try to force the remembering, but to let it happen of its own accord. It closed its eyes. Elizabeth waited patiently.

The child dropped its face forward and cleared its thoughts, and at last a doorway seemed to open in its mind.

9

The child gave a huge, profound sigh, through its entire body. It turned to Elizabeth.

'Isabella,' it said. 'My name is Isabella Margaret Leland.'

Elizabeth hurried back to the town. Already the afternoon was gloomy, the evening swiftly drawing in. Elizabeth's dress was sooty, and mud clung to the hems of her skirt. Her excitement, however, exceeded her worries about the scolding she expected when she got home. She had left Isabella at the hermit's cell with the rest of her own bread and a warning not to stray from the shrine. Elizabeth wanted to keep this extraordinary discovery to herself. A green girl! Perhaps she was a faery or a changeling. How strange she was – moving like an animal. And the way she smelled – of mud and earth, mixed in with some peculiar sweet and exotic perfume.

Elizabeth had to think carefully what to do next. If anyone else found Isabella, they might take her away before she had a chance to work out a plan. She had heard of wild children before, like the story of Romulus and Remus, who were raised by wolves. Had Isabella been raised by wolves? But Isabella had learned to talk. Not a snatched baby, then. Perhaps a lost child.

Elizabeth trotted back to the muddy highway through the forest. Not far ahead the trees gave way to fields, the crossroads, and further on, the town on the hill. The sun was sinking. Light reflected on long puddles in ruts left by cartwheels. Threads of smoke rose from the houses on the hill. The broken ruins of the old abbey were plain to see, rising above the level of the rooftops. Elizabeth was hungry, having given all her bread to the wild girl, but it was hard to

10

think about food when her thoughts were taken up by the fact of her marvellous discovery.

At first she had been afraid, spying the low shape leaning over the spring. She had thought it was a wolf. The creature she had seen peering into the water was dun-coloured, from a distance, with a thick pelt hanging over its back. Then the animal began to beat its head with its hands, and Elizabeth feared it was something unholy, a goblin, or a lunatic. She was torn, between fear and curiosity. Elizabeth was brave though. She didn't run away. Slowly she inched her way around the creature, trying to get a better view, to find out what it was. And then Elizabeth realised she was looking at a human being. It was a girl. And the girl threw herself on the ground in a kind of tantrum and Elizabeth stepped closer. Clumsily, she had broken a stick beneath her boot.

The wild girl's hair was very long, hanging in heavy brown clumps right to her knees. And her skin was green. Yes, it was truly green. The girl was wearing a torn brown tunic, very ragged and too small for her. This left her arms and legs bare, and the skin was mottled with the greens of moss and oak. Green dapples on the pale face. Patches over the backs of her hands, though when Elizabeth handed over the bread she saw the girl's palms were white. And the wild girl – Isabella – had huge long nails on her hands and feet. Like claws.

She guessed Isabella was about twelve – the same age as herself. It was hard to be sure because the wild girl was very thin. She didn't look frail though. She looked strong. She would have to be tough to survive on her own in the forest.

Elizabeth hurried through the crossroads. The place was haunted. Several years ago a robber had been hanged and

11

buried here, outside the town, and after darkness people avoided it. But Elizabeth was nearly home now. She walked at the edge of the highway, trying to avoid the mud. She passed two fields full of cows, crossed the bridge over the river, and ran up the steep cobbled hill to the marketplace.

She lived in a house on Silver Street, among the other merchant families. Her house was the largest on the street, with coloured glass in the front window. Despite appearances, however, the family was not prosperous. Their stubborn loyalty to the Roman Catholic Church had cost them dear. Elizabeth's father, Edward Dyer, was away on business but never made any money. No-one wanted to work with him. The house was cold and quiet, only one servant left, which meant Elizabeth, her mother and younger sister Esther had to take on the work of the household. They scrimped and saved to educate her brother Robert at the university in Oxford.

Elizabeth opened the front door and took off her muddy boots. Inside, the house was dark, the candles not yet lit.

'Elizabeth? Is that you?' A voice came from another room.

'Yes, Mother. It's me,' she called out, quickly brushing gluey crumbs of dirt from the bottom of her skirt. She put her boots to one side and replaced them with a very old pair of woollen slippers.

'Elizabeth, come here!'

She hurried through the living room to the kitchen at the back of the house where Mary, the housekeeper, was tending a pot over a fire in the large hearth. After the chill of outdoors, the kitchen was hot and bright. Elizabeth's mother, Jane Dyer, was standing beside the long wooden table with her head in her hands. Elizabeth's younger sister Esther was sitting on a stool by the side of the fire, fussing over a piece of embroidery.

Jane looked up when her elder daughter came in.

'Where have you been?' she said. 'I was afraid for you. I shouldn't have sent you on your own. What was I thinking?'

In a miniature portrait, painted when her mother was just sixteen and engaged to be married, Jane was a beautiful young woman with a wide, pale forehead and curls of golden hair. Twenty years later, it was hard to see the remains of the glowing girl in the tired woman. Jane was thin but her body was saggy. Her face was always grey and tired. Life had been difficult for them all, and Jane, more than any of them, had to deal with the difficulties. This wasn't the life she had expected to lead.

Elizabeth's father was often away from the town with his business, and Robert was at the university. It wasn't easy for the girls when the other merchants' daughters paraded in new dresses and Elizabeth still wore her mother's cast-offs. Elizabeth's hands had grown red and chapped from scrubbing vegetables and helping with the laundry while the other girls read poetry and learned to play the lute.

'Did you find the saint's shrine? Did you go the way I told you?' Jane said.

Elizabeth nodded. Mary glanced over her shoulder, still stirring at the pot.

'What is it like?' Jane said.

'Broken. Deserted. I tidied it, as you said. Swept out the leaves.'

'Did you pray?'

Elizabeth nodded, but she looked away from her mother. She hadn't prayed. The wild girl had distracted her. The prayers had been forgotten. Jane looked at her closely, perhaps sensing the untruth. Elizabeth's cheeks burned.

'Did anyone see you?' Jane said softly. 'It was a foolish undertaking, but I wanted it done. Did anyone see you?'

Still staring at the table, Elizabeth shook her head. Isabella did not count. This second falsehood was perhaps only half a lie. Isabella didn't belong to the ordinary world. She wasn't a threat to them.

Jane still regarded her carefully.

'Well done,' she said. 'Go again, but not too soon. Take your basket and if anyone asks you, tell them you're looking for mushrooms, or firewood. People know we haven't the servants to do all the work any more. And the Virgin Mary, she will see we haven't forgotten her. Saint Jerome will pray for us.'

Jane crossed herself, and the servant, by the pot, nodded and crossed herself as well. It was a risky, secretive business, clinging to the old faith.

Elizabeth helped her mother and the housekeeper prepare supper. If her father were home, they would light the fire in the main room. Tonight, though, Elizabeth would eat with her mother and sister in the warmth of the kitchen. Edward had been away a long time. He had travelled across Europe to Venice, hoping to make money importing silks and spices. His letters were infrequent and his family missed him dreadfully. Somehow the straitened circumstances didn't matter so much when they were all together – and Edward rallied their pride in the Catholic faith, telling them how generations of

14

Dyers had served the great abbey. And they cherished a great secret — a trust bestowed upon the family by the Catholic Church long ago, a secret they would protect even unto death. Pride in the importance of this trust helped them bear the persecution and held them all steadfast in the faith.

Elizabeth sighed. Sacred trusts were all very well, but they didn't ward off the cold or help pay the fines they faced for not attending Protestant church services. When Edward and her brother were away, only Jane and her sister were left. The glamour of their faith had faded. Life was falling apart at the seams.

They dined on a broth of barley, onions and root vegetables, with pieces of coarse bread. Elizabeth was very hungry. Mary lit a tallow candle that cast a dim yellow light on the table, and brought them stewed apples and a handful of dried raisins to follow. Esther was chatting on and on about her afternoon helping with the baking but Elizabeth could see her mother wasn't paying attention. She wriggled on the bench, trying to keep warm by the fire, her mind full of Isabella.

After the meal they sat together in the warm space before the hearth and Jane told them a story from the Bible. Then they bowed their heads and prayed for a blessing, for the health and safety of their father and brother, for the forgiveness of their own sins and the restoration of the true Church. When the candle began to die the girls left the sanctuary of the kitchen and made their way through the dark, cold house and up the stairs to the bedroom they shared.

Elizabeth lay awake beside her sister for a long time. They went to bed early now, because candles were expensive. She couldn't stop thinking about the wild girl. What would she be doing now? Where did she sleep? How cold and dark it must be sleeping alone in the forest. Elizabeth shivered, pulling the blanket closer around her body, sensing the warmth of Esther close beside her. Elizabeth had to find some way of bringing Isabella back to life – to human life, a home and a family to be with. She had to rescue her. This would not be easy.

Outside Elizabeth could hear the voices of men, as they walked home from the taverns. The moon rose into the space of the little window. A dog barked. Esther gave a tiny snore and hiccup in her sleep. The stairs creaked as Jane made her way to bed.

Elizabeth tried to will herself asleep but she was wound up tight, thinking about the wild girl and what she should do. Tomorrow she would go to the forest again, with food and something for Isabella to wear. Complicated plans unfolded inside her head. She tossed and turned, growing hot and itchy.

She drifted into sleep for a while. She dreamed the wild girl was eating the sheaf of papers they found in the fireplace. Elizabeth scolded her for destroying a piece of the old religion and the wild girl was sick, bringing up long shreds of parchment with the words still written upon them, except that the words didn't make sense any more. Then the wild girl began to beat her head again. The sounds of her blows were shocking and loud.

Elizabeth jolted awake, her heart thundering. Someone was knocking on the door.

She was afraid. Who was it, coming in the night? The

moon had sunk from the window. It was very late. The knock came again, a low, insistent thud.

She climbed out of bed and hurried into her mother's room, the floorboards icy beneath her bare feet.

Jane looked very peaceful when she was asleep, as though her worries had fallen away. Elizabeth didn't want to wake her up but the knocking came again. Elizabeth ran to the window and looked down to the street in front of the house. Two men were standing there, heavily cloaked. A face turned up, to the window. Her heart seemed to jump to her mouth.

'Robert!' she said aloud. 'Mum, wake up. Wake up. Robert's here.'

Jane's eyes flicked open.

'Robert?' she said. 'What's happened to him?'

'He's here! Outside the door!'

Not waiting for Jane to climb out of bed, Elizabeth ran out of the room and down the stairs. She drew back the bolt on the front door. The servant, Mary, was behind her now, coming from the kitchen, where she slept, tugging a shawl over her shoulders. Elizabeth flung open the door.

'Robert!' she cried. The two men stepped over the threshold. They were well wrapped against the weather. Robert's companion was swathed around the neck and face with a woollen scarf. Elizabeth flung herself into her brother's arms, not minding the icy cold of his coat against her warm body. He laughed, ruffling his hand through her hair.

'Robert!' Jane was standing on the stairs, a blanket over her long white shift. She stretched out her arms and reached out for her son.

17

'Robert,' she said again. 'Quick, Mary, light a candle. Revive the fire. It's so dark. I want to see my son!'

Mary nodded and hurried into the kitchen. Little Esther emerged from her bedroom, very sleepy. Robert and his guest were given the chairs to sit on, close to the kitchen fire, while Mary warmed beer and food for them. Jane perched upon a stool, beside Robert. Her pale blonde hair was loose over her shoulders, her face bright and happy. Elizabeth stood to one side, hopping from one cold foot to another, as the men slowly warmed and took off their hats and coats and scarves. How grown up Robert looked now, hardly like the brother she remembered. At nineteen he was a man, with a man's voice and a man's confidence. He was not as blonde as his mother and sisters. His eyebrows were dark, his hair wood-coloured and trimmed to the shoulders and he had a neat beard. How handsome he looked to Elizabeth, aglow with the adventure of his night ride.

The womenfolk waited patiently while the men dined, bursting with curiosity about the man Robert had brought home with him, and the need for a journey by night. But it would be rude and disrespectful to ask before they were ready. Esther clung tight to her sister's skirt, intimidated by the stranger, but eager not to miss any of the excitement. Elizabeth watched her mother stare at Robert, her face so keen and hungry she looked as though she wanted to eat him up. But Elizabeth sensed the change between them, Robert a man now, his mother an old woman who must wait on him.

'I'm sorry to wake you so late,' Robert said at last. 'I think you will understand the need for discretion and for speed. I want to introduce you to a very important friend of mine.'

He gestured towards the other man.

'This is Thomas Montford. He is a priest and a Catholic and he has come from the seminary at Douai in France. He has a mission to bring the English back to the true faith. He has spoken secretly to Catholics at the university and celebrated Mass in private rooms. But the church authorities got wind of him, and what he was doing, and it was necessary for us to leave as soon as we could.'

Jane drew back, and put her hand over her mouth. Elizabeth looked at the priest, this Thomas Montford. He was older than her brother by some ten years, strongly built, like a wrestler, with black, curly hair and a beard. When Robert finished speaking the man leaned forward, resting his elbows on his thighs.

'Thank you for the shelter you've provided me,' he said. 'I understand your family follows the true faith. Your son has been an ally and support for me these last months and when I was in danger he offered me the safety of your home.'

Jane nodded, her hand still over her mouth. Elizabeth could see she was afraid. Jane didn't look at the priest. She turned to Robert.

'Do you know what danger you bring upon us?' she whispered. 'Do you know what would happen if it was found out we harboured this man? For pity's sake! Do we not suffer enough for our faith already? What about your sisters, Robert, what about them? And your own safety? Do you understand what they would do to you?'

Robert stared at his mother and his lip trembled. For a moment he looked like the boy Elizabeth remembered. He was about to speak when the priest put up his hand.

'Do you think I don't know the danger I bring with me?' Thomas said. His voice was rich and warm, and his eyes, fixed on Jane, were passionate.

'I have celebrated Mass in people's homes, and I have spoken out for the need of England to return to the Catholic faith, and against the heretic Queen,' he said, in a fierce, low voice. 'If the authorities catch me I will be tried and convicted of treason. Do you think I do not understand the penalty for treason? That I should be tormented to reveal the names of my fellows, and then I should be executed?'

Jane couldn't draw her eyes from the priest's face. Her breathing was fast and shallow. Elizabeth lingered in the shadows. Her mouth was dry. She couldn't swallow.

The man spoke more gently now.

'If the people of England aren't taken back to Rome they will not find salvation,' he said. 'They will be doomed to an eternity of torment in hell. Our Lord Jesus Christ was beaten and executed for his faith, to save us, and I am prepared to take the same risk, to follow in his footsteps. All I ask of you, is to hide me here for a time, until the furore in Oxford has passed and I can move on again. There are more Catholic sympathisers in the north, and that is where I will head.'

'We must help him,' Robert said.

Jane nodded. She wiped her nose on the sleeve of her shift, and crossed herself. The priest sat back in his chair.

'Of course we must,' she said. 'Forgive me my doubt and fear. We will do whatever we can. Will you pray for us?'

The priest nodded. They all fell to their knees and the priest spoke a Latin blessing over their heads.

Brothers

Robert got up early the next morning and dressed by candle-light. He ate a generous breakfast with the priest Thomas. Together the men polished off pork chops, nuts, cheese and apples, while the women hovered around them, anxious to give them a good meal. The small store of food was stripped bare, in honour of the guests. Robert told his mother and sisters about life at Oxford, the long lessons in Greek and Latin and mathematics, his cold lodgings and the miserable landlady who grumbled about the hours he kept. He moaned about the poor clothes he wore, compared to the bright silks and furs adorning the richer students, though Elizabeth noted his poor clothes were still warmer and finer than her own. She loved her brother, but listening to him, she wondered if he truly understood how hard it was for his mother and sisters, to live on the meagre money left over. His battle with student poverty seemed like an adventure – not the day after day grind endured at home, the endless cutting back, the poor food and hard work.

Elizabeth sighed. It was hard to be cross with him for long. He looked so happy to be home and their mother had come alive, to be with him. And now he was leaving again, heading back to Oxford and entrusting Thomas to their care. He would walk to the crossroads and take the coach on the long, muddy journey to the university. After the meal Robert and the priest shook hands, and embraced awkwardly. Then Robert threw his arms around his mother and kissed her hard, on the cheek.

'Goodbye,' he said, unwilling to let her go. 'Take care of Thomas, and yourselves.'

He turned to his sisters, embraced Esther and patted Elizabeth on the head.

'Be good,' he said. They all stood together a moment, the mother and her three children, and the priest who had come from France. Elizabeth squeezed her eyes shut, wanting the moment to last, this circle of precious people, believing the feelings they had for each other might protect them. 'Please, God, please, Holy Mother, please, take care of them,' she prayed silently, longing for safety, for the family to be together again.

'I have to go,' Robert said, breaking the spell. His face was tired and white and his eyes watered. For a moment Elizabeth thought he was about to weep, but Robert coughed loudly and turned away from them. Then he straightened up, becoming a man again. He opened the front door, stepping out into the bitter cold air. He looked back and waved awkwardly. Beyond his head, the sky was washed out, a pale dawn with a powdering of red over the rooftops. One last star twinkled. Robert picked his way over the mud along the cobbled street, and disappeared down the hill. The priest returned to the kitchen but Jane stood a long time in the doorway, until he had disappeared from sight. Even then, she didn't come in. Elizabeth pulled Jane's sleeve, wished her mother loved her as much as she loved Robert.

'Come in, it's cold,' Elizabeth said, still tugging. 'He's gone now.'

Jane pressed her lips together. Her body was stiff and resistant, like a piece of wood.

'Mum, please.'

Jane shivered. 'I'm sorry,' she said, still staring through the doorway. 'Elizabeth, I'm so afraid. I have a terrible feeling.' She pressed her fingers to her chest, above the heart. 'I don't know why – but I can't help it.'

'What? What is it?'

Jane stared over Elizabeth's head. 'It'll kill me,' Jane said. 'It will be more than I can bear. I've tried so hard. I've endured so much. But this, this will be the end of me.'

'What?' Elizabeth cried. 'What's going to happen?'

'I am so afraid for him,' Jane said. 'He's so young and brave. But I have a premonition. I don't think he will ever come home. I am not going to see him ever again.'

Elizabeth swallowed.

'You don't know that,' she said. 'How can you say so?'

But Jane wasn't listening. Her eyes were fixed to the point along the street where her son had disappeared from view. Tears leaked over her face.

'You don't know that,' Elizabeth repeated. 'You mustn't say it. And we're still here,' Elizabeth whispered. 'Esther and I. And Father will be home soon.'

Jane nodded, holding her daughter against her. But her eyes were still on the doorway.

Elizabeth went to the kitchen to eat her own meagre breakfast. The priest was sitting on a stool by the fire, staring at the flames and lost in thought. He didn't seem to notice her, as she ate and observed him. Was he afraid? What was he planning? Elizabeth had heard the stories about other heretic priests, who had been captured and charged with treason, suffering terrible torments and a bloody execution. And now Thomas Montford had brought those dangers to her own home, and like a cloak, the threat spread out to cover them all.

The priest sat up straight, and turned to Elizabeth.

'Your brother has told me a great deal about you,' he said. 'Robert told me you were very clever and lively, never stopped talking – but you are quiet this morning. Are you afraid, Elizabeth?' The priest's cheeks were ruddy from the fire, his lips still moist from his breakfast. Nothing about Thomas's appearance suggested priestliness. He wasn't lean from fasting, or pale from hours in prayer. Instead he looked like a man who could wrestle and ride to hounds, who would spend his days in the sun and weather, and his evenings relishing hearty meals.

Elizabeth put down her crust and tried to swallow the half-chewed ball of bread in her mouth. The priest intimidated her. She looked at the table and swallowed. The bread seemed to lodge in her dry throat like paper.

'Yes,' she said simply. 'I am afraid.' But she lifted her face and looked directly at the priest. His eyes were green, lines curving from the corners in a way that suggested he was a man who often laughed. He smiled now, and his face looked

24

so warm and generous Elizabeth's shyness melted away. She smiled back.

'Aren't you afraid?' she said.

'Of course.'

Elizabeth continued to look steadily in his face, trying to understand him.

The priest continued. 'What I have to do is so important I have to put my fear to one side. I see my fears and I say how-do-you-do to them, and then I put them behind me. Do you understand? My fears are still there, but I don't let them worry and gnaw. The job has to be done, Elizabeth. I heard God's voice, and he wasn't to be put off.'

Elizabeth's eyes widened. 'God spoke to you?'

The priest nodded. 'He speaks to all of us, if we listen hard enough.'

Elizabeth looked at him. Had God ever spoken to her? She prayed every morning and night, counting off the prayers on the clay beads of her precious rosary, the blue paint worn away beneath her fingers. No, God had not spoken to her yet, and perhaps she was glad he had not, if the voice might ask her to risk her life as the priest risked his. Of course she should be prepared to die for the Lord, as he had died on the cross for her. But Jesus hadn't wanted to die either. Even he was afraid, as he prayed in the Garden of Gethsemane before the crucifixion and asked for the cup of death to be taken from him. Elizabeth's eyes filled with tears, to think of it, Jesus all alone while his friends slept, Jesus knowing what would be done to him, how he would suffer. Her heart was already in turmoil, missing her father, seeing Robert, and losing him, and now talking to the priest who risked death every day he remained in England.

The priest's smile was gentle now, seeing a tear slip down Elizabeth's cheek.

'There,' he said. 'God is with us. Take heart. You have a job too, you know. Take care of your mother, Elizabeth. Help her and be kind to your sister. Say your prayers. Wait for God to speak to you too.'

Elizabeth wiped her nose with the back of her hand. In the hearth the fire crackled and spat. The servant pushed her way through the back door, dragging a basket of logs and cursing under her breath.

'Don't forget, you have to go to Spirit Hill today,' Jane said as she stepped into the kitchen, carrying Esther on her hip. Jane's face was very pale from crying. Esther had her face pressed against her mother's neck.

Elizabeth was dismayed. She had forgotten all about her visit to Lady Catherine.

'Today?' she said. 'I can't go today.'

She was aching to escape to the forest, to see the green girl again.

'You have to go, Elizabeth. They'll be expecting you.' Jane looked to the priest for his support.

'Where does she have to go?' he asked.

'To the manor at Spirit Hill. The lady has taken an interest in her. A surprising interest, considering.'

Thomas frowned.

'Very surprising.' He looked to Elizabeth. 'You serve the lady? You wait on her?'

Elizabeth nodded, glumly. Usually the visits to the manor

were a treat, a chance to escape the less than charming conditions at home. Lady Catherine simply required her presence. Sometimes Elizabeth read to her, or wrote letters, or helped her in the little studio where she painted. Lady Catherine had also given her lessons in Greek or Latin, when the money ran out for a tutor at home. More often than not, Lady Catherine wanted someone to talk to. And Elizabeth was paid for her trouble, an important consideration when the family was so short of money.

'Does she talk to you about your faith? Is she spying on the family? Trying to convert you?' the priest asked. Elizabeth shook her head. She thought Lady Catherine still asked for her because, simply, she liked her.

'The lady is proud and unconventional,' Jane said. Then, disapproving: 'She is a painter. And she is childless.'

The priest looked from mother to daughter, sensing Elizabeth's reluctance to go and wrongly concluding it arose from his arrival, because he said: 'You must go. Don't worry about me. Behave as though everything is normal and you'll be fine.'

Elizabeth thought of Isabella alone in the forest and bit her lip. She had promised the wild girl she would return. What if Isabella went away, or someone else found her? She imagined her waiting all alone, in the cold, for Elizabeth to return. How long would she wait before she gave up and went away, feeling betrayed by her new friend? Elizabeth sighed. There was nothing she could do.

The manor at Spirit Hill was a four-mile walk from Maumesbury and when the weather was bad it took Elizabeth the best part of two hours. Today the sun was bright, but pale mud stewed the road from three days of rain. The roads around the town were paved with white limestone, a mire in the winter, dusty in the summer. She walked down the hill and over the bridge out of the town. The walk seemed particularly long and arduous, with the double layering of unease twisting and twitching in her mind. She kept thinking of Isabella waiting in the forest, with nothing to eat. And when she wasn't thinking of Isabella she thought of the priest hiding out in their house, and what would happen if anybody found out. As if life were not difficult enough, talked about in the town, ignored, treated with suspicion.

She followed the highway for two miles, before turning off through ploughed fields and meadows of cattle to the gentle rise of Spirit Hill. She passed through a gateway with stone columns, and at last the manor house rose ahead of her.

Lord Cecil and Lady Catherine Melibourne were very prosperous. Their house was new with carefully arranged gardens laid out with mazes of low shrubs and archways which, in the summer months, were covered with roses. The manor was a world in itself with a dairy, granary and bakehouse – and a horde of dairymaids, farm labourers and servants. Elizabeth walked to the back of the house and pushed open the door into the kitchen. The room was crowded and Elizabeth was shy, making her way through. A fire danced in the wide hearth, and half a dozen men stood in front of it, warming their backs. These men were better dressed than labourers and filled the room with their presence. The perfume of the bitter night still lingered about them, an aura of frost and mud. They were Lord Cecil's men, part of his household. They spoke together in loud, masculine voices, joking and boasting.

Their big boots were caked with mud, and carelessly they soiled the flagged kitchen floor. Two hounds, brindled brown and white with long noses, stared up at them, mindful of heavy feet on thin tails and paws.

The cook spied Elizabeth edging her way around the crowd of men and beckoned her to step forward. She was busy preparing a late breakfast for the men and had no time for conversation. She thrust a tray into Elizabeth's hand.

'Take it upstairs to the mistress,' she said. 'You're late. She's waiting for you.'

Elizabeth was well aware the servants were suspicious of her, because of her Catholic faith. They were all civil enough, because Lady Catherine expected it, but none had extended Elizabeth any kind of friendship. Probably they didn't understand why the lady should bother with her at all. Elizabeth took the tray and nodded, grateful to escape, and hurried along the corridor and up the stairs.

Lady Catherine was seated at the window when Elizabeth knocked and opened the door. The sun was shining upon one side of the lady's face, and on her long, white hands which drew a needle and thread through a piece of linen. For an instant the sunlight picked out the blood red strand of the lady's yarn.

Elizabeth gave a quick curtsey and placed the tray on a table beside her mistress. Upon it, three tawny eggs nestled in a dull pewter dish, beside two thick slices of bread skimmed with golden butter. Beside them, in a blue china bowl, lay half a dozen dark purple plums. Illuminated, in the shadowed room, the colour burned in the fat plums, and the smooth-shelled eggs, enclosed like a secret, and the rich Wiltshire

29

butter. The lady gave a little smile, putting her embroidery aside. Sensitive and insightful, she had observed that Elizabeth was admiring the colours of her breakfast. Lady Catherine passed her hand over the tray, throwing a shadow over the dishes, momentarily putting the colours out.

'Beautiful, aren't they?' she said. 'It seems a pity to eat them. Then again, the sun will have passed away from the window in another hour, and by then the eggs and bread will be cold.' She picked up a boiled egg and passed it to Elizabeth, who closed her fingers, feeling the weight and heat of the egg in her cold hand.

'Eat up,' the lady said, looking into the girl's face. 'You look very tired. Did the walk tire you today?'

Elizabeth nodded. She felt exhausted. Her legs were trembling. She hardly dared to speak. Her secret pressed too hard. The fugitive priest. A heretic, hiding out in her own home. Surely Lady Catherine would guess – wouldn't the secret be obvious in her face, in the windows of her eyes? If she opened her mouth, perhaps the words would just tumble out, giving everything away. In a fever of anxiety, she didn't trust herself.

'Sit down. Sit down. Eat,' Lady Catherine urged. Elizabeth sank down upon the wooden stool beside the window seat. Her mistress took up another egg and cracked the shell with her slim, clever fingers. Lady Catherine was dressed in a dark yellow gown, with a high collar and a froth of starched lace around her neck. The gown was thick and warm, decorated along the sleeves and bodice with intricate embroideries of birds and flowers. Her dark red hair was brushed back from her forehead, tucked inside a velvet cap. Her skin was fair and fine, unlike the tough, coarsened complexions of the servants and the women who worked outside, in the summer sun and the biting winters. But the lady wasn't young. There was a tiredness in her face, a disenchantment. After four years of marriage there were no children, and Lord Cecil had taken her from the court, where she was celebrated as a painter of portraits, and closed her up in the quiet country manor. The life of a court painter was not suitable for a married woman, and the wife of a lord, Lady Catherine had told Elizabeth with a lightness in her voice that did not marry up with the sadness in her eyes. She still painted at home, undertaking commissions for portraits of fine ladies and friends of her husband when they deigned to leave London, but life seemed to have ebbed away from Lady Catherine over the years of her marriage, despite her manor house and fine dresses. Perhaps this was another reason she had taken on Elizabeth to be a companion, her own sense of being an outsider.

When the meal was over, Lady Catherine took up her sewing again and told Elizabeth to read to her. She opened the pages of the *Iliad*, and recounting aloud in ancient Greek, transported them to another place, to the sun-baked islands studded in a sapphire sea, and the male world of fierce friendships and passionate enmities, of blood and triumph and grief. Elizabeth read for an hour, and for a time she was so caught up in the tale she forgot about the priest and her brother and Isabella waiting alone in the woods. For a moment – just a moment – she was somewhere else.

Lady Catherine lifted her head.

'Who's that?'

Elizabeth looked up from the page. Then she heard it – a clatter of hooves, as a horse skidded to a halt at the front of the house, and men's voices shouting. Elizabeth took a breath and the blood seemed to stop in her veins. All the worries rushed back – the weight of her secrets. She dropped the book.

'What – what—' she stammered. Lady Catherine stared at Elizabeth.

'It's only horses,' she said. 'Someone has arrived.'

Words were called, hard to make out. Elizabeth and Lady Catherine stood up and left the room, hurrying to a window at the front of the house to see who had come. They looked down upon two men on horses, the animals tugging at their bits, pawing at the ground with their muddy, fragile legs, necks slicked with sweat. The men of the household stepped out to meet the visitors and confronted them now. An unspoken communication was taking place between them, Lord Cecil's men and the visitors. Elizabeth could see it, the sizing up. Lord Cecil's men eyed up the visitors, sauntering, displaying how numerous they were, how strong. The first of the newcomers, on a tall grey horse, announced he had come from court on the Queen's business, that his name was Christopher Merrivale. The other man, presumably a servant, waited behind his master. Everyone hesitated for a moment, no-one moving, except for the grey horse tossing its head and sidling. Then the chamberlain stepped forward and nodded, extending his hand. Christopher Merrivale dismounted, handing the reins to his servant, and walked to the house. Just before he crossed the threshold he looked up to the window where Elizabeth stood, beside Lady Catherine. His big, feathered hat tipped back, revealing the oval face framed by long, black hair, a single pearl earring glinting. He

32

had spotted the watchers, and smiled. Lady Catherine drew a breath, fluttering beside Elizabeth.

'Oh, what a fine-looking man! Who is he?' she said. But Elizabeth pressed her teeth together, and her lips trembled. Her whole body felt cold. He had looked at her directly, Christopher Merrivale, and she was certain he could see who she was and what she had to hide.

The wild girl curled up in the corner of the hermit's cell. Her stomach growled and churned, struggling to digest the bread Elizabeth had given her. She hadn't eaten for such a long time and her belly hurt, as though the food had tied itself in a hard knot. It was cold at night, but Isabella was used to the cold. She had endured many winters in the hollow tree, lying beneath a blanket of snow. In that enchanted sleep Isabella had not been entirely a part of the ordinary world. If a man had climbed the tree and peered down into its hollow depths, he would not have seen a girl curled up, covered in ivy, dappled with frost. Perhaps he would only have noticed a shape in the bark or a pattern of leaves. Isabella had been only partly in the wood, as she slept.

Now she pressed herself against the walls of the hermit's cell and wrapped her rug of hair around her, as best she could. It rained in the night and Isabella listened to the patter on the lumpish thatch of the roof. Here and there leaks let the cold water through, and it lay in puddles on the floor. Isabella had no desire to sleep that first night. Her mind didn't want to let go, playing on the memories of the day – climbing out of the tree, meeting Elizabeth at the cell, remembering her name – remembering who she was.

Isabella Margaret Leland. She repeated the words over and over, until they stopped making any sense. She had a different name in the other place, the shadow land of the crow people. There was still so much to remember of her earthly life. She held on tight to the fragments she already had.

Isabella Margaret Leland.

Would Elizabeth come back? Isabella hoped and hoped that she would. Elizabeth had warned her to stay close to the hermit's cell and Isabella had no intention of leaving if her new friend was coming back to see her again.

The night was very long. Outside the leaky hovel, the forest was quiet, except for the low moan of the wind in the trees. Once she heard the rustle of paw steps outside, and smelled the sharp, rank scent of a fox. Near dawn, far away, the long, sad call of a solitary wolf wound among the trees. As the light rose through the forest, Isabella stepped outside. She spread her fingers, so her hands were stars, and drew a deep breath, filling her lungs, her body, with the breath of the forest.

She was glad to be back, despite the cold and the danger. She had stayed with the other people a long, long time, and her brother John was with them still. And Isabella missed him. She missed him very much. He was her only family, even if he didn't remember her very well any more.

Could she find him again, and bring him home?

She watched the sun rise, sensing the response of the trees, as they stretched their branches to the warmth and light. She felt the threads of energy flowing through each and every one, from the tips of their highest leaves, down to the furthest, deepest tendrils of roots in the moist, black earth.

34

She ate Elizabeth's apple. Afterwards she drank from the spring and washed her face and hands. The cold water stung her skin. Isabella rubbed her arms with a wet wad of scratchy moss but the green did not come off. Her face, she saw in the reflection, was a dappled leafy colour. How strange she looked.

Isabella spent the morning acquainting herself with the wood in an area around the shrine. She didn't stray far away, in case she missed Elizabeth. The movement stretched out the kinks in her joints and muscles, so she could stand upright. The exercise made her warm, and brought colour to her cheeks. It was good to be awake again, to be alive.

The day passed quickly enough but Isabella was always looking out for Elizabeth and when the light began to fade in the late afternoon she felt her happiness seep away. The sun descended into the treetops and Isabella knew it was too dark now for the girl to find her. She was deeply disappointed. Why hadn't Elizabeth come? Would she never come back? Had she changed her mind? Isabella retreated to the hermit's cell and sat huddled up against the wall. She felt empty inside, utterly alone. Now Elizabeth had abandoned her she knew no-one in this strange new world. She didn't know how long she had been asleep, but judging by the changes in the forest, the dereliction of the hermit's cell, anyone she might have known from her last visit would be long dead.

When the moon rose she went to the spring. The wind had died. The slice of moon reflected on the surface of the spring. How still it was, how eerie. Fragile feathers of ice formed over the stones and painted white the fallen leaves. Isabella crouched low, shivering, trying to wrap her arms about herself to keep warm. She was lost and adrift, totally alone. She remembered, with an empty ache, her mother who had died, and her brother, John, who was far away in the other land with the crow people. Now they were both out of reach. Isabella closed her eyes, conjuring up the memories of her life at home with her mother and baby brother. The stretches of time with the crow people lay between that time and now, like a long dream. A hundred years with the crow people might seem like a single night. On the other hand, the time it took for the Queen to raise a golden cup from the table to her dark red mouth could last for a dozen days. That time, in the shadow land, was a dark, formless mass, a great chasm she had to leap in her mind to reach the ordinary, long-ago time of her first home, her real and only home. And how long ago was it? Two hundred years? Three hundred? What year was it now?

1240

It was summer, the first time Isabella saw the crow people, and it was a sweltering day. Her mother, Ruth, had tucked baby John into a shawl and tied him on to her back so they could work in the vegetable garden, weeding between rows of beans and cabbages. Their tiny cottage, a single room under a messy thatch, was built on the fringes of the forest. From the front Isabella could see, in the distance, the town on the hill with its busy abbey, and at the back, beyond the neat vegetable garden, the darkness of the trees.

Isabella saw the man urging on the galloping horse from a long distance. The horse's hooves kicked up a white dust from the dry road. The drumming of hooves, almost impossible to hear at first, grew louder and louder as the rider approached. Then, all of a sudden, the horse was upon them, skidding to a halt, labouring for breath.

'Mistress Leland!' the man called. Slowly Ruth stood up straight, John asleep on her back. She mopped the sweat from her face. The horse, excited from the long ride, danced its flinty hooves on the road beyond the garden.

'It's Mistress Watts, she's having the baby, they need you,' he said.

Ruth nodded. She was a small, slight woman with dark brown hair that twisted into long, slippery curls. Even when she plaited it and tucked the shiny plait under her woollen cap, strands escaped and prettily framed her narrow face, with its pointed chin and dark brown eyes. She smiled now, and turned to the cottage.

'Hurry,' the man said. 'She's in a terrible way.' The man's face was pink with anxiety. His voice was unsteady. His horse pirouetted, eager to be off again. But Ruth unhurriedly entered the house to collect her things, leaving Isabella staring at the man. She had been about ten then, small for her age. The horse looked impossibly tall. Isabella noticed how the man gave quick little glances at the cottage, curious and nervous at the same time. People were afraid to come too close. It was a strange place, Isabella's home. Nothing untoward ever happened, but the shadows seemed to fall in the wrong places. From time to time the bundles of dried herbs hanging from the beams began to nod, without any discernible draught. A wooden bowl placed on the table might be found, the next morning, upon the doorstep.

'Please hurry,' the man said again, as Ruth emerged from the cottage with a leather bag. 'You'll ride with me.'

Ruth nodded and smiled. She lifted the baby from her back and handed him to Isabella. She bent over the baby and kissed his forehead tenderly.

'Follow me on foot,' she said to Isabella, tying the shawl around her daughter's shoulders. 'You know the place?' Isabella nodded. Ruth stepped up to the horse, and its dangerous dancing feet, but the animal settled when she drew near, reaching out its frothy nose to snuff at her. The man leaned over, and easily pulled her up behind him. He clapped his heels against the horse's sides and they were off again, flying up the road towards the town.

Within minutes, a huge, hot hush again. Only a few motes of dust still spun in the air where the horse had been.

Isabella sighed and wiped her face on the back of her hand. It would take about half an hour to walk to the town on foot, carrying the baby. And the sun was relentless. She awkwardly adjusted the shawl to cover John's head, and began the journey.

The town reared before her, the houses sheltering in the shadow of the huge abbey, home for hundreds of monks and a centre of learning renowned across Europe. Maumesbury Abbey owned much of the town, the vast library, the granaries, trout ponds, vineyards on the flanks of the hill – even the leper hospital on the edge of the town.

Mistress Watts was in a terrible way. The whole town was beaten into silence by the heat and the sound of the labouring woman's screams, which could be heard a street away. Even the dogs cowered and whimpered in the shadows. Isabella stopped by the house in Silver Street. The upstairs window was open, to provide some fresh air for the poor woman, but this only served to make her sufferings more public. John shifted on Isabella's back, as though the ripples of distress from the bedroom had woken him. Isabella went to the back of the house. An old woman in the kitchen scowled.

'What d'you want?' she said. Then she seemed to guess who Isabella was because her expression changed to one of grudging respect.

'You're the midwife's girl,' she said. 'Go on up.'

Isabella stepped past, noticing from the corner of her eye how the servant stared at baby John and made a gesture, perhaps the sign of the cross.

The bedroom was busy with women, all fussing around the central actor in the drama of birth giving, Mistress Watts, who struggled and bellowed on the high bed. Isabella had seen it before, many times, in low hovels, the grand houses – even once, at the side of a road. Mistress Watts was a big woman, with huge white thighs and a belly like a mountain. Beside her, small and neat, Ruth was the only element of calm in the room. She held Mistress Watts's hand and smiled, offering words of comfort. The woman held on to Ruth's hand and arm with both hands, squeezing till Ruth's skin must be bruised, but Isabella knew her mother would not complain. Isabella had seen so many women, wretched with exhaustion and pain, gripping her mother's hand as she encouraged and reassured them, giving them a beacon of hope and comfort to cling to.

Then, a moment of calm, the pains sinking away. Mistress Watt stared into Ruth's face, placing all her hope of delivery onto the slight shoulders of the midwife. After a few seconds, the pains came again, in a great wave, and then baby was born all at once, pink and red and slippery, the umbilical cord glittering like a string of jewels. In an instant the mood of the gathered women turned. There was a cry of delight.

'It's a boy, Mistress. A lovely boy!' And they all came close, the women relatives and servants, to peer at the baby and marvel at him, to pat and congratulate the new mother who smiled as she panted, her eyes bright with delight.

With quick, deft movements Ruth cut the umbilical, checked and wiped the baby, wrapped him in a clean cloth and handed him to his mother. Mistress Watts, her thick hair tumbled over her shoulders, gave the midwife one deep look, full of gratitude. Mistress Watts looked beautiful, Isabella thought, the struggling animal she had been just minutes ago transformed into something magical, almost luminous, like the picture of the Virgin Mary in the church window when the sun shone through. Isabella felt so proud of her mother, who was so generous and modest. Already she was packing up her things, so the family might celebrate together. She called Isabella to help her sort out a concoction of dried raspberry leaves for the new mother to drink, to help her recover. One of the servants tapped Isabella on the shoulder.

'Go to the kitchen,' she said. 'The woman will give you a drink.'

Isabella glanced at her mother, who nodded. 'I can manage now,' she said. But Isabella hesitated. The tone of Ruth's voice troubled her. Was something wrong?

'Go on,' she urged.

Isabella was reluctant to go on her own to the dour woman in the kitchen, who had made a sign at her, to ward off evil, but she was too shy to protest before so many strangers. Slowly she made her way down the stairs. John weighed very heavily upon her now. She was tired.

40

'They said you'd give me a drink,' she whispered. The kitchen woman frowned.

'Sit down,' she said. Bent over, shuffling, the old woman drew a mug of small beer from a barrel. Isabella untied the shawl and sat baby John on her lap. He waved his arms up and down, and grinned at the old woman. Isabella took a sip. The drink was cool and earthy. Isabella savoured the taste, moving the beer around her mouth. The old woman smiled at John, despite herself.

The news of the safe delivery had already circulated the house because the old woman said: 'Your mother will be well rewarded. This child has been a long time coming. She has always miscarried before.'

Isabella drank again, not knowing how to answer, wishing the woman wouldn't stare at her so hard.

'They tell me your father died,' the old woman said. 'Your mother couldn't heal him then.'

'It wasn't her fault,' Isabella flashed suddenly, unable to hear Ruth criticised unfairly.

Her father, John Leland, had died when she was very young, after a battle on the Welsh borders when he was compelled to fight for the Lord Marchers, powerful nobles who guarded the frontier between England and Wales. He hadn't died fighting, Ruth had told her. He was wounded and contracted an infection on the journey home. A pointless death Ruth could have prevented if she had been at hand. When she spoke of her husband, and the manner of his death, Ruth's eyes darkened. It was the only subject likely to put her out of humour.

'Beg pardon.' The woman's voice was cold, and she still stared, making Isabella shy again. She gazed into her cup, hoping to

41

escape the woman's scrutiny in the swirl of beery fragments floating in the dark liquid.

'So who's the baby's father?' the woman persisted. It occurred to Isabella this was the question the old woman had wanted to ask all along. And it was one she could not answer. She continued to stare into the wooden mug and simply shrugged, squeezing tight the mug in her hand. She wanted the old woman to leave her alone. Only Ruth knew who baby John's father was. It was the one subject she would not discuss with her daughter. Sometimes Isabella speculated who it might be, among the men of the town and outlying villages, but she had no real idea. Single women were vulnerable and she suspected someone might have taken advantage of her mother. Once she had overheard someone suggesting the father was a devil from the woods, and repeated these evil tidings to her mother, but Ruth had dismissed this suggestion with a laugh. To all intents and purposes, the pregnancy had come from nowhere.

At last Ruth came downstairs, her face pale and damp from the heat. She picked up her baby, took Isabella's hand, and they left the house in Silver Street. Nobody there needed them any more.

Both mother and daughter brightened as they walked away from the town. They talked as they went, John high on his mother's back and soon fast asleep, the side of his face pressed against his mother's shoulder. Ruth began to smile again and her words were cheerful, but Isabella sensed something wasn't right. Her mother was always laughing, always in good spirits – even when she was treating patients with terrible afflictions, setting broken bones or bathing filthily infected wounds. Perhaps this was part of her success, because her good humour and happiness

42

were themselves so infectious. Isabella had already attended the delivery of babies with her mother, and assisted when labourers or soldiers needed muscle and skin stitching. One day this job would be hers and although the spectacle did not upset her any more, she wondered, could she ever be as strong and generous as her mother? It was hard to believe it. Despite the heat, Isabella gave a little shiver and a knot of nerves tied up in the pit of her stomach. Ruth glanced across.

'What's the matter?' she said.

Isabella shook her head. 'Nothing. Just – just thinking about how clever you are. I'll never be as good as you.'

Ruth smiled. 'Yes, you will,' she said. 'You know so much already.'

'It's not the knowing I'm scared about, it's how you are,' Isabella said. 'You help people just by being with them.'

Ruth's face clouded again, with the worry she was trying to hide.

'What are you thinking about?' Isabella said. 'What's wrong?'

Now Ruth sighed.

'It's the baby,' she said, looking at the road and not her daughter. 'The new baby. When I placed my hand on his chest,' she cupped her fingers in the air to demonstrate, 'there was something wrong with his heart, Isabella. I didn't tell them. I couldn't bear to. They've waited so long for this baby and she was so happy. But the rhythm of his heart was all wrong.'

Isabella looked at her mother's face. Plenty of babies died before they were a year old. Illnesses picked them off – the flux, measles, bouts of fever. But this baby was more important than most. This was an only child and the Wattses were a powerful family.

43

A vague sense of unease haunted them the rest of the day. In the long, midsummer twilight Ruth, Isabella and John left their little cottage and walked into the forest at Ruth's bidding. The lanes were closed in under the cover of young leaves, making emerald tunnels, with thin blades of sunshine cutting through. Ribbons of perfume trailed from honeysuckle clasping the branches. Flat pink dog roses bloomed on tough, thorny tendrils.

On the way Ruth told Isabella about the properties of herbs and plants, pointing out examples as they walked – which leaves might be eaten as a salad, what bark could be brewed as a tea to treat the pains of toothache, which roots might be dug up, dried and ground to provide a cure for stomach cramps. These lessons had been often repeated, so that Isabella could soak it all up. Ruth's mother had also been a healer, and hers before that. Ruth Leland had inherited a wealth of herbal and medical lore from generations of wise women. Everyone came to her for help. Even monks from the abbey, many of whom were accomplished doctors and surgeons, sought her out.

Isabella absorbed the beauty of the forest, decked in golden green. Her mother stopped talking as the sun slowly declined. Leaves gently stirred in the treetops, and then became still. Everything was silent – not a note from a bird, nor the stirring of a squirrel in the branches. The forest held its breath. Ruth followed the little path to a brake of holly and elder trees, which gave way to a clearing where bright, cold water bubbled into a shallow pool. An old willow stretched its branches over the water. Dozens of strips of coloured cloth and ribbon had been tied to the willow tree. In the still air the strips hung limp, some stained with age and weather, some glossy and new. It was a part of the old religion, this offering to the tree and the spring. Even now, women from the town and the villages made wishes when they tied up their ribbons, though the priest had forbidden it. Sometimes they tried to ease their consciences, claiming the shrine was dedicated to the Virgin Mary, but Ruth had said the spring had received offerings long before the Christian religion came to England.

Ruth took John from her back and handed him to Isabella. She looked very serious.

'You see the rowan tree to the west,' she said, pointing out the slender sapling. 'I want you to take John and wait with him over there, in its shadow. And whatever you see, and whatever happens, you must stay there and you must be especially careful your brother stays within the shadow of the tree. Do you understand?'

Isabella nodded. She knew about the crow people, the faeries who lived in the wood. Her mother had told her stories about them all her life. Even lying in her cradle, a tiny infant, Isabella had learned about the Queen of the Faeries and her court. Perhaps she had dreamed of them too, before she could walk or talk. Never though, never, had she seen them. Sometimes at night her mother had gone to the forest, occasionally with other women from the village, more often alone, to return with a curious perfume on her cold skin, her hair tangled with twigs and leaves. But she had never allowed Isabella to attend before. Why had she changed her mind now? Was it to do with the new baby and its broken heart?

Isabella took John beneath the rowan tree and watched as her mother washed her hands and face in the cold water of the spring. Isabella was excited, and frightened too. She had longed to see the crow people for so long. But she knew they were powerful, sometimes cruel. The rowan tree offered protection, because the faeries didn't like it, and hiding in its shadow she and John would be safe from them.

Isabella's family had a long connection with the faeries. Mother to daughter, through hundreds of years, they had carried the colourful history of the faery people, a treasury of tales. Before Christian times, Isabella's great-grandmothers were priestesses, a link between mortals and the crow people, held in high esteem. Of course it was different now. People came to Ruth for help when they were ill, but they also treated her with suspicion. She wasn't part of acceptable society.

A curious ripple passed through the forest, and Isabella snapped to attention. Nothing had changed – except for a charge in the atmosphere, like the moments before a bolt of lightning strikes. She remembered what her mother had explained to her. Across the ordinary world lay a web of silvery connections, holding stone and seed, bone and fur, ice and wood, in the pattern of the wood. And behind the web, beyond the pattern that made up the wood, was the shadow land, where the crow people lived. And the crow people could pass through spaces in the web to the earthly side. Sometimes mortals passed to the other side but they rarely came back again, and if they did, a hundred years might have passed.

For the very first time, Isabella was aware of the web her mother had told her about. She could see it in the glint on a stone, in the coils of a barbed bramble, the pattern of veins in a leaf. The forest seemed to fill her mind – more real than ever. It was frightening, and exciting, how the forest crowded inside of her, too much to hold all at once. At the same time she sensed how the entire scene could be pulled aside, like a curtain. And what would lie on the other side?

Ruth stood up straight, her long hair loose and blowing in a wind Isabella couldn't feel. Ruth raised her hand, and an arched doorway appeared in the picture of the forest. Lying on the ground beside her, John became agitated, waving his arms and legs in the air, but he didn't cry.

'It's all right,' Isabella whispered, stroking his soft cheek. 'We're safe here. Don't worry.' She stared out, trying to see beyond the doorway, scenting on the air the potent and alien perfume of the land of the crow people, cold stone, and dust and roses. Isabella was afraid for her mother and thrilled by her power, as she stood by the black mouth of the door.

Then the faery appeared. It stepped through the archway.

The faery was taller than a man, and very slender with long, white hands. Glossy black feathers poured over his shoulders and back, and over the long wings folded on his back. The faery, which Isabella sensed was a male despite the extraordinary beauty of his face and the dark red colour of his mouth, had long, silk black hair down to his thighs. He wore a soft leather cloth around his waist, and a large quantity of gold jewellery, which glinted dully – a necklace of engraved coins, thick bracelets, a host of rings, and about the waist a plated belt.

The creature turned his head, perhaps sensing Isabella's presence. The yellow eyes sought her out. The shape of the faery wasn't consistent. From time to time it changed momentarily into another form, a beak pressing out from the face, the long, white feet becoming wicked claws. Then he found her – the blank yellow eyes fixed on Isabella's, holding her.

Isabella froze. It was only an instant. She felt the faery look into her mind, her trove of memories – her ten years of life, bright, colourful, passionate life. The faery seemed to taste them and spit them out again. From the faery's perspective, she was nothing, she knew it. Less than nothing. Her life was of no importance at all, as the life of an ant might be nothing to her. The faery looked away, forgetting her, and Isabella was overwhelmed by a sense of her own smallness and unimportance. She was nothing.

Ruth still stood before the faery. She wasn't afraid. She was proud, confident of her own worth and power, the daughter of generations of wise women. The faery stretched out his hand and placed the palm on top of Ruth's head, in a gesture of blessing. Did they speak together? Some kind of communication seemed to pass between the crow man and the mortal woman. Ruth shook her head and gestured to her children, sheltering beneath the rowan tree.

Isabella watched. She felt so empty and dreary now the faery had turned away from her. Heavy as a clod of clay. She wanted to get close to the beautiful creature again, so she could cover up her own sense of smallness by worshipping him. She ached to be close to him, to bathe in his majesty, to fall on her knees before him.

She remembered her mother's words, the promise she made to stay by the rowan tree with her brother. The words rang clearly in her memory. But she was hollow inside. She wanted – she wanted so much – more than anything . . .

She rose to her feet, and John gave an agitated squawk. Her fever of longing grew. Yes she had promised, but the promise meant nothing now. Nothing was important except for the faery. For a moment, she wanted to throw everything away, mother, brother, life, to be close to the crow man.

She stepped forward, one foot moving from the shadow of the

rowan tree. A blast of moonlight washed across her face. It was a shock, like cold water. She hadn't noticed nightfall, or the moon-rise. The grove around the holy spring glowed with faery light. She hesitated, and baby John grabbed the edge of her skirt with his tiny hand. When she tried to step forward again he tugged and gave out a squeal. Furious, Isabella whipped round to pull her skirt free but John's fingers held on tight. She wanted to push him away, kick him, hurt him — anything to make him let go. But John turned his face to hers, looked into her eyes. His mouth curved into a toothless smile. Isabella softened. She looked at his smooth, chubby face, the perfect new skin, the unique and special person John already was.

Now she felt ashamed of her anger. She remembered, with horror, how just a moment before she'd wanted to kick him and throw him away to be close to the faery. And so the spell fell away and Isabella scooped up the baby in her arms, pressed her face against him, and burst into tears.

Isabella woke up, still sitting by the same spring where her mother had called up the crow man so long ago. Of course the spring now had a wall of stone about it, and a niche where a statue of the Virgin Mary had stood for many years. The willow tree was long gone. It took a moment for Isabella to remember what she was doing here. Past and present were confused. She didn't know how long she had lived in the shadow land. She had visited the ordinary world from time to time. But this visit was different. She didn't want to go back again, except to get John. She wanted them both to stay here. The chilly grey dawn spread over the forest and Isabella rubbed her cold arms. She waited for Elizabeth.

49

Kit Merrivale

The chamberlain escorted Christopher Merrivale into the long hall. A young man wearing a leather apron hurried after them with a basket of logs to feed the fire. Lady Catherine hesitated before she entered the room, touching her hair and her face. Merrivale took off his hat and gave a sweeping bow. He took Lady Catherine's hand and kissed it.

'I am your servant, my lady,' he said. 'I come here on the Queen's business, but I'm a friend of your husband's. He sent his greetings, and a letter.'

Merrivale unbuckled a pouch on his belt and drew out a sealed, folded letter. Lady Catherine took the letter, without looking at it, and slipped it into her pocket, without reading it. She invited Merrivale to take a seat by the side of the fire and ordered the chamberlain to bring hot beer and food for the visitor, and to make sure Merrivale's companion was well cared for. The chamberlain bowed and left the room. His voice could be heard, shouting at the other servants. Elizabeth hovered in the background, wishing she could slip away, but Merrivale paid her no attention.

The long hall at the front of the house, where the

household dined, was full of sunlight. Wooden panelling lined the walls, adorned with a tapestry of knights fighting dragons. The coloured threads glimmered. Fresh straw and rushes were spread in a carpet across the floor, with sprigs of dried rosemary, which gave off a tangy perfume underfoot. Merrivale left a trail of mud across the room. He signalled to the young man feeding the fire to pull off his filthy boots, and then he stretched his stockinged feet to the fire, with a sigh. Already this young man treated the house as his own. And he was indeed young – probably about the same age as her brother. Elizabeth glanced at Lady Catherine, but she didn't seem bothered by Merrivale's manners, instead drawing up the second chair to sit on the other side of the fire.

'May I ask what business it is that brings you here?' she said. 'Are you passing through, or will you stay? And how is Her Majesty? And life in the court? You know, I was a portrait painter in the court, before I married.'

Elizabeth felt a little embarrassed for her mistress, because she was so transparently desperate for news and excitement.

Merrivale held up his hand and laughed, cutting off the stream of questions.

'Lady Catherine's fame lives on at court, even though her husband has buried her in the country,' he said smoothly, looking sideways at his hostess to see how she blushed at this piece of easy flattery. His voice was lazy, his expression calculating.

'Where shall I start?' he said. 'Your husband is hard at his work, ministering in the Queen's treasury, trying to raise money for the navy and battles with the Spanish. I cannot

51

speak of my own business but I intend to stay here a few days – if you are happy to offer me your hospitality.'

'Of course,' Lady Catherine said quickly. She blushed again, and twisted her hands together.

'Of course,' she repeated, trying to regain her dignity. 'We are a loyal and devoted household, and we shall render any service we can to a man on the Queen's business.'

Merrivale nodded. 'I'm grateful,' he said.

A serving girl bustled into the room with a bowl of hot spiced pork and vegetable broth. Merrivale ate with good appetite as Lady Catherine and Elizabeth watched. Elizabeth supposed he would be considered handsome, with his fine, pale face and grey eyes with long, dark lashes. He had a narrow moustache and a small, pointed beard. And he dressed well, in a burgundy velvet jacket, trimmed with black fur and fastened with a dozen tiny pearl buttons. His stockings had the sheen of silk, and his long boots, drying by the fire, were finely fashioned from soft red leather. His pearl earring shone. But Elizabeth didn't like him, for all his pricey clothes and the effort he obviously lavished on his appearance. There was something about the colour of his skin that made her think of the belly of a dead fish. And his eyes were like stones, flat and closed, as though he had trained himself to hide his thoughts – though this was a talent, right now, that she wished she possessed as well.

When he had eaten, Merrivale satisfied Lady Catherine's thirst for court gossip. He told her who was in and out of favour, which of the Queen's ladies-in-waiting had married, and to whom. He told her about the theatres and concerts, the entertainments laid on for the foreign ambassadors at the

52

court. Lady Catherine drank it up, asking for details, wanting to hear about the fortunes of the friends she had left behind. Finally Merrivale shook his head and laughed. He was tired, he said. He would speak with his servant and check the horses, then he would take a rest. When he left, Lady Catherine was silent for a few moments, still absorbing all the news, spellbound by their fashionable court guest. Outside, the evening was approaching. Elizabeth was bored and tired, wanting to go home and get away.

'Elizabeth,' Lady Catherine said, remembering her presence. 'Isn't he a wonderful young man? Isn't it exciting to have a visitor?'

'Yes, my lady,' she said. 'May I go home now? It's getting late, and I don't want to walk in the dark.'

Lady Catherine frowned and bit her lip, lost in thought.

'I would like you to stay here tonight,' she said. 'I shall send a message with one of the men to your mother. We have a special guest and I would like you to attend me. I need a lady-in-waiting.'

Elizabeth paled. 'Please,' she said. 'My mother needs me. I want to go home.'

Lady Catherine sat up straight. Her face stiffened. 'For one night, Elizabeth. I'm sure your mother doesn't need you as much as I do. You will do as I say.'

Elizabeth swallowed. She felt numb. What could she do? She was helpless. The lady did so much for her, and was her superior. She was not to be gainsaid. Elizabeth thought of her cold, quiet home, her mother and sister sitting by the fire, with the priest who trusted them to hide and guard him. She wanted to be with them. And what about Isabella, out in the wood? Elizabeth clenched her teeth together, trying to hold back the tears that pricked her eyes. She shouldn't cry. She looked away from her mistress, to hide her feelings, but she needn't have worried. Lady Catherine wasn't paying any attention. Her head was full of thoughts about the evening meal, and how they might entertain their visitor.

That night Elizabeth slept on a straw mattress with the cook, in a room off the kitchen. She slept badly, disturbed by the cook's snores and her stink of sweat and spiced meat. Elizabeth's mind would not be still, thinking about Isabella and wondering if the wild girl had already run away. She obsessed about Merrivale, convinced he had come in pursuit of the priest, that already he knew where Thomas Montford was hiding, and that he was trying to trick her and trap her too. And she ached to be in her familiar home, with her mother, to be lying beside her little sister instead of the rank, farting cook who scratched and dribbled in her sleep.

The cook got up before dawn to shout at the girl who laid the fires and to supervise the making of breakfast. Her absence from the bed was a huge relief. For a while Elizabeth lay alone, as the rain beat against the window. Eventually the sound lulled her off to sleep, until the commotion in the kitchen woke her, the men calling for their food, cursing at the weather.

As the day went on she realised why Lady Catherine was so eager for her to stay at the house. It would not be proper for the married lady to spend time alone with Master Merrivale, but the constant presence of a lady-in-waiting made everything respectable and proper. Elizabeth helped her mistress dress and tied up her hair. Merrivale seemed in no particular hurry to get on with whatever important business he had to attend to, and put off by rain, he sat by the fire in the long hall with Lady Catherine and they played cards together. Elizabeth sat to one side on her stool, a piece of embroidery in her hands. They talked about the court again, and discussed people Elizabeth didn't know. Merrivale told Lady Catherine to call him Kit. It was tedious, to attend them. Lady Catherine, whom she liked so much, began to irritate with her bursts of girlish laughter. Thoughts of Isabella went round and round in Elizabeth's head, as well as worries about the danger her family faced – was Merrivale looking for the priest? The suspense was unbearable, the not knowing.

In the afternoon, when the rain finally stopped, they walked outside and Lady Catherine showed Merrivale the gardens and grounds. The sky was bright and blustery, with rags of cloud and intervals of vivid blue sky. Lady Catherine was proud of her estate, acquainting her guest with the stables, and the dozen satin-coated horses bedded in deep straw, and then the kitchen gardens, where a lad and an old man hacked at the heavy soil among ranks of cabbages and ribby turnip tops. They walked in the orchards and among the ranks of medicinal herbs, dying back now in the cold weather. Lady Catherine explained how the estate included so many farms and tenants, how many thousands of acres.

'Of course all of this belonged to the abbey before the Reformation,' Merrivale said. He didn't look at Elizabeth, who was trailing after them, but Elizabeth couldn't help but think the statement was dropped into the conversation for her sake. She shivered in the breeze, pulling her shawl closer around her shoulders.

'Yes,' Lady Catherine answered. 'The abbey was very powerful. Its lands stretched to Cornwall. Of course it had grown corrupt. The monks had forsaken their vows and taken wives. The abbey's wealth was used to buy power.'

'But the abbey's great library was destroyed,' Merrivale said. 'That was a dreadful thing. Five hundred years of learning was lost.'

Lady Catherine nodded. 'They say for years the town was awash with books and manuscripts from the abbey library. People used them to line their boots, and light fires and keep out the draughts from their homes.'

Elizabeth shuddered, to think of it, the scale of the destruction. Even now the last remnants of the library could be found, slips of illuminated parchment squeezed in the gaps of window frames, or lining the thatch of the poorer houses on the town slopes. So much had been lost. She sighed. Her hands were cold. And somewhere out in the forest perhaps Isabella was waiting at the shrine.

Merrivale and Lady Catherine slowed to a halt at the end of the orchard. In the sunlight the lady looked older. The bright light picked out the stitched skin around her eyes and her lips were pale with cold. Elizabeth saw Lady Catherine's hands were shaking. Lady Catherine touched her face again, a nervous gesture. She looked at Merrivale, colouring as she spoke.

'What do you really know about me, Kit?' she said. 'What do they say at court?'

'Your portrait of the Queen is greatly admired. People still marvel that a woman should be so accomplished, and with such powers of expression.'

'My father was a painter,' she said, her voice trembling. 'We were not a rich family and I was his student. That is the reason I took up such unusual employment. And it turned out I had some natural talent. But I am married now – a marriage to a lord. It was a remarkable marriage for an artisan's daughter.' She swallowed, and touched her face again, very quickly.

'I have no children. At court they say I'm barren,' she said. 'They think my husband's long absences stem from his disenchantment with me.'

'No, everyone knows he is devoted to you,' Kit protested.

Elizabeth looked away, across the fields, embarrassed by the intimacy of the conversation, surprised that Lady Catherine should lay herself open to this stranger.

Far away, beyond the garden walls, a boy in a ragged coat stood in a field of cold, chalky soil and chased away crows that came to peck at the seed. Elizabeth shivered. Even she had not realised how lonely Lady Catherine was, living in the manor. Even with the great herd of servants, the remarkable gowns, and the powerful husband at the court of the Queen.

Elizabeth was ordered to stay for a second night. Her worries about Isabella dulled. There was nothing she could do now. The manor was in a state of excitement. To celebrate their court guest, the entire household would dine together at the table in the hall. Musicians were summoned from the town, an elderly man and his son, playing the lute and dulcimer. In her husband's absence Lady Catherine sat at the head of the table, Elizabeth tucked in close to her right and Merrivale to her left. The lord's men sat about them, then

57

further down the servants in their varying ranks. They dined well, all of them. Thick slices of bread served as trenchers to soak up the spiced gravy of roasted, sugared meats and stewed vegetables. Afterwards, they ate fruit puddings and cheese. The servants drank small beer, but the lady and her husband's men drank pitchers of red wine. Lady Catherine sipped discreetly, the men were less judicious. Their voices grew louder. Tallow candles burned on the table, filling the room with warm, yellow light and a thick, meaty smoke. Elizabeth's eyes watered and she was drowsy with so much food, and the weariness of two broken nights. The men quizzed Merrivale about the goings-on at court, where their fellows waited on Lord Melibourne. Elizabeth was too tired to pay much attention, until Merrivale began to talk about plots by members of the Roman Catholic seminary in Douai.

'They are sending priests over to England,' Merrivale said. 'This is nothing to do with matters of faith. These men have one aim. They are heretics who wish to remove Elizabeth from the throne and replace her with a Catholic monarch.'

The room was thick with smoke and noise, but Merrivale's words were distinct to Elizabeth, as though he had spoken just to her. He was addressing Lady Catherine, but the other men turned from their boasting and jeering to listen as well. Elizabeth stared at the platter before her, the remains of her meal. She forced herself to breathe.

'These men are not just Catholic troublemakers. They are trained to foment revolution.' Merrivale spoke with great seriousness now. The other men, red in the face from drink, turned to each other and murmured. The table, a pool of yellow candlelight in the dark space of the room, swam in front of her eyes. As the men whispered one to another, light and shadows slid over their faces, alternately revealing and hiding eyes, noses, mouths moist with wine and words. They looked like demons, leering and grimacing. Elizabeth's heart thundered. She felt faint, hot and cold at once. She sat back on the long wooden bench, wishing the shadows would swallow her up entirely. She tried not to think of the priest in her own house, of her brother caught up in plots, and her father far away in Italy, trying to rebuild the family's fortune. She pressed her hands into her lap.

'Is there evidence of this?' Lady Catherine asked.

One of the men harrumphed. Merrivale nodded. 'Walsingham's spies have uncovered them, intercepted letters. They've caught a number of the priests.'

'And they have confessed?'

'Walsingham is persuasive,' Merrivale said. Lady Catherine shuddered, and the men too. Tales of the Queen's spymaster and torturer had spread across the country. Elizabeth felt sick, thinking of her brother and the man hidden in her house. Had the captured priests told Walsingham about Thomas Montford? That was why the priest had fled from Oxford to Maumesbury, maybe. He needed somewhere to hide now his cover had blown away. How dangerous it was.

The meal she had eaten lay like a great weight in her stomach. Elizabeth picked up her cup, but her hands were shaking and she couldn't swallow.

The men, drunk and keen to prove their bravado, began to speculate about methods of torture and the spectacle of a heretic's execution they had witnessed on a trip to Tyburn in London, when they had attended their lord at court. Elizabeth tried to block out the sound of their voices, the images their words created in her mind. She pressed her nails hard into the palms of her hand, trying to distract herself with pain. Her stomach heaved – she would be sick. The room was so hot now – she could hardly breathe. Then, the blood seemed to fall from her head. The hall, the men, the voices, were all snuffed out. Elizabeth fainted.

For one long, pure moment everything was calm and dark. Her terrors dropped away. All was perfectly, delightfully still. Then her eyes flicked open. Half a dozen dark faces stared down at her.

Where was she? What had happened? Then she recognised Lady Catherine, who fussed with water to splash on Elizabeth's face. Behind her, Kit Merrivale was also on his feet. He looked down at Elizabeth on the floor, with his eyes like stones. He smiled.

Isabella crept on her hands and knees to the doorway and stared out at the night. It was the end of the second day of waiting for Elizabeth. The wind whipped up the tops of the trees, but the sky was clear, stars glittering, and the warped hoop of a moon high above the forest. Isabella sniffed the air, rich with the scent of old leaves and fresh earth. It was safe in the forest. She had places to hide. It was best to stay here, where people couldn't find her, or be afraid of her. Best to linger among the other creatures of the forest, the deer who let her move among them, the fierce wild pigs, the bears and wolves. But Isabella rubbed her face, blinking away tears. It was not good. No matter how often she thought it through, and however safe she might be in the forest, she didn't want to be on her own any longer.

When she lived with the crow people, they had provided company of a sort but they were not friends, not like Elizabeth. She wasn't one of them. And her brother John, who had only been a toddler when they were taken to the shadow land, was taken away from her and became more and more like the crow people himself.

The hermit, Jerome, had been a good friend to her, when she had visited the ordinary world some time ago, but he was long gone. Only his writings remained, tucked behind the brick in the fireplace. Time was different for the crow people. A night with the faeries might be a year in the forest. The stories were true, that a man might wander into the shadow land, and return to find everyone he knew in the ordinary world had died. Or else he might leave his wits behind, returning as a mad man. In this world she was alone and vulnerable but Isabella hungered to be with people like herself, for talk and a warm fire. She had to find Elizabeth. She had to take the chance.

Isabella stepped out of the cell. The moonlight striped her face. She shivered, though she didn't feel cold. The town lay to the north. It would be easy to find the way. Elizabeth's tracks still disturbed the forest litter, and anyway, towns were inevitably obvious to the eye, as well as the nose and ear. Like an animal, she could see well enough in the dark, so she set off at once through the trees, until she reached the muddy track.

All was quiet. It was too dark for people to be about, but occasionally men went hunting in the wood at night, poaching the deer. Isabella could not afford to be careless. She emerged from the lair of the wood, stooped over, turning her face upwards to sniff the air. Her sheaf of matted hair lay heavily on her back, like a wolf's pelt. All she could hear was the drip of moisture from the trees to the soft, decaying fabric of the forest floor.

Keeping close to the tree line, she crept along the muddy track through the trees, to the crossroads. This was the critical point for Isabella. Beyond the fields the town rose blackly on the little hill, houses heaped up the sides and over the top in a swarm, and above them the broken walls of the old abbey. Numerous ribbons of smoke twined from the mass of houses.

The town had grown since Isabella's last visit. The clutter of buildings had entirely covered the green hill now like some kind of disease, but the abbey was greatly diminished. Isabella frowned, shifting her weight from one foot to the other, trying to match up the new town with the memory she still had of a Maumesbury past. She would have to leave the forest behind and pass along the highway through the fields.

Isabella lingered at the crossroads, reluctant to leave the trees behind and commit herself to the open spaces of the fields and the dangers of the town. The forest was familiar, riddled with hiding places. She switched from one foot to the other again, trying to work up her courage. But what choice did she have? She could return to the forest on her own, or she could try to find Elizabeth.

Isabella took one tentative step forward, and then another. The wind rose, a sound like a sigh in the trees. The moonlight was very bright and cold, casting grey shadows behind the hedges. In a little field half a dozen cows were dozing. They stirred as she passed, tossing their heads, shifting hooves on the muddy turf.

Creeping along the roadway, she felt very small. After so long in the closed-in forest, the vast sky threatened to swallow her up. Like a little beetle, she tried to hide in the shadows of the hedges.

She approached the town. A stone bridge humped over the river at the town's feet, and the cobbled street rose from the bridge into the houses. Where to go now? So many houses. Where did Elizabeth live? How would she find her? Isabella bit her lip. How much more chilly it seemed among the houses. And many smells – damp stone, cooked food, the open sewers full of excrement, all overlaid with the ever-present smell of woodsmoke from the fires keeping out the November cold.

She crossed the bridge. At the bottom of the hill were the poorer houses, many of them shacks of stick and thatch. Further up, the houses were more substantial, rough stone or wattle and daub. The grandest houses of all stood on the top of the hill in the centre of the town.

Isabella came to the marketplace, staring at the warm yellow light burning in the glass windows of the merchants' houses. Would she find Elizabeth here? She heard footsteps – and spun round. On the other side of the marketplace, three dark figures were walking from an alehouse. Men, by the tone of their voices. One of them laughed. Isabella held her breath but they didn't see her. She crept up to one of the grand houses, and pressed her face to the window.

63

A scene opened before her. A fire burning in a wide hearth, a family sitting together. A tapestry hung on the wall, a blur of blue and red to Isabella beyond the thick glass. It seemed a very happy scene to her, alone in the cold and staring in. She scanned the faces and couldn't see Elizabeth. This was not the place.

Isabella slipped along a little alley between this first house and its neighbour. The back door of the next house was open and Isabella caught a glimpse of a kitchen. The servant woman had stepped out to throw rubbish into a cesspit at the end of the yard. The woman huffed and puffed, grumbling to herself. Isabella tried to peer inside. Dared she speak to the servant? Could she ask where Elizabeth lived? Isabella touched her green face and the heavy rug of her hair. She would be chased away, or worse. The servant bent over, tipping out the contents of her bucket. Then she straightened up, still grumbling, and headed back to the house. Isabella took a deep breath.

'Excuse me,' she called out. 'Could you tell me where I might find the home of the Dyer family?'

The woman halted. She turned her head, looking for the source of the question.

'Who's there?' she said, suspicious. 'I can't see you. Who's there?'

Isabella stuck her head above the wooden fence, so the woman could see her face. The woman, illuminated by a splash of warm light from the kitchen, stared at the girl.

'Who are you?' she said. 'What are you doing out at this time?'

'I'm looking for my friend Elizabeth Dyer,' Isabella said. 'It's very late and I need to find her.'

The woman screwed up her eyes and stepped closer, trying to make out who this visitor might be. But Isabella drew back into the shadows.

'The Dyers,' the woman said. 'Who are you?'

'Isabella Leland,' she said.

The woman stepped forward again, peering into the darkness, intrigued by the girl's voice and unable to make out who she was.

'Stand forward,' she said. 'Let me see you.' Inside the house someone called out. The servant sighed.

'Silver Street,' she said. 'The big house, with the red glass in the window. The Dyers,' she repeated with a sniff. 'Godless, Catholic folk. Take yourself over there.'

Isabella smiled to herself. The woman closed the door, cutting off the dusting of light. She remembered Silver Street very well. She skipped back along the alley and into the marketplace.

'Hey,' said a voice. 'Hey!'

A lantern was held aloft, and suddenly men were all around her. She panicked, trying to break away, and tripped over someone's rough-clothed leg. Voices started up, a shout of alarm.

'Who's that?' said one. 'Quick, catch it. Don't let it get away.'

Isabella struggled on the ground, trying to stand up, but the cobbles were slippery and the men leaned over her, trying to grab. Their beery breath puffed warmly into the night air,

65

and the sharp stink of their unwashed bodies. A hand seized her upper arm and Isabella turned to bite. The hand was swiftly withdrawn.

'Little beast,' the man cursed. 'Get your stick, Will. Whack it!'

A stick came down, as Isabella wriggled on the ground, a painful blow on the shoulder. She cried out.

'Steady on, it's a girl,' said another voice. 'Don't hurt her.'

'She bit me! Sorry sort of a girl.'

The stick was withdrawn, but the men were standing all around her, six or seven of them, in a tight circle. Someone raised the lantern over her head, and as the light picked out her face and features, the voices died away. They stared, the men who had spent their evening keeping out the cold with ale.

'What is it?' A boy peered at Isabella. She looked from one face to another, looking for a way out. She jumped at the boy, trying to push him back, but one of the bigger men grabbed her and wouldn't let go.

They couldn't take their eyes off her.

'Look at the colour of her,' one murmured. 'Come out of the forest, ain't it? Something unnatural.'

'What shall we do?'

Isabella stood up straight. Her heart was hammering. She had to think. How would she get away now? She took a deep breath, forced out the words.

'My name is Isabella Leland,' she said. 'I have come to see my friend Elizabeth Dyer.'

They looked at one another, then back at the green girl.

'She speaks funny,' one said.

'The Dyers. Heretic people,' said his neighbour.

'Let me go,' Isabella said. 'Let me pass.'

But no-one moved. She was almost in tears now, choked with fear and frustration.

'Shall we take her to the priest?'

'Too late. Lock her up, somewhere safe, till the morning. Then we'll take her to the priest. He'll know what to do.'

They seized her, a man to either side, pinching her bare arms with their hard, strong fingers. It was hard to tell them apart, one from another, this succession of lined, masculine faces with their hats pulled low. They disputed where the best place to keep her might be, then dragged her away from the marketplace, up a narrow lane, where one of the men owned a cooper's workshop.

'In the storeroom at the back,' he said. 'I can bolt the door.' She was thrown in without ceremony and heard the bolt drawn. It was a tiny, airless place with broken barrels and slices of wood heaped haphazardly. Outside, she heard the men's voices as they drew lots for who should keep guard during the night. The discussion went on a long time. Finally there were goodnights and a departure. Two men were left behind.

Isabella curled up among the barrels and hugged her legs. Would Elizabeth come to her rescue? No, Elizabeth had gone. She was utterly at the mercy of her captors, and men could be unspeakably cruel. Behind a locked, barred door in her mind, the memory of her mother's terrible fate rattled and called for attention. But Isabella pushed the memory away, as always. She wouldn't go there. Not now, as she waited for daylight, and judgement.

Faery

Isabella was too afraid to sleep. Curled among the broken barrels and splinters of wood, she shivered. Isabella strained her ears to hear the men the other side of the bolted door. She could make out their murmurs, but not what they said. At last they fell asleep, so she hoped, and Isabella began to look for a way out. She pressed against the door, looking for a weakness in the wood. She scraped at the walls and even poked at the roof space. But the old, muddy thatch was solid and the door refused to budge. So she closed her eyes and thought of the crow people, sending a wish for their help. But the town was a cold place, with its churches and houses, far away from the woods and springs where the crow people moved from realm to realm.

On her hands and knees, Isabella walked round and round the tiny space, like an animal in a cage. Charged with fear, her body ached for action – to fight or run – and frustrated, she turned and turned again within the storeroom, till her mind went blank and empty.

How long the hours of darkness were. From time to time Isabella tried to sleep, but whenever she tried she just felt more awake, and more afraid, so she shuffled and turned and paced within the confines of her little prison till her body was so tired it hurt.

Just before daybreak the town began to stir all around her. Isabella could hear horses shifting and stamping their feet in stalls nearby. A cockerel crowed from far away, then another in the middle of the town, perhaps from someone's backyard. A dog barked. The first light leaked into the cooper's workshop and beneath the Isabella's bolted door. Outside in the street she heard the tread of boots, the sound of voices.

Then, closer to hand, she heard her guards begin to wake and stir. Their voices were hard and loud and they smelled, with their sleepy, sweaty bodies and the stale beer on their breath. And they sounded nervous, wondering perhaps, sober and in the clear light of day, what they had caught the night before.

'Shall we have a look?' one said. 'Make sure it's still there?'

A moment's hesitation, and murmuring.

The bolt drew back slowly. Isabella stood up straight. The door opened a few inches, and a slice of a face became visible in the gap. A brown eye, a bearded cheek. The eye blinked and the door closed again quickly.

'No doubt about it,' the man said, to his companion. 'Green as moss. A goblin girl, from the forest.'

Then more waiting. Isabella was thirsty now, and she needed to pee. Her head ached. At last, she heard other men arrive, though she couldn't work out from the voices how many there were. They sounded excited, shouting to be heard, one over the other.

'Fetch the priest,' one said. 'Bring him here to see her.

That's the safest, in case she escapes. We don't want everyone else to know, coming here to take a peek.'

More arguments, and finally one of them left again to fetch the priest. While they waited, the men broke bread to share amongst themselves and swigged from a bottle of beer. The scent of the bread leaked into the storeroom, making Isabella's mouth water. She pressed her hands together, and gnawed her fingers.

At last the priest arrived. Isabella heard him from some way off, grumbling in a loud voice along the street. Evidently the men had got him out of bed. He had hurried his breakfast, and obviously didn't believe what they had to tell him. The workshop door swung open, the men's voices died away when the priest stepped in.

'Come along,' she heard the priest say briskly. 'Let's see what you have. Wasting my time like this. Your creature had better be good.'

The men replied in lowered voices, deferring to the priest as though they were his children. He had great authority in their lives.

Isabella, helpless, shrank to the back of the cooper's store cupboard, till staves of wood pressed into her back. The bolt drew back once more and the door swung wide open. Daylight flooded the dim cupboard, and Isabella covered her face with her hands. She heard the priest gasp. Slowly she peered through her fingers, still shrinking to the back of the store.

The scene revealed itself – the stout priest in a dark robe, surrounded by the other men, squeezed close together to catch a glimpse, these dozen faces all turned towards her. The priest crossed himself, and crossed himself again. They were silent for a few moments, all of them, as though even the men who had caught her in the marketplace couldn't quite believe their eyes either.

The priest swallowed. Shaken out of his composure, he now had to pull himself together.

'Can she speak?' he asked abruptly.

'She spoke last night. Said she had a name.'

The priest leaned towards her and held out a hand.

'Good day,' he said gently. 'What's your name?'

Isabella shook her head, and the long rug of draggled hair fell over her shoulders. She peered up at the priest, through her fringe.

'Tell me who you are,' the priest said. 'Come along now.'

Isabella didn't know what to do. There had been priests before, and they had not been kind. However, Jerome, the hermit in the old cell by the well, had fed her and befriended her, and done her a great service. She shook her head, a quick, animal movement, like a dog with a gnat in its ear.

'Speak to me,' the priest coaxed. He turned his head to the men, all gawping at Isabella.

'Has she been given any food?' the priest said. 'Anything to drink?'

The men looked at one another, each expecting the other to make a reply and take the blame.

'No, no,' one said. Another ran off quickly to pick up the remnants of their breakfast of bread and small beer.

'Give it to me, give it to me,' the priest snapped impatiently. He snatched the crust and held it out to Isabella.

'Are you hungry?' he said. 'It is good bread.'

Isabella reached out her hand to take the crust, and at the final moment the priest drew it away from her.

'Tell me your name,' he said. 'Then you can have the bread.'

Isabella retreated again, shifting her weight from one leg to the other, left to right, right to left. She was trapped now, between anxiety and hunger. She could smell the bread, sweet and warm, and she licked her lips.

'Isabella Leland,' she said. 'My name is Isabella Leland.'

The priest nodded. She stretched out her hand again for the crust but the priest held on to it.

'How long have you been in the forest?' he said.

Isabella stared at him. How long? She had no idea. Time with the crow people didn't count as time in the so-many-Sundays sense. She couldn't answer.

The priest shrugged. He handed over the crust and Isabella crammed it into her mouth.

The priest turned to the men. 'Remarkable,' he said. 'You were right to bring me.'

The men relaxed and nodded, and whispered to one another. A sense of excitement rose.

'What d'you think she is?' one asked the priest. 'A faery girl? Look at the colour of her. A green girl.'

The priest shook his head.

'No,' he said. 'Nothing unnatural. She's been living in the forest.'

'Reared by wolves,' the man suggested.

'Like Romulus and Remus?' the priest responded. 'Then how did she learn to speak? Clearly she's been living on her own for some time. For years, probably. But she is remarkable, for all that, because she has survived.'

'But the colour!' Another man pointed to Isabella's face. He reached out with a grimy hand to touch her cheek, but she drew away, as though his fingers would scald.

'I think the colour would wash away, in time,' the priest mused. He rubbed his own very clean, soft hands together. Another of the men offered Isabella a leather bottle. She took it gingerly. The bottle stank of small beer, ripe and fruity, also of the accumulated sweat from the man's hand. His spittle glittered on the neck. Isabella held the bottle for a moment or two, wondering if her thirst outweighed her sense of revulsion. Slowly she raised the bottle and tipped a drop of the contents into her mouth. It was foul stuff, and although her mouth seemed to soak up the liquid before she had even swallowed, the taste made her cough and gag. The men laughed, to see her reaction to the beer, but the priest frowned and shushed them, with a little gesture of his hand. Isabella clutched the bottle, wanting to be rid of it, looking from one face to another.

'What shall we do with her?' The man took his bottle back, grinning and leering at Isabella.

'We must find her somewhere suitable to stay,' the priest said. 'I'll think about it. Give the girl some milk to drink and more food. Nothing rich, mind. She must be docile. We do not know how she will behave. She looks' – he wrinkled his nose – 'and smells like an animal.' The priest stared at Isabella one last time, drinking her up with his eyes, committing the very sight of her to memory. He nodded, with some satisfaction. Then he turned away. The door was closed and locked.

Now the threat seemed temporarily abated, Isabella relaxed a little. She was so tired, her nerves strung out tight after the long night. Beyond the storeroom door the noise of the men died away. Isabella curled up tight on the floor, closed her eyes. Sleep drowned her, like a deep black well, without the chinks of dreams. When she woke up, minutes or hours later, the door opened and a hand dropped in a rough wooden platter with bread and cheese, and a bowl of milk, still warm. Isabella ate and drank, till her stomach felt tight as a drum. Then she sank again into sleep, swallowed up, exhausted.

She didn't wake up until the door opened again, the bolt making a great noise. Isabella jumped, scrambled to her feet. Yet another visitor?

Lavender perfume billowed into the room, in a cloud. Isabella saw a fine dress, a pair of white hands, and last of all the quaint, oval face with its high forehead, curls of golden hair pinned back under a soft black cap. A gold ring glinted on the woman's gloved finger. Isabella took a deep breath, her heart beating hard. Had the crow people sent her, to set Isabella free?

No, she thought, shaking her head. The lady was beautiful and finely dressed, yes. But she wasn't really like the faeries. Beneath the perfume of lavender, her flesh gave off the familiar sour, mortal stink.

Beside the fine lady, a young man dressed in mud-splashed leather and velvet leered at Isabella. He carried a riding crop in his hand, and wore a pearl in his ear. His dark hair hung

74

to his shoulders. The man stepped forward, as though to grab Isabella, but she scurried back to the wall, evading his gloved grip.

'Leave her!' the woman said. The young man glowered, to be reprimanded, then leaned back on his heels, smirking. Isabella raised her face cautiously, peering at the young man in case he should try to grab her again. But the lady spoke again, more gently now.

'Isabella,' she said. 'They told me that was your name. Isabella Leland. Will you speak to me? My name is Lady Catherine. I want to take you to my house. We have room for you there and can take care of you.'

Isabella trembled. The gentle tone of the lady's voice was appealing but Isabella was suspicious. She couldn't trust anyone. Instinctively, without meaning to do it, she drew back her lips and snarled. The sound was so wolf-like, the lady made a quick, startled sound. The young man stepped forward again, hand raised now, ready to strike. Isabella regarded him directly and snarled again.

'Shall we see if she bites?' the man said.

'No,' Lady Catherine said, gently pushing the man aside. 'You're frightening her, can't you see?' She stretched out her hand to Isabella, the small, white-silk gloved hand reaching for Isabella's rough, green fingers.

'Come along,' Lady Catherine said. 'I shan't hurt you. We can find you somewhere nice to stay.'

Isabella stared at the white hand, now opened to her. She knew she might face the harder fists of the man if she didn't do as she was told. Maybe the chance for escape would come later, and she didn't want to stay in the cooper's storeroom for a minute longer. She took the white hand in her own green one, and squeezed the lady's fingers.

'Come along,' Lady Catherine said. She turned to reveal the crowd gathered in the room, with the priest at the front, nodding graciously. The crowd parted before them, leaving a pathway through the low workshop to the open door. Two saddled horses were tethered outside, and a third was harnessed to a low cart. Lady Catherine led Isabella to the cart and gestured to her to climb up, where hay and sacks were piled. When Isabella was safely on board, the young man helped Lady Catherine onto her horse, where she sat side-saddle, tucking her skirts about her legs to keep them out of the mire of the street.

'Don't be afraid,' Lady Catherine said. 'I shall ride right beside you, Isabella. We'll be home before dark. Be glad! We shall take care of you.'

Beside her, the young man wrinkled his nose, scornful of the kindness Lady Catherine was lavishing on Isabella, a little beast from the forest. Quite a crowd had gathered now, to stand around the cart and the lady on her horse. Apparently word had spread, about the green girl. The men had told their friends and wives. Everyone stared at Isabella, her moss-coloured skin and pelt of hair. One or two of the men dared themselves to touch her, reaching out their hands, but Lady Catherine's man shooed them away. The women whispered to one another behind their hands. Then the carter flicked the reins on his horse's brown rump, and the cart lumbered away, over the muddied, cobble street to the marketplace, down the hill and out of the town.

Both Lady Catherine and her companion kept a close eye

on Isabella, as they travelled. In the distance Isabella saw the wood, dark and enclosed, and she considered jumping from the cart, trying to fly to her old home. She thought she could dodge the man on the horse, though she was afraid of his fists and riding crop. But something stopped her. She simply didn't want to be alone any more. The crow people had left her behind, flying away like the swallows at the end of the summer, dumping her in the forest. It was possible they would come back again, as they had done before. But Isabella wasn't sure she wanted to return to them again, a toy to be picked up and thrown away as it pleased them.

Elizabeth woke fighting for breath. The darkness seemed heavy, as though it were pressing on her chest and limbs as she struggled to move. For a few moments her mind was a blank, she couldn't remember where she was, or why she had to be afraid. She couldn't see anything. Her thoughts whirled. Then something shifted beside her, with a grunt and a tug on the blanket covering them both – and everything fell into place. She was lying beside the cook, in the house of Lady Catherine, and she feared her beloved family was in the greatest danger. She forced herself to take deep breaths, once, twice. This sense of panic, that froze her thoughts and paralysed her body, would not help her face the dangers that beset them. She remembered the priest, Thomas Montford, telling her how he said how-do-you-do to his fears and then put them behind him. But her fear was like a pack of wild dogs, constantly biting and worrying and tugging and gnawing. How could she put them to one side? She took another deep breath, closed her eyes, and tried to pray. She wasn't alone. God was with her, if she opened her heart to him. God's love would take the place of the fear. In her mind she recited the Our Father and the Hail Mary, trying to focus on the words. Then, she went over the events of the previous evening, step by step, trying to assess the danger she faced, and what she could do about it.

When she had revived from the faint with the ring of faces looming over her, Merrivale, golden in the candlelight, had a curious cold smile on his face. Lady Catherine fussed, and had the servants help Elizabeth to the cooler climes of the next room, away from the fire, to recover. Lady Catherine blamed the heat and smoke for Elizabeth's faint, and shooed the others off so Elizabeth could have space and air. Elizabeth was horrified. Had she given herself away? Had Merrivale understood why the conversation had frightened her so much?

When the household retired to bed, Lady Catherine stayed up late with Merrivale. Elizabeth lay down beside the cook, unable to sleep or close her eyes, fearing what Merrivale might say. But she must have slept for a short while, because the next thing she knew Lady Catherine was standing over her with a candle in her hand.

'Wake up,' Lady Catherine said. 'I need you to help me undress, Elizabeth. Come to my chamber.' Lady Catherine looked tired in the candlelight. Her hair had come loose from her cap. Elizabeth hurriedly clambered to her feet, dressed in her white shift, and followed Lady Catherine up the stairs to her chamber. A chilly draught blew along the corridor, nipping at Elizabeth's ankles. The house was silent, except for the sound of Lady Catherine's shoes and

Elizabeth's bare feet. The solitary candle sent long, wavering shadows along the floorboards.

Lady Catherine closed the door behind them, and set the candle down on her little table. She drew the curtains.

'Unbutton the dress,' Lady Catherine said. Elizabeth's fingers fumbled with the buttons and ties. Lady Catherine sighed.

'You will have to stay here, at Spirit Hill,' she said. Elizabeth's clumsy fingers stopped altogether. She swallowed.

'What?' she said faintly.

'Merrivale is a priest hunter,' Lady Catherine said, keeping her voice low. 'Your family has come under suspicion. It is likely your mother will be arrested and questioned. I am very fond of you, Elizabeth. Your wit and company has been a gift for me – stuck out among so many ignorant and insensitive country people. I appreciate you are only a child, and you have been obliged to follow the religious path your family set down for you, and I wish to protect you if I can.

'Kit is a good man, but he has a duty to the Queen and to England, and his dearest wish is to protect her.'

Elizabeth's mouth felt cold. Her lip trembled. 'Why has my family come under suspicion?' she said. Her voice sounded odd. 'What are they supposed to have done?'

'A heretic priest, come from Douai, has fled from Oxford where he celebrated Mass in secret for Catholic students. Several of the students have been arrested and questioned, and their evidence suggests this traitor priest was heading for Maumesbury.'

Elizabeth swallowed. Lady Catherine turned to face her.

'You've been a loyal friend to me,' Lady Catherine said.

'You are so bright and clever and friendly. I have come to love you.' She looked into Elizabeth's face, as though she were searching for something. Elizabeth waited for the inevitable question, for Lady Catherine to ask if she knew the whereabouts of the priest. But Lady Catherine didn't ask. Perhaps, she already knew the answer.

'I don't wish to see you caught up in this,' Lady Catherine said. 'I understand your loyalties to your family and their faith, but I want you to stay here with me, for your own safety.'

Elizabeth was hardly listening. Her mind was a whirl of images, men coming for her mother and sister, the priest being dragged off for torture and execution. She rocked on her feet, afraid she would faint again.

'Elizabeth? Elizabeth, are you listening to me?' Lady Catherine said. 'Kit is an honourable man, and I think' – a smile strayed across her face – 'I have some influence over him. He will listen to me. Stay close to me. Stay at Spirit Hill.'

In the morning, Elizabeth lay beside the hot, smelly cook and racked her brain for an answer. She was forbidden to leave the house, and her family were in danger. What could she do? What? How could she warn them?

She got up at the same time as the cook and dressed in the half-light. In the kitchen the sleepy servants revived the fire, cleared up the dinner of the night before, and prepared a breakfast. The lord's men got up late, nursing headaches. They loafed in the warmth of the kitchen, in their tall, muddy boots. They all had bristly faces and long hair. Their voices were loud. Elizabeth avoided the men as much as possible, paying them as little attention as they paid her, but

80

over the months she had come to know them better. There was a father and son in the company, and one of the men, very gaunt and scarred with smallpox, was often the butt of jokes from the others. Three lean dogs cringed at their feet, or else growled and scrabbled for scraps thrown down. She suspected the men were bored in the long, quiet winter. Doubtless they wished they too were attending the court with their master.

The other servants gave her sidelong glances but nobody spoke to her – except once, to tell her Lady Catherine and Kit Merrivale had gone out early on their horses. So Elizabeth loitered in the kitchen. One of the maids struggled with the fire that filled the room with smoke.

'Can I help?' Elizabeth asked the cook. 'I prepared food at home, for my mother.'

The cook turned to look at her. The woman's arms were red to the elbow, streaked with dark blood. A pearl of moisture hung from her nose, which she wiped with the back of her hand. Now the tip of her nose was smudged with red, and snot mingled with the blood on her hand. The cook sniffed.

'This is kitchen work. Not for you, Dyer. Go and wait for the lady. You're nothing to do with me.'

'Where shall I wait?' Elizabeth said.

But the cook had turned away from her now, and merely shrugged, plunging her arms into a wooden tub of lamb's entrails. The air was perfumed with the hard-iron odour of liver.

Helpless, Elizabeth turned away. She ached to be at home, in a familiar place, where the faces were friendly and she

81

belonged. Never in all her life had she slept away from home for two nights, and it was agonising to know how much danger her mother and sister faced, while she was unable to help them or warn them.

Slowly she made her way to Lady Catherine's empty room, where a little girl, a couple of years younger than Elizabeth, was industriously sweeping the hearth. The maid at the fireplace puffed up clouds of ash as she shovelled the cold remains of the fire into a basket. The maid sat up on her knees and coughed, waving away the dust with her hand. Then she turned and grinned at Elizabeth, her face now white and grey with ash.

'You're the Catholic girl, aren't you?' she said. 'Your name's Elizabeth Dyer.'

Elizabeth nodded.

'Everyone knows who you are,' the girl continued brightly. She put down the brush and basket, and wiped her eyes with her fingertips. 'The lady's keeping you here. She feels sorry for you cos you're a Catholic.' She stared and grinned at Elizabeth, as though she were deciding for herself if Elizabeth merited pity.

Elizabeth said. 'What's your name?'

'Deb Glover,' the girl said. 'Are you really a Catholic? That means you'll go to hell.'

Elizabeth shrugged uneasily. 'Yes, I'm a Catholic,' she said. They didn't speak further because Deb Glover was called away to tend to another fire and Elizabeth was left alone again. She sat at the window, worn out by anxiety, and homesickness. The wild dogs of her fears gnawed again. She tried to put them behind her, to think clearly.

Distantly she registered the sound of hooves. Perhaps it was the lady returning. A few minutes later, she heard doors bang, loud voices, and some kind of dispute in the long hall. One of the dogs was barking. A ripple of excitement flowed through the household. Elizabeth could detect it, even sitting alone in the lady's chamber, the quiver of expectation. At first she was afraid to move. Had something terrible happened?

The door burst open. It was Deb Glover – a huge grin on her face, dying to tell the news to someone – to anyone.

'Come and see,' Deb said. She was out of breath from running up the stairs. 'They've caught a faery. Out in the woods. They've brought it here. It's bright green like a cabbage, with a wolf's coat, and sharp teeth, and wings. It's the strangest thing! They've locked it in the stables so it won't escape, and the men have got sticks – in case it attacks. Come on, come and see.'

Elizabeth stood up. She couldn't breathe. The floor seemed to plunge beneath her feet.

Isabella.

They had captured Isabella. What would they do to her? Had they hurt her? Deb was already off again, running down the stairs. Elizabeth hurried after her, out of the house to the stables. The entire house was agog. The cook came running heavily from the kitchen, wiping her hands on her apron.

'This way,' Deb called, prancing ahead. She was quick and elfin, eyes alight.

Elizabeth shivered in the bitter cold. She folded her arms and trotted after Deb. She looked to the fields. Could she run away now, back to the town, to warn her mother and the priest? Or would that simply confirm their suspicions? How

83

much did Merrivale really know? Was he setting her some kind of test, to see what she would give away? No, there had to be another way to warn them. She had to be secret and circumspect. She turned away from the fields and set off after Deb.

The stables stood behind the house, in a courtyard. They were solid and stone-built, like the manor itself. Inside a long, low building the horses were stabled in stalls separated by wooden panels. The floor was bedded with straw. It seemed the entire household was crowded around the entrance, fighting to get into the doorway. The men were at the front, pushing the others out of the way. Deb hopped up and down at the back, like a little bird, trying in vain to see over shoulders.

'Stop pushing!' Kit Merrivale shouted the order. At the sound of his voice the tight bunch of bodies at the stable doorway began to loosen and back away. Elizabeth wondered why they all deferred to him, even Lord Cecil's men, this young upstart who had only arrived two days before. But it was the men who were allowed to see the faery first, while the lesser servants waited outside. Elizabeth sidled up to Deb, white-faced with cold.

'Please tell me about the faery,' Elizabeth said. Deb drew up straight, stiff with importance to be the custodian of secrets.

'They say it came from the woods,' Deb whispered. 'Some men caught it in the town late last night. I expect it was up to some wickedness. Tying up people's hair, or sucking from the cattle.' Deb made a curious little gesture, bunching her fist and sticking her thumb through her fingers. It only lasted a moment, Deb's instinctive signal of protection against the Evil Eye.

The men took a long time, surveying the faery. Outside, the other servants could hear their voices, the occasional burst of laughter or heated exclamation. Finally the men emerged, shaking their heads, animated and excited. Then the dozen or so servants swarmed in to see the captive creature.

Elizabeth hung back at first. She was afraid to see Isabella. Had they truly beaten her? Was she hurt? And what would Isabella do if she saw Elizabeth? So she crept in behind everyone else.

After the wait in the bitter cold yard, the stables were warm, with the heat of the beasts. In the stalls further up, three horses were restless, disturbed by the presence of so many people. The air was sweet with hay, the scent of long-gone summer preserved in the dried meadow grass. Deb was trying to push her way in, bobbing up and down to get a better view.

'It's true,' she cried, in her high, shrill voice. 'It's true.' She made the little sign again, covertly, and probably without thinking, before making the sign of the cross.

'But it hasn't got wings,' she added, disappointed. 'They said it had wings.'

The others craned to see. Elizabeth crept forward, keeping herself obscured by the cram of other bodies. Then she leaned forward and peeped through a gap in the planks of the stall partition.

She saw Isabella. The wild girl was crouching in the corner, pressed against the stone wall on a fresh mound of straw. A platter with bread and cheese waited on the floor beside her, but this was untouched. Elizabeth could make out the rise and fall of Isabella's body as she breathed. How green she looked. How small too, as though she had shrunk, away from the forest.

'It's a girl,' one of the women said. 'Poor thing. It's only a girl.'

'But look at the colour of her,' another said. 'That's not like any girl I've seen. It isn't natural.'

'Come from under the hills,' one of the older men had piped up. 'A goblin girl. One of the faery people.'

Isabella looked up, her eyes flared, her attention snagged on the man's last words. A murmur rose among the gathering.

'You're right,' the first woman said. 'She knows what you said.'

But Isabella's interest didn't last. The light seemed to fade from her eyes again. She stared straight ahead of her, indifferent to them all.

'Come up here, Elizabeth, come and see.' Deb's voice was loud. Elizabeth shook her head, still trying to hide from Isabella. At the mention of Elizabeth's name, Isabella looked up again.

'Come on,' Deb insisted. 'You can't see properly from there. Don't be afraid! She won't hurt you.'

Elizabeth sighed. She took a deep breath and stood up, revealing herself to the green girl sitting on the pile of straw in the stall.

They stared at each other, one long moment, Elizabeth and Isabella. And in that instant, Elizabeth tried to communicate her apology, her sense of failure, her continued loyalty. I'll come back, she thought. I'll help you escape, Isabella. I want to be your friend.

Did Isabella understand? It was hard to know. She didn't say anything or give any sign that she knew Elizabeth. Instead she turned away again, apparently lost in a dream of far away.

Finally Lady Catherine shook her head, to see everyone gawping, and she shooed them out, like so many chickens – all except Elizabeth.

'What do you think, Elizabeth?' she said, nodding to the green girl. Elizabeth swallowed, not wanting to give anything away, and afraid to be deceiving Lady Catherine about her relationship with Isabella.

'She is a remarkable creature,' Elizabeth said. 'What will happen to her now?'

'I think we should take care of her. She can speak well enough, and told me her name is Isabella. She needs to be cleaned and made respectable again, brought back into Christian company.'

'Do you think she is a goblin, or a boggart, or something from under the hills, like the men said?' Elizabeth asked, careful not to stare at Isabella.

'I don't think so,' she said. 'Perhaps she has simply been living alone in the woods for a long time. She is an uncanny creature, nonetheless. I don't know what to make of her. Perhaps Isabella will tell us, in her own good time.'

At the mention of her name Isabella blinked and shifted on the straw. Something clinked when she moved. A chain – Elizabeth saw – with a clasp about the girl's wrist and fastened to an iron hoop on the wall. She gasped.

'It's for her own good, Elizabeth,' Lady Catherine said. 'For her protection, you understand. She might not realise what is best for her, yet. And if she escaped, she might be misunderstood and badly treated. She will only be chained until we know we can trust her to stay with us.'

Elizabeth nodded, but her heart was heavy. Lady Catherine shivered, and tucked her fur collar more tightly about her neck.

'Isabella will need a blanket,' she said. 'She doesn't shiver though, do you see? I'll fetch one for her. Come along now. It is time for us to eat.'

Raid

In the afternoon Kit Merrivale ordered his servant to saddle his horse and rode off alone, beneath a clear sky. From a window, Lady Catherine and Elizabeth watched him trot up the drive. He turned and waved his hat in farewell. Lady Catherine smiled and lifted her hand in reply. Elizabeth responded with a cool stare. Lady Catherine wouldn't tell her why he had to leave or where he was going, and Elizabeth suspected the worst. He was gathering intelligence, on the trail of the Oxford priest, and this trail would surely lead him to the single Catholic household in the town, her home in Silver Street. Elizabeth shivered and rubbed her arms. Lady Catherine, obviously torn between her affection for Elizabeth and her infatuation with the young gallant from court, patted her lady-in-waiting on the shoulder.

'Don't worry,' she said. 'You're safe. I'm sure everything will be fine.'

These words must have sounded as hollow to Lady Catherine as they did to Elizabeth, because Lady Catherine patted her again, a little harder, and turned away from Elizabeth.

'I'll take a rest,' Lady Catherine said briskly. 'I'll send for you later.'

Elizabeth remained at the window, watching Merrivale disappear down the long, gentle slope of Spirit Hill. In the distance, Maumesbury rose from the bleached, level landscape like a clenched fist.

Downstairs, the servants were busy preparing another lavish evening dinner to impress the London guest. Nobody took any notice of Elizabeth, when she stepped into the room. Despite the rigid pecking order, and the insults freely traded amongst them, the servants were a close family and Elizabeth, a Catholic and an outsider, was not part of it. Even Deb Glover, busy gutting fish, didn't manage a smile. She was sniffing and wiping her eyes, Elizabeth noticed, doubtless from another scolding. Poor Deb was the lowest of low in the female servants' hierarchy. Still Elizabeth envied her, that she had nothing more to worry about than the cook's bad temper. It would be pleasant to belong, to know what was expected and to be safe. Elizabeth edged her way to the back door. The servants stepped aside to let her past. The atmosphere in the kitchen was warm, the women trading gossip and jokes. A brace of pheasants hung from a hook near the door, the dead, stiff wings still glowing with feathers of red and gold. Mud and vegetable peelings mingled in the floor. The stinging perfume of cloves and nutmeg threaded through the pervading atmosphere of pig's blood and smoke.

Elizabeth stepped through the door, into the fresh, chilly November sunshine. Nobody stopped her. She waited a moment just outside, to hear what the servants might say.

There was a moment's silence, then she heard someone mutter: 'I don't like to have her creeping around.'

Someone else responded: 'The lady's favourite. Don't know why she has to take in a papist. Did you see her faint when the talk turned to heretics? It's not right. They side with the Spanish, the Catholics. We'll be overrun. None of us is safe. And we have to put up with a spy in the house.'

'I have to share a bed with her. What do you think about that?'

The servants' venom was a shock. Elizabeth stepped away, not wanting to hear any more. Already she was trembling. Did they hate her so much? She imagined the servants' poisonous feelings pooling in the house, and choking her, and she longed to be home, with her family. Many people in the town were suspicious of them too, but not everyone. And at least she had her loved ones to shore up her morale against the surly comments of the townspeople. Here she was alone. Slowly, she headed for the stables, looked around, to make sure no-one was looking, and unlocked the door.

Isabella sat up straight when Elizabeth stepped inside the stable. For several long moments, neither girl spoke. They just stared at each other. At last Elizabeth swallowed nervously.

'Isabella,' she said. 'It's me. Elizabeth.'

Isabella nodded. 'Yes.'

'They've chained you up.'

Isabella shook her head. 'No, they haven't.' She folded her hand, thumb to little finger, compressing the bones together. The manacle slid off easily. She was limber, like a cat, her joints flexible. Elizabeth stared.

'How can you do that?' she said. 'Why do you stay chained up if you can escape? Who are you, Isabella?'

Isabella gave a shy smile. 'Why didn't you come back? I waited for you in the wood,' she said.

'I couldn't. I tried! I was forced to come here and they wouldn't let me go home, and I was thinking about you and worrying, and now my family is in terrible danger and I can't warn them, and everything is going wrong.' Elizabeth dipped her head, helpless tears flooding her eyes and dripping onto her cheeks. Isabella stepped towards her, and hesitantly held out her green hand. Elizabeth, blinded by tears, didn't see the gesture, so Isabella stretched out her arms. With only the slightest hesitation, Elizabeth stepped into the stall and embraced her. Isabella's bare arms were smooth and warm and Elizabeth was aware how rough and chilly her clothes must feel to Isabella, but they held each other tight, Elizabeth's hot, wet cheek on Isabella's shoulder.

Finally, Elizabeth pulled away, and the two girls sank down onto the straw bedding in the quiet stall. They sat arm to arm, backs pressed against the wooden partition. Nearby the horses tugged at racks of hay. The sound of their munching teeth was soothing. Elizabeth wiped her face on her sleeve.

'When I saw you in the wood, you gave me your food,' Isabella said. 'It is such a long time since anyone has been kind to me. I knew then we would be together again. I never gave up hope, even when you didn't come back. That's why I went to the town. I was looking for you. Was I right? Did I understand properly? Will you be my friend, Elizabeth?' Isabella hesitated then. 'I've never had a friend before,' she said. 'I had my mother and my little brother John, but nobody ever wanted to be my friend.'

'I've never had a friend either,' Elizabeth said. 'My family are Catholics. Nobody wants to associate with me, except for Lady Catherine, and that is a kind of pity. And in any case, I'm her servant.' She looked sideways at Isabella, wondering if Isabella would change her mind about this friendship once she knew about Elizabeth's dangerous faith. But Isabella did not make any obvious response to this revelation. She just looked puzzled.

'What are the others, if they're not Catholic?' she said. 'I thought everyone was a Catholic.'

Elizabeth was agog to think Isabella didn't know about the Church of England. How much of her life had she spent with the beasts in the forest?

But the green girl was obviously thinking about something else, winding herself up to speak.

She took a deep breath. 'Elizabeth,' she said. 'You ask me who I am. Well, I am almost afraid to tell you, because you will either think I am mad or, worse, you will think I am something terrible.'

Elizabeth shook her head, not understanding. 'I will never think you are terrible,' she said. 'I know already you are something strange. The way you move, and look. And taking off the manacle.'

Isabella sighed again, and Elizabeth sensed she was preparing herself for her own revelation.

'Who is King of England? What is the year?' Isabella said.

The question took Elizabeth aback. 'The king?' she said. 'We have no king. England is ruled by Queen Elizabeth,

Isabella.' She looked into the green girl's face. 'Living in the forest, you didn't know this?'

'Listen to me, Elizabeth. Please listen. I used to live in a cottage on the edge of the forest and the king was Henry III. I saw him once. He came to Maumesbury to visit William of Cullerne, the abbot at the monastery, and the year was 1239. Then my mother sent John and I into the shadow land, and gave us to the crow people, and asked them to care for us. From time to time I returned to the ordinary world because I missed it, because I belong here. But it has never been safe to stay long.'

Elizabeth stared at Isabella, her mouth slightly open. She frowned, and without realising what she was doing, moved away from her. She didn't know what to think. Isabella's words slowly sank in.

'Isabella, it is the year of our lord 1586,' she said. Isabella's words buzzed in her head, nothing making any sense. 'Who are the crow people?'

Isabella swallowed. 'They used to have lots of names,' she said. 'Boggarts. Faeries. The Old Ones.'

Elizabeth went cold. 'Faeries?' she said. 'You have lived with the faeries for more than three hundred years? That's what you're saying, isn't it?'

Isabella's face seemed to close up, and Elizabeth realised how cold her voice had become. Confusion and fear wrestled inside her. She wanted to reassure Isabella, but something held her back. Could this be the truth? There were old stories about the forest, and once, about five years back, three women were hanged for practising witchcraft and under torture had confessed to cavorting with demons and spirits in the wood.

The story had become much embellished over time and was often repeated to youngsters, to frighten them into behaving themselves. Elizabeth didn't know how much truth survived in the tale, but the townspeople were credulous and superstitious. Few of them liked to stray alone in the woods.

What did Elizabeth believe? Sitting beside the green girl, who could free herself from an iron manacle, it was easy to believe she possessed an unholy power. For God made man and the heavenly host, but the unclean spirits of the wood drew their magic from another source.

'Devils,' Elizabeth whispered. She turned to Isabella. 'Magic, sorcery – it is the work of the Devil.' Should she tell the priest, for the sake of Isabella's soul? The girl should be confessed and shriven, her sins wiped away. Otherwise she would be damned. Earthly life was brief and full of trouble and suffering – a trial and a preparation for eternal life with God and the angels. But Isabella would tumble into the eternal fire with Satan, to face unending punishment, if she was allied to the powers of evil. Perhaps sensing her thoughts, Isabella turned away from Elizabeth.

'You think I'm evil?' she said. 'Like everyone else thinks you are evil? Do you think I'm something wicked? And doesn't everyone think you're bad too, because you don't believe the same as them. Explain to me why they don't like you.'

Elizabeth gathered her thoughts. Where to start? Slowly she explained about the Reformation, how the Queen's father Henry had torn down Maumesbury Abbey and established the Church of England, how his elder daughter Mary had restored Catholicism for a few brief years, only for Queen Elizabeth to turn the tables once again. She explained the fate of heretics, and the crippling fines the family paid for their refusal to attend church services. It was a long, complicated business and soon Elizabeth realised she had lost Isabella some way through this rambling account.

The green girl shook her head. 'It is very hard to understand.'

Elizabeth wrung her hands together, tugged at her fingers. She longed to tell Isabella about the priest, to ask for her help. But this revelation seemed a step too far. But what Isabella had told her was enough to have her tried and executed for witchcraft – she had placed her life in Elizabeth's hands.

She fretted. After so many years of fear and secrecy Elizabeth couldn't help wondering if this was all a trick. What if Isabella was in league with the priest hunter? Wasn't Thomas Montford a secret too potent to reveal?

'I don't know,' she said. 'I don't know what to think. Nothing makes sense. So why are you green, Isabella? Is this an enchantment?'

'I think the colouring is part of my faery self – and I've spent so long in the shadow land, it has become a part of my earthly body as well.'

'And the way you can move?'

'Yes. And all my senses have become acute. I think if I stayed here in the mortal world a long time, the colour would fade. I would become ordinary again. Maybe we all have a self in the faery land but mostly we aren't aware of it. Except perhaps in those odd moments when everything seems particularly bright, and the world shines, or a shadow makes you shiver for no reason.

'When you pass properly into the shadow land, you leave a part of your earthly body behind – your mortal remains,' Isabella said. 'This might take the form of a handful of bones, or a hank of hair, or a skull or your finger- and toenails. It is this that binds you to the place you belong.'

Elizabeth didn't know what to think. This talk of other selves, of toenails and markers of bone, conjured up horrible images of witchcraft.

Isabella took hold of Elizabeth's hands. 'Look at me,' she said. 'How do I know you're not evil, because you're a Catholic, and all the others are – whatever they are now. They believe you're evil – how do I know if that's true or not?'

Elizabeth stared at Isabella, longing to trust her.

'Look at me, Elizabeth. Do you think I'm wicked? Do you think I'm a devil? In my time everyone was a Catholic, because there was only one Church, but even then I was different from the others because of the shadow land. Don't let your mind be clouded by what other people have told you. Judge me with your heart.'

Elizabeth's eyes filled again. What did she feel about Isabella? She looked into the girl's clear eyes, her bright, vulnerable face. 'I don't think you're evil,' she whispered. 'Of course I don't. God help me, I can feel how good you are. It gives me strength just to talk with you, to hold your hand.'

A smile stole across Isabella's face, and despite her tears, Elizabeth began to smile too.

'Then we are friends,' Isabella said. 'Tell me what's happened, and I can help.'

Elizabeth nodded. She had made her decision. 'And I can help you too,' she said.

They talked for a long time, until the long November evening deepened and the darkness crept over the fields. Elizabeth worried she would be missed in the house when she realised how late it had become. She gave Isabella one final hug, and pressed her faded rosary beads into Isabella's green hand. Then she hurried away.

Isabella watched her through the window, the pale form running across the yard and through a door into the house. She waited another hour or so, and polished off the food she had been given. Then she left the stable herself, heading off into the darkness away from the manor, and along the highway back to the town.

She covered the ground swiftly, running fast and low, her feet barely leaving an impression on the muddy road. The moon was high and bright, casting long shadows. Isabella startled a posse of sheep, in a huddle by a signpost. They jumped to their feet and hurtled away, across a field. Inspired by her purpose, warmed by Elizabeth's offered friendship and the real evidence of her trust, Isabella felt vital and alive, as she ran across the fields. She enjoyed the sensation of blood moving around her limbs, the flood of light from the moon, the moist earth under her bare feet. She was afraid, yes, but for the moment, the fear had transformed itself and she felt exhilarated.

Isabella moved confidently. She knew where to go, and she had no time to lose. Elizabeth had explained where the house could be found, and Isabella, moving like a wolf, could travel more quickly and easily than her friend. She loped over the bridge and up the cobbled hill into the town. She found the house in Silver Street belonging to the Dyer family. She identified the stained-glass panel in the front window.

Shadow-like, slinking, she made her way to the back door and knocked gently. She knew she looked strange, so she kept back, in the darkness, when the door swung open and a face peered out, with a candle.

'Who's there?' The elderly female voice was suspicious.

'Mary?' Isabella said. 'Are you Mary? Don't be afraid. I have a message from Elizabeth. I need to speak to her mother.'

'Who is it?' A second anxious voice, another woman.

Isabella crept forward, so the wavering candlelight fell upon her. The two women gasped, and Mary drew back, crossing herself quickly.

'Elizabeth sent me,' Isabella said. 'Please – please let me in. I need to speak to you.'

Mary shook her head violently.

'Don't listen,' she said. 'It's a trick. The creature wants to be invited into the house. Don't, Mistress. Send it away.'

Isabella's heart sank. She had to convince them.

'Please,' she said. 'For Elizabeth's sake. I'm her friend, you see. She sent me to you. From the manor.'

'Is she in trouble?' Jane said, stepping forward suddenly. 'What's happened to her? Why have they kept her there? What is it?'

'Elizabeth is fine,' Isabella said. She shifted forwards, to the doorway. 'She said to give you this, so you would believe me.' Isabella fumbled for the rosary.

Elizabeth's mother stretched out her hand and took the

wooden beads. She held it on her palm, staring. Then she nodded.

'Come inside,' she said. 'Quickly now.'

Mary shook her head, reluctant to move from the threshold and let the creature in – but she couldn't gainsay the mistress and Isabella passed her by, creeping into the kitchen at the back of the house. Mary shut and locked the door behind her.

In the light from the fire burning brightly in the hearth, Isabella knew the women would see her more clearly. She hid her long-nailed hands behind her back, pushed the mat of hair back over her shoulders. Jane Dyer and the housekeeper stared, but Isabella ploughed on. She didn't have much time.

'Elizabeth said to warn you the priest is in danger. Some of the others, from Oxford, have been captured and examined. She said Walsingham had taken them to the tower and a plot had been discovered. She is afraid they will have confessed under torture and may have named your priest, and your son. And now there is a priest hunter staying at the manor. A man called Kit Merrivale.' Isabella took a deep breath. Had she remembered everything correctly? Would they believe her, or suspect another trap? Even the rosary could be a trick – for Elizabeth might have been arrested and searched. The circle of suspicion and secrecy was dizzying.

Jane raised her hand to her mouth, her eyes bright with tears. Mary murmured something Isabella could not make out.

'What shall we do?' Jane said at last, her hand still pressed to her lips. 'Oh,' she moaned. 'Oh, Robert. What shall we do? What shall we do?'

The housekeeper stepped forward, and placed her hand on her mistress's arm. In the face of Jane's indecision, it was Mary who straightened up and made the choice.

'I'll get the priest, to speak to her.' She gestured towards Isabella. Jane nodded, tears on her cheeks. Isabella swallowed hard. Elizabeth's mother didn't seem able to manage. Perhaps the priest would know what to do, and would help Mistress Dyer to cope. The woman moaned again, her cheeks glittering.

'My Robert,' she whispered. 'If only Edward were home. If only I were not on my own, always on my own. And they've taken Elizabeth from me too.'

Isabella waited respectfully. Mary hurried out of the kitchen and in a moment she fetched the priest. He was well built and strong, his face bearded. He looked at Isabella directly, his eyes quick and clever. And passionate too. A man, she sensed, who would not crumble like Mistress Dyer, who would be strong in the face of a challenge.

'What are you?' the priest asked.

'My name is Isabella Leland, and I'm Elizabeth's friend. She sent me with information she heard at the manor. There is a man, Kit Merrivale, and she thinks he is hunting for you, and knows where to find you. She asked me to warn you that some of your friends have been captured and tormented, and she is afraid you will be uncovered too. And her brother, who helped you, and the rest of the family.'

Mistress Dyer moaned again. The priest stretched out a hand, not quite patting her, his mind intent on the news Isabella had given him. His eyes gave a curious blaze, an emotional light rising up in his face. Grief or anger, she couldn't tell which. The priest glanced at Isabella. And they stared, making an assessment of each other.

'What manner of creature are you?' he said.

Mary interrupted: 'Sir, she must be the goblin. All day the town has buzzed with the news of it.'

'The buzzing of the town is not my concern,' he said. The priest's voice was firm but Isabella could detect no malice. The man was focused, wanting to get to the pith of the matter.

So quickly she told him her name, and that she had been living in the woods. The priest stepped forward and seized her hand. He examined the green skin, the horny nails springing from her fingertips. He peered into her face, and her hair. Then he dropped her hand again, and stepped away.

'She's a girl, Mary. Neither more nor less,' he said. 'She needs to be washed and trimmed, that's all. Pay no attention to the superstitious fools in the town. Now' – he turned again to Isabella – 'tell me everything you know. How did you meet Elizabeth? What exactly did she tell you, and what do you know of Kit Merrivale?'

Half an hour later, Isabella slid from the back door of the Dyers' house and began the journey back through the town. She had to get back to the manor before anyone discovered she was missing. But she was tired now.

The town was quiet. Although light flickered in the windows of the grander houses, most of the little cottages and the poorer dwellings were dark and quiet, the eternal ribbons of smoke twining from a hundred fireplaces. A cat tiptoed through along the footway, soundless, and frost crystallised on the rooftops. The stars wheeled over her head. Isabella

102

reached the bridge over the river at the town's feet, where the water jostled and chattered over the stones, tumbling to the mill wheel further downstream. She rested for a moment, staring at the black water, the reflection of the stars a stew in the tumult of the river. How loud it was, in the quiet night. A bird flew overhead, a little owl, a dead shrew pinched in its beak. Isabella lifted her head. She could hear something else, too.

She strained to hear, above the noise of the river. What was the distant sound? She turned her head, trying to catch it. Louder now, she identified the dull vibration of hooves on the wet, heavy ground. Horsemen, travelling fast for the time of night. A minute passed. Another. The sounds grew more distinct.

As the horsemen drew nearer she heard the clink of bits, the words cast between the men, the laboured breathing of the horses.

Then, all of a sudden, they were upon her, the horses clattering over the bridge. Six, eight, ten of them. She pressed herself against the wall, to escape the trampling hooves. One of the horses shied to see her, the rider lurching in his saddle and cursing, whipping up the reins. Iron shoes bit the cobbles, throwing up sparks. Sweat lathered the necks of the animals, their sides sore from the prick of spurs. The men were cloaked and booted, hats pressed over their brows. The moonlight picked out the silver blade of a long dagger lying across a rider's thigh. They hurtled up the street, pell-mell, horses slipping and skittering over the muddy cobbles.

Isabella took a quick breath. Her heart contracted, then her pulse beat fast and clear, right into the chambers of her brain. Frozen to the spot, in the shadow of the bridge wall, she feared the worse. Who else would be riding, in the depths of the night?

Weariness fell away. Isabella turned back to the town and ran up the hill, after the riders, to Silver Street. She peered around the corner.

The horses milled in the narrow street in front of the Dyers' house. Several of the men had dismounted, and the leader banged on the door with his fist. Isabella caught a glimpse of his face. It was Kit Merrivale.

The hammering on the door was loud enough to wake the town. Nearby, a dog began to bark, and a second. Isabella waited at the end of the street to see what would happen. She was torn by indecision. Should she go to the back of the Dyers' house and try to help? Too late, three of the men now jumped from their horses and strode along the alley to block the escape route. Merrivale banged again on the door.

'Open up,' he called out, in a low, hoarse voice. 'Open up in the name of Her Majesty Queen Elizabeth. Open the door, or I shall break it down.'

Across the town now, dogs were barking. Isabella sensed the awakening of the nearby townspeople in their homes, the eyes peeping through windows, or the cracks of doors opened just wide enough for a pair of eyes to see out. But no-one came into the street. They were all too afraid. And perhaps some were not surprised by the night raid, pleased the Roman Catholics were getting their comeuppance at last, these traitors living among them.

At last, many long moments later, Elizabeth's mother opened the door. Her face was white and grey, in the light of the candle in her hand, her hair disarrayed as though she had just climbed out of bed. Isabella was afraid Mistress Dyer would give way to her feelings again, dissolving into tears, but the woman's face was hard as stone.

'What do you want?' she asked, her voice clear and cold. Merrivale didn't wait for an answer. He pushed Mistress Dyer out of his path and strode into the house. He shouted out to the men who had entered the house at the back. Others trooped inside. Three riders remained in the street, holding the reins of the horses. One rider cursed the cold weather.

The little herd of restless horses twisted and stamped their hooves, the steam from their hot bodies and the clouds of their breath creating a miasma all about them in the darkness. Bits clinked. Isabella crept nearer. She had to see more. Dodging the hooves, she scuttled behind the horses and pressed herself into a doorway, so she could peer across the street into the wide front window.

It was hard to make out exactly what was happening. The house was a dark box where the brilliant red and gold light of the men's torches flared and died away as the men walked back and forth through the room. Merrivale stood beside Mistress Dyer. Mary cowered at her side, gripping her shawl with her hand like a child. The other men called out to each other in loud voices. Presumably they were searching the house. And they would find him of course, the priest Thomas Montford. Isabella didn't want them to find him – for Elizabeth's sake, and because she liked him too. She wished for his safety. She prayed for it, for a miracle. But how could he escape? There hadn't been time to get away. Isabella screwed up her eyes, trying to see what was happening inside. Someone was coming downstairs now. One of the riders was carrying a child in his arms. It was Elizabeth's little sister, surely, sleepy in her white nightgown. Yes, the man was holding Esther, taken from the warmth of her bed.

The little girl stretched out her arms to her mother but the man kept a hold, restraining her. Then he passed her to Merrivale who jogged her up and down, a cruel smile on his face. Mistress Dyer's impassive expression faltered. Her mouth moved, but through the glass and the distance of the street, Isabella couldn't hear what she said. The little girl was crying now, her hair spilling from her white cap over her shoulders. Isabella shivered. Would Merrivale hurt her? The spectacle filled her with cold horror – the man holding the little girl, the mother powerless to stop him. He spoke again, and Mistress Dyer shook her head. Esther was blind with tears, eyes screwed up, her face turned towards her mother, arms stretched out. Merrivale wiped the tears from her cheek, but the act wasn't comforting. Mistress Dyer shook her head again and again, but he wouldn't let the child go. Isabella clenched her hands together, taut with helpless frustration. Put her down, she willed. Leave them alone. Why hadn't they found the priest yet? There were only so many places he could hide – unless he had already escaped from the house. But the riders had approached so fast, and Isabella had left them just minutes before. Surely the priest hadn't had time to flee?

The front door swung open, and the loud voices of the men spilled into the street. They were angry now, the search apparently unsuccessful. Merrivale stepped out, beckoning to the men with the horses. He shook his head. One of the riders bent down low, and Merrivale whispered to him. The horse stamped its foot, tossed its head, teeth grinding noisily on its bit. The rider sat up straight and nodded.

Esther had been dropped to the ground. The little girl clutched for her mother but the men pulled Mistress Dyer away. Esther and the servant woman held on to each other instead, desperate for something to cling to. Still dressed only in her shift and shawl, Jane Dyer was pulled into the street and placed on one of the horses. Esther ran after her, shrieking.

'Where are you taking her? Where? I want my mother!' She launched herself at one of the men, waving her arms, trying to kick out, but the men were impatient and angry, and one simply pushed her over into the muddy street, rolled her out of the way with his foot. The other men streamed out of the house and mounted their horses. One had Elizabeth's mother in front of him on the saddle. They called out to one another, then they all wheeled their horses around, and clattered back over the cobbles. Isabella feared for the small, vulnerable body of the little girl still lying, curled up, on the icy ground, in case she was trampled. Then the horses were gone, the sound of their hooves receding into the night.

Isabella ran forward.

'Esther!' she whispered. 'Did they hurt you?' She tried to pick her up, but Esther's body had tensed into a tight, white ball, the sound of sobs low and indistinct. Isabella tried again to unfold the tense little body but Esther resisted her.

'Mary, help me,' she called. The servant woman was caught

in the same abstract shock as Esther, gazing into space, her mouth opening and closing.

'Mary!' Isabella said. The irritation in her voice seemed to startle the servant from her terrified dream. The old woman gasped and crossed herself, then crossed herself again. She started to cry too, as she hurried out of the house to help Esther.

'Come along, little one,' she crooned, voice wavering. 'You can't lie out here. We've got to get you inside. We have to clean you up and put you to bed or your mother will be angry when she comes home again.'

This mention of her mother brought another bout of sobbing, but Esther's body softened. Mary picked her up, and Esther clung to her, arms and legs. Mary struggled to stand up, burdened by the limpet body, but she carried her inside the house, to the kitchen.

Isabella followed. The house had been turned upside down. The long table and benches were tipped over, the wooden chest emptied, pewter plates tipped over the floor. In the kitchen every pot, bowl, knife, cup, had been thrown onto the ground, jars of flour and dried fruit scattered over the flagstones. Even the fire had been extinguished, and the house stank of them, the men and the pitchy torches, their stale breath, the cindery scent of their anger and frustration.

Isabella righted a bench and Mary sat down, moaning and rocking, holding Esther against herself till the girl fell asleep.

'What am I going to do?' she said, over and over. 'What'll I do without the mistress?'

'Where do you think they've taken her?' Isabella said.

The old woman shook her head.

'What happened to the priest? Where did he go?'

At this, Mary gave a low, bitter laugh. 'Oh, the priest,' she said. She stood up, still cradling Esther. 'I'll show you.'

They walked through the house. In the front room a tapestry had been ripped from the wall and lay in a heap on the floor. A chest had been overturned. They stepped over the spilled contents, heading for the stairs. Mary laid Esther down in her bed, in an exhausted sleep, and led Isabella into the large bedroom at the front of the house, where the master and mistress slept. She dropped to her knees by the fireplace, pressing her hands on the bare floorboards near the hearth. Then she ran her fingertips over the nubbed surface of the floor, reading the grooves and runnels in the wood.

'There it is,' she said. A stab of a finger in a knothole, and a piece of a floorboard was levered out. She put her hand underneath this first piece and lifted away a longer section, revealing under the floor the face of the fugitive priest, Thomas Montford.

'They've gone,' Mary murmured. 'They've taken the mistress, but you are safe.'

Isabella detected a repressed anger in the servant's voice, that their guest should be free while her mistress had been taken away in the night to God knows where. Mary removed another slim plank, revealing the tiny hiding place. Like a coffin, there was barely enough room for the big man, the floorboard just above his nose. No room to move, while the boots of the Queen's men tramped just an inch above him. How horrible, to be wedged in such a tiny space, unable to do anything but wait and hope. His eyes were full of dirt he had not been able to brush away.

Thomas struggled out. Mary glanced across at Isabella.

'It's an old priest hole,' she said. 'It was built in the house years ago, when the monastery was dissolved. And then I never thought to see the day it would be used again.'

The priest straightened his clothes, and wiped the dust from his face. He looked from the green girl to the muttering servant woman.

'Where's Esther?' he said. Mary gestured to the door.

'I've put her to bed, but she won't be able to sleep,' she said. 'And Miss Elizabeth is safe at the manor, God be praised. But what about the mistress? What about her?' And she moaned again, powerless, overcome by the loss, and pressed her apron to her face.

The priest stood up straight, becoming master of the situation. He placed his hand on the old woman's sagging shoulder.

'Don't lose faith,' he said. 'I don't believe she's in danger. They can prove nothing against her. She will be questioned, that is all.'

This prospect did not seem to reassure Mary, who wept more copiously into her apron. Thomas turned to Isabella.

'I shall leave immediately,' he said.

'Where will you go?'

'I was hoping you might be able to help me,' he said. 'You have lived in the forest. There must be secret places nobody knows about but you. Until I can send a message for help and another safe place, I'm in your hands, Isabella.'

Portrait

When the household had settled down for the night, Elizabeth sneaked out of the house. She told the cook, who was already bedded down to sleep, she needed to pee. The cook only grunted a response, not caring either way. Elizabeth hurried across the yard to the stables and curled up in the straw of Isabella's stall, waiting for her friend to return.

The wait seemed to last for ever, and Elizabeth spent the time chewing over the events of the evening. She was still racked with indecision. One minute she was furious with herself for confiding in Isabella – what if she took the information straight to Kit Merrivale? The next minute she was berating herself for putting Isabella in danger, involving her in a life-and-death matter that had nothing whatsoever to do with her. What if Isabella was caught at the house in Silver Street? When this conundrum had been exhausted Elizabeth tormented herself with worries about Isabella's tales of the forest spirits. Was it right for Elizabeth to trust herself to a girl who consorted with devils? Had she let her judgement be clouded by some kind of charm, some demonic sorcery? For the Devil had the power to assume a pleasing shape, did he not? Maybe Isabella was tempting her into a diabolic contract, luring her into evil-doing. Then she remembered how Isabella had offered to help, even putting herself in danger, and Elizabeth felt guilty for thinking such terrible things about her friend. However much she wrestled with the facts, she couldn't find an answer. She had nothing safe to cling to, all alone, with no-one to help or advise, and no-one to trust. And beneath the constant toing and froing in her head, there was the huge and unavoidable concern for the safety of her loved ones. For Robert at the university, for Mary and Esther and her mother Jane worrying in the cold house, and for the priest who faced a terrible death if he were caught by the priest hunter.

Merrivale hadn't returned to the manor yet. Earlier in the evening Lady Catherine had anxiously looked out for him, delaying the serving of the meal until it was certain he wouldn't be back. Then she was tetchy and restless, snapping at Elizabeth, shouting at the servants. She retired to bed early, complaining of a headache. Elizabeth helped her undress, untying the stiff corset and skirts, and then she brushed Lady Catherine's long hair. But Elizabeth was distracted and Lady Catherine was waspish with disappointment, so the comfortable companionship the two usually enjoyed with one another was absent.

Now Elizabeth curled up in the straw. She wished Isabella would hurry and return. Soon the head groom would check up on the horses, giving them a final supper before turning in to bed, above the stables. She didn't want him to discover that Isabella was missing. It was warm, lying in the straw wrapped up in Isabella's blanket. Eventually Elizabeth dozed, weary of thinking and worrying. She dreamed of the green girl dancing in a circle with creatures possessing the bodies of men and the legs and feet of birds. The spectacle filled her with horror, and when the dream Isabella beckoned her to join in the ugly, disjointed dance Elizabeth cried out. But a cold hand pressed over her mouth. Elizabeth's eyes flicked open. It was very dark, but dimly she made out a mossy face and swag of hair belonging to Isabella. The green girl was hot and out of breath. She raised a finger to her lips, and then withdrew her other hand from Elizabeth's face. The stable door rattled. In a moment Isabella had drawn the blanket over her friend and partly across her own body. She slipped her wrist back into the irksome iron manacle.

Elizabeth couldn't see who had come, but she heard the clank of a wooden pail on the flagstones, and she could smell the tallow from the groom's lanthorn. The horses moved about restlessly, anticipating their supper. A man spoke in a low voice to the horses, moving from one stall to another. Isabella squeezed Elizabeth's arm. It didn't seem the groom had noticed anything amiss. The door opened and shut again, as the groom went out, and everything was quiet, except for the sound of the horses chewing their meal of bran and oats. Isabella threw back the blanket.

Elizabeth waited for her friend to speak, but the green girl hesitated.

'What happened? What is it? Did you see them?' Elizabeth said.

'Elizabeth,' Isabella whispered. 'I'll tell you. Just be patient – listen to me.' Elizabeth tried to make out the tone of her voice. What was it? A mixture of compassion and anxiety, a

113

struggle to find the right words to tell her what had happened
. . . She could not be patient.

'What is it?' Elizabeth demanded again. 'Tell me!'

Isabella swallowed. She took up Elizabeth's hand in her
own, but Elizabeth pulled it away again. She didn't want
comfort now, she wanted to know.

'They came in the night, Elizabeth. Merrivale and his
men, on horses. They went to your house and searched it.
They took your mother.' Isabella's voice was level, imparting
these brief, terrible details. Elizabeth stared. She struggled
to breathe, then she began to suck in quick, deep breaths. It
couldn't happen. How could it happen? Hadn't they prayed
for God's help? Weren't they faithful enough? She pictured
her mother, dragged into the street and bundled on a horse.
Where would they take her? What would they do? Terrible
images rose up in Elizabeth's mind. The authorities were
cruel, and the punishments meted out even to petty criminals
were swift and savage. Elizabeth began to shake. She tried to
speak, but the words wouldn't come out.

'Elizabeth, Elizabeth,' Isabella said, putting her arm
around her friend. 'It might not be as bad as you think.'
She lowered her voice. 'They didn't take the priest – they
couldn't find him. And Esther is safe, with Mary.

'The priest said they would only question your mother.
They found nothing! They have no evidence against her.'

Elizabeth turned to Isabella numbly, trying to absorb her
words.

'Esther?' she repeated. There were no rules making
children exempt from questioning, or even torture.

'She's safe,' Isabella reassured. 'At least for the time being.'

Elizabeth nodded. But her mother – what about her mother? And Robert – had he been taken too?

Isabella hugged her, and pushed the hair from her face, trying to comfort. Elizabeth blinked and sniffed. She looked at the green girl.

'Why are you so kind to me?' she said. 'You're risking your life, helping me. Why should you do that?' She remembered worrying that Isabella was a demon and felt a pang of guilt.

'You're the first friend I've had, Elizabeth. I want to help you,' Isabella said. 'You found me in the wood and fed me and protected me.'

Elizabeth shook her head. 'It was a small thing I did.' She frowned, trying to get the better of her feelings, to think straight.

'So where is the priest?' she said. 'Do you know where he went? Is he safe?'

She sensed, rather than saw, a smile on Isabella's face. 'For the moment, yes,' Isabella said. 'That's why I took so long. We headed out to the wood and I led him to the shrine by the spring, where you found me. The priest seemed glad to be there. And he is a kind and brave man, Elizabeth. I wanted to help him.'

Elizabeth nodded. It was not a place Merrivale and his men would find in the night, but it wouldn't be safe for long. In the daytime, the local people foraged for fuel in the woods, and drove their pigs among the trees to feed on nuts and roots. They would have to find somewhere more secure.

'It was a good choice,' Elizabeth said. 'Thank you. It was an excellent choice. But tomorrow he'll have to move again, until we can find another safe house.' She hugged Isabella

115

again, bade her goodnight, and ran back into the house. The cook was already snoring when she climbed beneath the blanket. But she didn't sleep, her thoughts fixed on the task ahead, considering the options, making plans. She must have fallen asleep in the end because she didn't even hear the cook get up and the usual morning noise in the kitchen didn't disturb until the chamberlain himself came in to wake her.

'Lady Catherine wants you,' he said abruptly, as Elizabeth struggled out of bed. She quickly arranged her hair, still tucking the stray locks into her cap as she hurried up the stairs and along the corridor. All the servants stared as she passed them. No-one said a word. Elizabeth knocked on the chamber door.

Lady Catherine was standing at the window, in the sunshine, already dressed. When Elizabeth entered, she gestured her to sit on the window seat. Lady Catherine frowned and pressed her lips together. Her hands were clasped nervously.

'Elizabeth, I have some bad news for you,' she said. Lady Catherine was not looking at her. Instead she gazed through the window as she continued to speak.

'Your mother was arrested last night, on suspicion of harbouring a fugitive priest. She is being held for questioning.' Lady Catherine gave Elizabeth a quick glance then, probably expecting tears or an emotional outburst. But Elizabeth remained still and cold, though her lip quivered.

'How do you know this?' Elizabeth asked, trying to keep her voice level.

'Kit supervised the arrest,' Lady Catherine said, staring out through the window, across the fields. 'He came back this morning. Of course this makes things difficult for me. It might not be wise to have a girl from a suspect Catholic family in my household, now an arrest has been made.'

Elizabeth squeezed her hands together. But Lady Catherine was not as chilly as her words suggested. She dropped to sit on the window seat, beside Elizabeth, and she grasped her shoulder tight.

'We've been friends, haven't we, Elizabeth?' she said. 'All the long days you've brightened up for me, when I was on my own. I haven't forgotten it.' Elizabeth nodded. It was true. For two years now she had come. Sometimes several times a week, to listen to Lady Catherine, helping in her studio, reading Greek and Latin, acting as a confidante for her grumbles about her life in the country, soaking up tales about life in court.

Lady Catherine drew a breath. 'Would you do something for me, Elizabeth?'

'Of course,' Elizabeth said. 'Anything. What do you want?'

'Would you convert to the Protestant faith? Would you stay with me here at the manor and be safe? Be a daughter to me? I am so very fond of you.'

'What?' Elizabeth said, in shock. She couldn't believe it. Was Lady Catherine serious? Convert to the Church of England? Abandon her family to save her own skin? Her thoughts tumbled over one another. This was too much. And if she said no, would Lady Catherine withdraw her protection, hand her over to Merrivale?

'Lady Catherine, I – I don't know what to say.' Elizabeth stumbled over the words, struggling to find a way out. Lady Catherine gave her a long, searching look.

'I appreciate this is a difficult decision, and you will need time to think and pray,' Lady Catherine said. 'We will speak of this again soon.'

Elizabeth knew her mistress was a clever woman. Her unusual occupation and dazzling success as a woman artist at the court had required huge reserves of cunning, tact and diplomacy. She had to know when to speak, and when to be quiet. When it was sensible to flatter, and when it was better to be honest. Had she come under pressure from Kit, to hand over her lady-in-waiting? Was Lady Catherine playing her own game, and giving Elizabeth a little space of time, with this invitation to think about conversion?

Elizabeth gave a little curtsey. 'Thank you. Yes, I will think on it,' she said gratefully.

Lady Catherine nodded. 'I have no sympathy with heretic Catholic priests, come here to stir up trouble,' she said. 'But I am sorry for you that your mother has been taken. I pray she will soon be released. The courts can't keep her if there isn't any evidence.'

Lady Catherine kept Elizabeth beside her all morning. Elizabeth dreaded the moment she would have to face Kit Merrivale again, but this happened soon after Lady Catherine had breakfasted on porridge and honey. Elizabeth herself was quite unable to eat.

'Kit wants his portrait painted,' Lady Catherine said, by way of a warning. 'Keep up your courage, Elizabeth. I shall need your assistance.'

Lady Catherine worked in a long, low room on the first floor, with windows to the south and west, which filled the space with light. It had been many weeks since Lady

Catherine had painted. Stepping into the room, Elizabeth breathed the familiar perfume of linseed oil, the base for the rich paints. The place was cluttered with canvases, some coloured with half-finished paintings, some newly stretched and primed. She helped Lady Catherine select a suitable canvas and set it up on an easel. Then she set to work grinding pigments, to make up fresh paint for the picture. The previous summer she had spent many happy hours with Lady Catherine, mixing up paints, talking to the mistress while she worked. It had been a soothing and intriguing distraction from the hard work and straitened circumstances at home. Then Lady Catherine grew bored and lonely, and her painting fell by the wayside. The studio had been shut up. It was strange and unsettling to return now, with her mother under arrest, having no knowledge of her brother's fate, and carrying the responsibility for the safety of the priest. The present fears polluted the good memories locked up in the room.

Ochre, for yellow and brown, cinnabar for red, and precious lapis lazuli for blue, Elizabeth ground the pigments in a cold stone pestle. The work was tricky and absorbing. She tried not to pay any attention when Kit walked in, dressed in his white shirt and wide leather breeches. Looking through her lashes, she quietly observed Lady Catherine stretch out her hands to his in a greeting, the smile on her face, the fluttering and flirting. It was all very well to be clever, thought Elizabeth, but cleverness was obviously no protection for a lonely woman, long deprived of attention and admiration, when a creature such as Kit came to call. Lady Catherine might understand what kind of man he was, and she certainly knew he was responsible for arrests and night-time raids. She was prepared to connive at her lady-in-waiting's protection, but still she blushed when he stepped into the room, and she smiled too much, and laughed a curious, giddy laugh. What was it about him that attracted her? His pretty looks, perhaps. His careless air and fancy clothes. His aura of confidence and power? Elizabeth lifted her face from the pestle and stared at Kit. What was she thinking? Why *wouldn't* Lady Catherine like him? He was handsome, respected, and undertook supposedly honourable work for the protection of the realm. But Elizabeth was still angry with Lady Catherine for being susceptible. Her mistress was making a fool of herself. After all she was older than Kit, and even though she hadn't seen her husband for months, she was still married.

Elizabeth watched Merrivale charm and flirt, and at the same time imagined him breaking his way into her home, seizing her mother, locking her up in a cold cell, bullying, threatening, taking full advantage of his strength and power. Elizabeth banged the mortar fiercely into the pigment, glaring at him with a profound hatred. God said to love your enemies, to pray for those who persecuted you, but she could not pray for Christopher Merrivale. Except to pray he might one day find himself cold, alone and friendless in a pit full of rats, awaiting the kind of fate he meted out now to Catholic priests and helpless women.

Merrivale turned to look at her, perhaps sensing the feelings burning inside her.

'I think your lady-in-waiting wishes she were grinding my

skull in her stone bowl,' he observed. 'A fine ivory colour it would make, wouldn't it?'

Lady Catherine smiled swiftly. 'Come and sit here,' she said. 'By the window, so I have the sunlight upon you.'

She had him sit at a desk, posed with a book beside him, and dagger visible at his belt, and on the desk, a flower, a candle and a skull, symbols of mortality. She fussed over his position, sideways to the painter with his upper body turned towards her and his face regarding her directly, so in the portrait he would look out at the viewer. It was a long process, and an hour had passed before Lady Catherine was happy. She settled his clothing correctly, brushed the hair from his face, moved his elbow forwards, and back again, seeking a perfect structural balance. For this space of time, caught up in her work, Elizabeth observed Lady Catherine was indifferent to Merrivale as a man. She was absorbed in the process of her work. Finally she stepped back to the canvas and made a swift, deft sketch.

'My men will continue the questioning today,' Merrivale said lazily. He addressed Lady Catherine, but Elizabeth knew the statement was made for her benefit. She tried not to hear, to make no response.

'We know well enough the priest was at the house. It is only a matter of time before we find him. I'm certain the woman will tell us where he is.'

Elizabeth turned away, but she made a curious gulp. Had Merrivale noticed? Lady Catherine didn't encourage him in this line of conversation. Instead she made a comment about the portrait but Merrivale ignored her.

'Do you know where the priest is, Elizabeth?' he said.

Lady Catherine broke in. 'Of course she doesn't!' she said. 'She's been here with me! Leave her alone. Isn't it bad enough for the poor girl to know her mother has been arrested?'

Merrivale rolled his eyes, fixed his gaze on Lady Catherine. 'You are not sympathetic to the Catholics, are you?' he said, teasing.

'No, I'm not,' she responded angrily. 'But Elizabeth isn't a heretic. She's loyal to me. Please, let her be.'

'Then she's your responsibility, Kate. I don't want her leaving the house or speaking to any of her family members. No letters, Elizabeth. Do you understand?'

Elizabeth nodded. Merrivale looked at her again, cold and assessing. When at last they left the studio for their midday meal, he reached out his hand to her, grasping a blonde curl that had escaped from her cap. Without a word he gave it a little tug, hard enough to hurt. Elizabeth stared at him. She knew what he was thinking. If Merrivale didn't get what he wanted, she would be next on his list and then Lady Catherine would not be able to protect her. Be afraid, little girl, he said without words. And Elizabeth was afraid.

The kitchen was full of steam, buckets of hot water plummeting into the wooden tub set up in front of the fire. The men were driven out, along with the dogs, leaving Lady Catherine, her dress covered in a white pinafore, presiding over a herd of female servants. A large brick of cream-coloured soap waited on the table, and a knife for trimming.

Isabella hovered at the edge of the room, knowing what the preparations presaged and dreading the inevitable scrubbing. It was the humiliation she feared the most, to be stripped and manhandled by these women, who seemed to think they were being kind. At least, she thought glumly, if I look more like them, I will be accepted and people won't be frightened of me any more.

Finally the preparations were complete. Lady Catherine turned to Isabella.

'Take off your clothes,' she said briskly. 'Come on now, Isabella. It won't be so bad. I take a bath at least twice a year and it does me no harm at all.'

Everyone stared. Isabella shivered, to be the focus of so much attention. What choice did she have? Retaining as much of her dignity as possible, she slipped off the old, leathery dress and stepped into the tub. She had never bathed like this before, and the slide of clear, warm water felt strange upon her chilly skin. Did she like the sensation? There was no chance to think about it. The women descended, armed with pieces of cloth and soap, and she was unceremoniously scrubbed, rubbed, tugged and rinsed. Caught up in the storm of enthusiastic washing, Isabella surrendered. Her eyes and ears were soon full of soap. Her hair was heavy with water, her skin raw from their endeavours to get through the green to her natural skin. Then her nails were trimmed with a paring knife, and the long rug of matted hair was cut off short. Isabella felt a pang to lose her hair. It had served as a cloak, a blanket – a form of protection. Now the hair lay in a greasy brown pile on the wet flagstones, like a soggy animal corpse. At last she was dried off with a blanket, presented with a linen shift and a long woollen dress to wear, and a pair of plain leather shoes. Lady Catherine tugged a white woollen

123

cap on her head, tucking the shorn ends of her hair under the hem. Then they all stood back, the manor women, to make an assessment of their work. There were murmurs of satisfaction, and self-congratulation. Lady Catherine smiled.

'A great improvement,' she said. 'At least you resemble a Christian now.'

Isabella gave a wry smile, trying to look grateful. Despite the covering of clothes, she felt bare without her hair. She shook her head, unused to its lightness. The dress felt itchy and constricting, and her feet felt trapped and awkward in the shoes. She peered at the back of her hands. The skin was still green, but the colour had faded a little. And how did she feel about this? Isabella tested her ambivalent emotions. She wanted to be human again, to live among her own people. At the same time, she was not entirely comfortable with her transformation – as though the well meaning women had washed away some of her identity along with the green stain. Still, she mustered a smile and made a clumsy attempt at a curtsey, which prompted a ripple of applause from the gathering.

Now suitably clean and dressed, Isabella was allowed to stay in the house. Lady Catherine gave her a tour, intrigued by her new toy, the girl from the woods. If she expected Isabella to marvel, she must have been disappointed, because Isabella didn't say very much. When they stepped into the studio, Isabella spotted Elizabeth mixing up paints. She nodded a greeting when Lady Catherine introduced them, but was careful not to give anything away.

At nightfall, a rainstorm drove in from the west and the household was grateful to shelter inside, as the fires were stoked. Outside, the animals in the fields would huddle as best they could under the hedges. Isabella was given chores in the kitchen – turnips to chop, beans to pop from their pods. She felt uneasy amongst so many people. She wasn't used to so much company. She stared out of the window and thought of the priest alone in the leaky shrine in the woods. He would be hungry, after a day without food. Doubtless, despite his courage, fears would be gnawing too. She had to find a way to talk with Elizabeth, to make a plan to see the priest and find him somewhere safer to stay.

When the household gathered for a meal that night, Isabella was the centre of attention, the marvellous wild girl brought in from the forest. Everyone wanted to talk to her, asking questions she refused to answer, or pinching her skin, wanting to see her teeth, jesting that she might have a tail or claws on her feet. They wanted to know how she had lived in the forest, and why she was green. But Isabella wouldn't speak to anyone. As the night went on, and the beer took effect, the questions became more intrusive, and louder. Isabella suffered, in the welter of people and the babble of voices, the claustrophobic atmosphere heavy with the scent of unwashed, heated bodies and the rich, spicy food, the baked meats and over-stewed vegetables. She was conscious of Elizabeth, similarly isolated in the crowd, and of Kit Merrivale, who drank and jested with the lord's men, but, she realised, still kept himself aloof and observant, never letting down his guard. She suspected he considered himself better than they were. His chilly eyes were disdainful.

At last Lady Catherine took pity on Isabella, bidding the servants to leave her alone. She asked Elizabeth to escort the woods girl to a straw mattress set up in the corridor close to Lady Catherine's room.

'You girls are about the same age,' she said. 'Perhaps you could be friends. Elizabeth, take care of her. See if you can draw her out.'

Isabella saw her friend suppress a smile. How fortunate was this turn of events? Elizabeth bobbed a curtsey and gestured for Isabella to follow her. Once outside of the long hall, they picked up their skirts and raced up the stairs.

'Come to the studio,' Elizabeth whispered, taking up a candle. 'We shall be private there. Hurry up!'

The room was cold and quiet. On the easel the painting of Kit Merrivale waited. Three colours blocked in the background, Merrivale's body, and the pale oval of his face. Elizabeth scowled as she passed it. The two girls sat down together.

'You look so different,' Elizabeth marvelled. 'I hardly recognised you at first.' She stretched out a hand to touch the blunt ends of her friend's cropped hair. 'Was it terrible, when they did this to you?'

Isabella shook her head. 'Not so bad,' she said. 'At least I don't look like a devil any more.'

'No, but you look more ordinary,' Elizabeth said, a little regretfully. She searched Isabella's face, uneasy about something.

Isabella said: 'You're wondering if I'll still help you.'

Elizabeth bit her lip. She looked on the verge of tears. 'Yes,' she said. 'Why should you help me? You're not all alone in the forest any more. You don't need me. You have lots of friends here now. They all love you. And they don't love me. No, they hate me. You can be one of them.'

Isabella shook her head. 'Just because they cut off my hair?' She ached, to see the pain in Elizabeth's face. It stirred too many locked up memories of her own. Could she help Elizabeth? Could she make up for the way she left her own mother behind, by helping Elizabeth save hers?

'You are an extraordinary person,' Elizabeth rambled. 'I don't know what it is. Just being with you makes me feel stronger. And d'you know? I'm ashamed to tell you this, I have wondered if you might be in league with devils, like a witch, but I know it can't be so. I think you're an angel, Isabella.'

Isabella shook her head, with a snort. 'Don't be silly,' she said.

Elizabeth, pulled up short, regarded her with surprise.

'I'm not an angel,' Isabella said crossly. 'We haven't time for this. What are we going to do about the priest? Where should we take him?'

Elizabeth opened her mouth, and shut it again. She blinked suddenly.

'I've put some food aside for him,' she said. 'When I took a meal to Lady Catherine and Merrivale in the hall at midday, I told the cook they needed extra because they were so hungry.' Elizabeth looked away, wrinkling her forehead. 'I don't think I've ever deliberately lied before,' she said, still looking at the wall. 'It's funny how much easier it is to do when you know the person you're lying to hates you.' She looked very tired and pale and old.

Isabella shook her head.

'They don't really hate you,' she said. 'They only hate the

127

idea of you being a Catholic. And they're afraid, because of all the fear being whipped up about Catholics. It isn't you. Try not to take it to heart.'

Elizabeth looked puzzled. 'How would you know?'

Isabella smiled sadly. 'I've been listening to the servants talk. And my mother said exactly the same thing to me, when they took against us.'

'What happened to your mother?' Elizabeth said. 'And what about your brother?'

'I don't want to talk about my mother. And John? You can help me find him.'

Elizabeth slowly nodded. 'I will do everything I can,' she said. But first they had to think about the priest and Elizabeth's mother.

'What do you want me to do, Elizabeth?' Isabella said. Her friend swallowed and took a deep breath.

'My family has a secret trust, with the old abbey,' she said. 'This is the most precious of secrets — but it might be of service now.'

Isabella nodded. She sensed how powerful the secret was — how much it cost Elizabeth to speak of it.

'It is a place where the priest will be perfectly safe,' Elizabeth said. 'You must tell him to wait for me in the old abbey chapel. It is the only place King Henry did not destroy. The people use it as their parish church for, for the Church of England.'

Swiftly, Elizabeth explained what the priest must do, and the nature of her family's secret.

'I swore to my father I would tell no-one, except my own children,' Elizabeth concluded bitterly. 'Now I have betrayed my father's trust – and his father's and grandfather's. But what else can I do?'

Isabella squeezed her friend's arm. 'It will be all right,' she whispered. 'You have the best intention. I think your father would have done the same. Have faith.'

They agreed it would be safer for Isabella to head out again. She travelled faster and knew the woods better. And in the event of her being caught out of the house, she might be scolded or punished, but in the same circumstances Elizabeth would certainly be arrested. So, when the household finally settled down for the night, and Lady Catherine had retired to bed, Isabella took off her punishing shoes, and tied up her skirt. Then, with Elizabeth's stolen food under her arm, she set off on the run through the night and the rain to the forest, and the hidden priest.

Despite the hurly-burly of the wind and weather, Isabella was relieved to be outside and on her own again. The storm was exhilarating. She could see in the dark as well as a fox, and passed over the mud with swift, light feet. The forest embraced her, like a long-lost friend, the trees a comforting shelter, a place where she felt at home.

'Thomas? Thomas Montford?' she called out, when she reached the broken hut by the shrine.

Peering into the murky shelter she spotted the priest crouched at the back, trying to avoid the worst of the leaks in the roof.

'Isabella? Is that you?' The priest unfolded, rising to his feet. 'I thought you were a wolf. You move like a wild animal.' The previous night, in the pitch black, she had guided him through the forest, hand in hand. He had been noisy and clumsy beside her, walking into branches, tripping over brambles.

'I brought you food, and candles,' Isabella said. 'Elizabeth stole them from the manor. She asked me to beg your forgiveness, for the sin, but she couldn't let you go hungry.'

Thomas laughed. 'Of course she is forgiven. Didn't the Lord tell us to feed the hungry?' He was ravenous, tucking into the bread and cheese and cold vegetable stew as though he hadn't eaten for a week. When he had finished, he wiped his mouth with the back of his hand and sighed.

'Now,' he said. 'I know of safe houses in York, but how I am to get to York is the question. It is a long way off and I don't have a horse.'

'What about Elizabeth's mother?' Isabella asked.

'She doesn't know where I am now. Even if she confesses I was in the house, they won't find me there. Don't worry about that.'

Isabella frowned. The priest's answer was chilling. Didn't he care what happened to Jane, who had sheltered him? Was his own safety his only concern?

'I didn't mean that. I want to know how we can get her released,' Isabella said coldly. The priest was taken aback.

'You think me uncaring?' he said. 'I am a priest, sworn to restore the true faith, Isabella. I would give up my own life for the faith like that' – he snapped his fingers – 'if it were needed.

'Yet I don't disdain life. No, indeed, I love it. Men are endlessly cruel and selfish. Everywhere there is death and suffering, but it is here the sun shines, and I'm greedy for it. But what does it merit a man to gain the whole world, if he loses his soul? Jane's fate lies in the hands of God, not in mine.'

Isabella was not convinced. She had suffered too much at the hands of priests and under the weight of their convictions. She would help him all the same, for Elizabeth's sake, and for the sake of her mother. But she understood the fever of faith in Thomas Montford, and knew he would have her tormented and burned if he learned of her relationship with the crow people. He would accuse her of witchcraft, as the other people had accused her mother, and think he was saving her soul when he assigned her to the flames. She had hidden for three hundred years, and nothing had changed. A weight of sadness settled on her heart and there was a moment of silence between them.

'Light the candle,' she said at last, in a low voice. 'I have something to show you.' The flame flickered in the draught blowing through the cell. In the wavering light, Isabella found the loose brick in the chimney breast, that Elizabeth had shown her just a few days before.

'Elizabeth told me to show you this. She said – the walls of the abbey were torn down, but the abbey was much more than stones and mortar.

'The abbey was a great centre for learning. Elizabeth has explained to me that much was destroyed, the books and parchments, but some of it has survived, hidden away in secret places – like this one.' She pushed her hand into the space behind the brick and pulled out the sooty rolls of parchment.

The priest looked from Isabella to the parchment in her hand. Excitement coloured his face. He nodded.

'Elizabeth knows one of these secret places, and she will show you where to go. She will meet you in the chapel in the old abbey, if she can get away from the manor. Wait there tomorrow in the middle of the day.'

'In the abbey chapel? I might be noticed – what if people ask who I am?'

'You have to take the risk,' Isabella said. 'If someone asks – make something up. Say you're a travelling merchant – you have business in the town.'

The priest stared at the thick, grimy papers rolled up in his hand.

'God bless you, Isabella,' he said.

Secrets

Isabella ran through the rain, her skirts catching on branches and brambles. Her legs were plastered with cold, clinging mud. Twigs swiped at her face. She was clumsy, not concentrating on the journey, thoughts knotted, the priest's words stirring up spikes in her memory.

She didn't want to think about the past. Three centuries had come and gone since that terrible time, and living with the crow people it had been easy not to remember. But thorns were still lodged in her heart, and now the priest had set them stinging.

1240

The day a baby boy had been born to the Watts family, Isabella saw a faery for the first time. She saw them again, after that, around the cottage she shared with her mother and brother, in the woods and fields. Not fully visible, not entirely in the earthy world, but present nonetheless. All her life she had lived in the presence of the crow people, without even realising, but the ceremony by the decorated spring had revealed them to her. She could sense them now, a glimpse out of the corner of her eye, a prickling of the skin on the backs of her hands, a thread of an enticing, other-worldly perfume. The other world, the faery land, was close at hand.

The baking, golden summer passed away. The nights closed in, the forest green fell into tatters of gold and scarlet. Men herded their pigs into the trees to feed on acorns.

For weeks after the birth of the infant, the Leland family were well provided. Mysterious gifts of food appeared by the garden gate – grapes from the abbey vineyards, sweet apples, tasty fruit cakes and nuts. Once, the day after the birth, a bolt of blue cloth Ruth made into a new dress for Isabella, who was growing fast. Isabella was thrilled by the gifts. Ruth made every effort to look pleased, but Isabella sensed her unease. For the first time, Isabella began to notice the deepening signs of age in her mother's face. There were fine lines around her mouth, and another across the bridge of her nose.

'What's wrong?' she would ask, when her mother sighed, but Ruth only replied with a smile and a dismissive shake of her head. The teaching went on as before, except that Ruth seemed more eager than ever to impart her store of knowledge, reminding her daughter, testing her, allowing her to take over the preparation of medicines for the people who came to the gate with their endless procession of ailments. And without any help from her mother, Isabella developed her knowledge of the crow people. Inside the cottage, when bowls moved on the table, or bundles of herbs dropped to the floor, Isabella knew the faeries were close at hand. She wasn't afraid of them. She strained her eyes to see, hungry to know them better. She remembered the creature, like a god, her mother had summoned at the spring, and sometimes he stole into her dreams, but always far away, always out of reach. Once, in the depths of the night, she woke to hear the beating of huge wings over the cottage, and imagined the faery, black and gold, dressed in his crow feathers, planting his thin, nailed feet upon the ridge of the reed-thatched roof.

In the twilight, at evening and dawn, when the shutters were folded back from the window at the back of the house, the expected view of the forest sometimes became something else — mountains beneath a cold stone palace, its windows ablaze with firelight, or a forest of black trees where a faery girl ran away, long golden hair floating over matt white skin.

Ruth did not comment or explain these happenings. She sat in the cottage's single chair — a gift to her grandmother for the long-ago safe delivery of a noble child — nursing baby John, or embroidering white daisies on the hem of Isabella's new blue dress. Already, in spirit, Ruth was far away. Isabella sensed it, the distance growing between them. For the first time, even tucked up in the warm with her family, she felt lonely.

Autumn darkened into winter. After the unseasonably hot summer, the winter retaliated with weeks of ice and snow. Even the river around Maumesbury froze, and children skated on the deep, murky ice. There was nothing to do on the long, dark nights but raise the fires, close the doors and huddle close to the hearth. It was too dark to sew any more, so Ruth recounted again the tales of the Kings and Queens of the shadow land, the adventures of faery knights, their loves and conquests, as the snow fell, and far away, Isabella heard the long, mournful howl of a solitary wolf, driven to the fringes of the forest by hunger.

The winter dug in its heels until Lent, and everyone was hungry. At last, on Ash Wednesday, snow gave way to rain, the river broke out of its skin of ice and flooded the neighbouring fields. Then mud everywhere, and an icy, driving wind. The animals huddled, shivering and forlorn, in makeshift shelters, and everyone was miserable, cursing the weather, the cold and damp that seemed to last for ever.

Then, just before Easter, the sun broke through at last. Eager leaves seemed to cover the bare limbs of the trees in a single night. And the servant came again from the house of Mistress Watts, asking Ruth to attend on the baby, who was seriously ill.

A shadow crossed Ruth's face when she heard the news, standing beside the servant's horse. She dropped her head forward, looked at the ground. She seemed very small now, shoulders bony from the long winter, the hungry spring.

'Will you come?' the servant asked. The tone of his voice did not suggest Ruth had any choice about this. She raised her face and nodded.

'Ride ahead,' she said. 'Tell them I'll attend on the boy this afternoon. I need to prepare.'

The man turned the horse around, and headed back to the town. Isabella watched the horse pick its way through the mire of the road. She didn't want to look at her mother, who was still standing exactly where the servant had left her.

'You're afraid he'll die,' Isabella blurted out, still staring into the distance.

Ruth didn't reply at once. The moments passed. Then she nodded. 'His heart isn't right. I'm surprised he has lasted this long – the winter.'

'Why're you so afraid? Lots of babies die.'

'Yes,' Ruth said. 'But this time is different. Mistress Watts – she won't accept it.'

Isabella chewed her lip. 'Perhaps he won't die,' she said.

'You're an excellent healer. The best. Maybe you can save him.'

'Maybe,' Ruth said.

Isabella insisted on accompanying her mother on the visit to the Watts house, even though Ruth suggested she stay behind with John. He was toddling now, his wisps of baby hair giving way to thick, dark curls, but Ruth hoisted him up on her back for the walk to the town on the hill.

They were let in the back door by the same dour servant who had questioned Isabella about John's father, in the summer. Mistress Watts was sitting in the front room of the house, a generous fire roaring in the hearth despite the arrival of warmer weather. The baby lay in a carved wooden cradle beside her. Other servants fussed about in the room, whispering, as Ruth stepped into the room. She handed John to Isabella and dipped in a little curtsey to the lady of the house. Mistress Watts had changed a great deal over the months. Her fleshy body had not thinned down – instead her figure seemed to have sagged. Her pretty face was pouchy now, grey under the eyes, as though from crying, and she had a rash of angry spots on her chin.

Ruth stretched out a hand, and touched Mistress Watts on the shoulder.

'I'm sorry he's ill,' she said. Mistress Watts lifted her face and sighed deeply. A brief smile crossed her face, as though even Ruth's presence was enough to soothe. Then she turned her attention to her child, Peter, and other feelings washed across her face. Grief, frustration.

'He doesn't thrive,' she said, quietly. 'He hardly feeds. He's nearly ten months old now, and he can't even sit up. I need your help.' Then she looked at Ruth and her eyes flared, issuing the challenge.

Ruth nodded. 'Of course.' She picked up the baby from the cradle, and loosened the blankets wrapped around him. Isabella drew a breath. How pale the baby looked — worse than pale. His lips, his skin were bluish, starved of blood. And how puny, for a ten-month child. His limbs were thin and undernourished, and his head flopped. He looked like a rag doll. The baby stirred, as Ruth examined him, and his legs gave a feeble kick. He whimpered, his baby face crumpling into an expression of woe. But it was too much for him, all too much. The body didn't have enough strength for him to share exactly what he felt. The whimper died on his lips.

Ruth ran her hands expertly over the child, feeling his chest, his hands and fingers. She pressed her ear to his ribs, to hear the heart. Everyone stared — the mother, the servants, Isabella holding her own sturdy baby brother. Ruth's face was warm with compassion for the sick baby, and he calmed beneath her touch. Then she wrapped him up again, and held him gently in her arms.

'How does he feed?' she said.

'A struggle, always,' Mistress Watts said. 'I have plenty of milk for him — but he doesn't have the strength to suck for long. I have to wake him up to nurse him — otherwise he would just sleep for ever. He doesn't even cry.' A fat tear welled in her eye and plopped onto her cheek. A gust of wind outside puffed a curl of black smoke back into the room from the chimney and the dim room was clouded. One of the servants stepped forward and fanned the gritty woodsmoke from the baby's face.

'His father despairs of him,' Mistress Watts continued. 'Thinks he should die, instead of lingering. But we've waited so long for this child. So long. I couldn't bear to lose him. I don't think

138

there'll be another.' A second fat tear dropped onto her cheek and Mistress Watts wiped it away with the back of her hand.

'You can save him, Mistress Leland. They say you are the best. You can save him.' She had all her hopes pinned on Ruth, and Isabella quailed under the weight of the rich woman's hopeless expectation. Ruth handed the baby to his mother.

'It's his heart,' she said. 'The heart isn't working properly. Put your ear to his chest and you will hear for yourself how weakly and oddly it beats. To be honest – I don't know how much I can do.'

The servants muttered again, indignant, and Mistress Watts's lips trembled.

'You can,' she said. 'You can do something. I understand – I have been told – you can work magic. Do what you have to. Anything – just as long as Peter lives.'

Ruth sighed. 'I've brought a tonic for him,' she said, drawing a pouch of herbs from her pocket. 'Brew them with boiled water and feed him drops from a spoon. This will stimulate the heart. Have you consulted the doctors at the abbey? They are skilled men. They would give you another opinion.'

Mistress Watts shook her head angrily. 'They say his heart is weak, that he will die,' she said. 'They've washed their hands of him. But you're different. You can resort to other powers,' she pleaded. 'I would reward you – whatever you wanted. Can you do something? Some magic? A charm?'

Ruth shook her head. 'What you're asking – it is beyond me,' she said. 'There is nothing more I can do.'

Mistress Watts's face clouded. 'What I don't understand,' she said, 'is how my son came to have a heart that doesn't work. How did this happen to him? Why was he born this way?'

The words hung like a threat in the smoky room, and the questions had no answer.

At the end of the summer, as reapers cut the first wheat in the fields, death made the small harvest of baby Peter, just two months past his first birthday. Isabella was surprised he had lasted as long. Ruth had seen the baby twice more, but the tonics she prepared simply delayed the inevitable. The whole town seemed weighted down by the grief of the Watts family. The funeral was lavish, conducted by the abbot, William of Cullerne, but Ruth was not invited to attend. Mistress Watts was hysterical, and couldn't be consoled. One day she rode out on a horse, flabby and awkward, to Ruth's cottage and screamed out abuse. She accused Ruth of cursing the baby at the birth, of working witchcraft, consorting with demons. She wound herself up into a passion, shouting about changelings and stealers of souls. Isabella and Ruth peeped out of the window through the chinks in the shutter, watching the bereaved woman rage. Isabella was shaking. She could feel the anger – like a storm – breaking over the roof of the cottage.

'Shall we go out and speak with her?' Isabella whispered. But Ruth shook her head.

'It won't do any good,' she said, her face drained and pale. 'There is nothing I could say. She has to blame somebody.'

'Shall we leave? Shall we run away? We could head off into the forest – never come back.'

'That would be taken as an admission of guilt,' Ruth said. 'They would ride after us, hunt us down. And how fast could we move with John to carry? Besides, our family has lived here for hundreds of years. Maybe longer. We have always cared for the shrine. This is our place, Isabella. Your place.'

140

Behind them, John began to cry, as though the vibrations of Mistress Watts's rage had disturbed him too. Isabella picked him up and shushed him. He stretched out his plump hand and pinched her cheek. His eyes were bright blue, curiously flecked with gold. His skin was soft and perfect, like a petal, radiant with health. Isabella's heart swelled with love for him. What wouldn't she do to prevent anything bad ever happening to her brother? How would she feel, if, like baby Peter, John was snatched away by death? Her blood ran cold to think of it.

Outside, the demented woman continued to shout and rant, till her voice was hoarse. She used terrible words, foul language, the most bitter of curses, calling down the wrath of God upon the heretic, the witch, the paramour of devils. And the Lelands cowered in the house, trying in vain not to hear, until evening fell and the husband galloped out in search of his wife and finally took her away. He was older than his wife, but strong and hale, richly dressed. He heaved Mistress Watts back onto her horse and led them away. As they departed, he looked back at the cottage and spat on to the ground.

No-one called on Ruth Leland again, seeking help for sickness or childbirth. No-one stepped near the cottage. Mistress Watts's angry voice had settled over the cottage in a venomous cloud.

If Isabella, out walking, passed one of the local people, they turned away from her and made the sign against evil, balling up their fists, poking a thumb through the fingers.

The tide had turned against them.

Running through the night, to the manor at Spirit Hill, Isabella was swallowed up in the remembering. It had happened more than three hundred years ago, but the feelings

141

were fresh and raw, as though it were yesterday. The images of the last days in her mother's cottage were bright and vivid in her head. The emotions of that horrible time washed through her, the isolation, the constant gnawing of fear. Her mother had seemed like the one permanent, essential part of her life – the root of everything, the sunshine, the source of all comfort and protection. But her mother had gone. The world was endlessly hostile, and now she was a lost child, alone and helpless, at the mercy of everyone.

The crow people had taken her in, but they didn't care for her. Or no more than a human might care for the birds they might throw crumbs for, pleasing for a moment but forgotten the next. Then Jerome the hermit had befriended her, when she returned briefly to the ordinary world many years ago, but he was dead and gone. Now she had Lady Catherine, who had taken her into the household, and she had Elizabeth. Lady Catherine was kind, but it was Elizabeth Isabella had given her heart to – the girl who had offered her food in the forest. So much about Elizabeth echoed Isabella's own life – the persecution, the mother and brother in peril. Isabella hadn't saved her own mother. Perhaps she could help Elizabeth save hers.

The manor crouched in the darkness ahead. Isabella stole into the silent, sleeping house. The dogs didn't bark at her, instead wagging their tails as she slipped past. But she was covered in mud, head to foot. There would be no way to disguise the fact she had been out and about in the night. Quickly she peeled off the sodden, filthy gown and lay down on the little mattress in the corridor where she was to sleep. She would be told off, certainly, but hopefully no-one but Elizabeth would have any idea what she had been up to.

In the morning, Elizabeth was sitting in the kitchen with a bowl of scalding hot porridge before her. The house was relatively quiet, the men out on some hunting expedition now the rain had stopped. The dogs had gone with them. It was hard to eat, because since the moment she had woken up, images of her mother and brother loomed up in her mind. Where were they? What was happening to them? It was hard not to imagine the worst. In her mind she saw dark cells, hunger, and cold, cruel men asking questions, the endless biting of fear, and helplessness. The images swam. Far away, at the other end of the house, she could hear the voice of Lady Catherine scolding Isabella for running out during the night, for the terrible filth on her clothes.

And then for a moment, Elizabeth smiled to herself, bent over the steaming bowl. It was a terrible telling-off, furnished with the threat of a whipping, but Isabella would bear up, she was sure. And the expedition had been a success, because Isabella had nodded and given her a secret smile when the two girls passed in the corridor, just moments before the scolding began.

Afterwards, as Lady Catherine continued to work on her portrait of Kit Merrivale in her studio, Elizabeth asked if she could return to the town to consult with the priest about her conversion to the Church of England. She asked if she could see her little sister Esther too. She kept her voice very level, looking directly at her mistress, without hesitation.

Lady Catherine looked to Merrivale, who was posed in the chair by the desk.

'I don't have any objection,' she said, turning from Merrivale to Elizabeth, and back again. 'What do you say, Kit?'

He turned his cold eyes to Elizabeth and looked her up and down, making some kind of calculation. Elizabeth stared straight back, with a chilly smile. Her dislike of the man had hardened into a kind of courage. She remembered the words of the priest, Thomas Montford, about putting her fears behind her. She understood him now. Fear would be useless. It would just hold her back from what had to be done. Say yes, she willed. Say yes, Kit Merrivale.

'Yes,' he said. 'I can't see that would be a problem. Who am I to stand in the way of a conversion? But she must be accompanied, of course.'

'Certainly,' Lady Catherine responded. 'I shall send one of the servants.'

Elizabeth felt a surge of triumph. She smiled again, and bobbed a curtsey.

But Merrivale shook his head. 'Oh no,' he said softly, returning the smile. 'I'll go with her. I need to visit the town. She can ride with me.'

Elizabeth froze. She looked to Lady Catherine for support, but the lady had her eyes fixed on Merrivale and she simply nodded.

'As you wish. I can continue the painting without you now. Take good care of her.'

'Oh, I shall,' Merrivale replied, gracious as ever. 'I cannot tell you how delighted I am she's prepared to renounce her faith and family to join the true religion.'

An hour later, Merrivale's elegant grey horse was saddled and ready. Merrivale mounted, and one of the grooms hoisted Elizabeth into the saddle behind him. Elizabeth was obliged to ride squashed against his back. It was appalling, to be so close to the man responsible for taking her mother. She felt as though her fear and hatred should burn him. She imagined it, willed it, that the strength of her feelings should poison him, infecting him as they rode away from the manor. But Merrivale gave no sign of it. He seemed remarkably sprightly, talking to his horse, fondly patting its graceful, muscled neck. Merrivale paid Elizabeth no attention at all.

It was a cold, bright morning, frost melting from the fields. The grey horse sploshed through the mud and puddles. Elizabeth tried to concentrate on her plan. Merrivale's attending made things a little more difficult, but she had known he would not have allowed her to visit the town on her own – of course not. She pushed back her fear, the worries about her mother and brother, and focused on what she had to do.

Despite the promise to her father, Elizabeth was about to reveal the secret library of the old abbey to Thomas Montford. No-one knew about the hidden places under the hill, except for her father, her brother Robert and herself. The secret was closely guarded – only revealed to direct descendants. Even her mother didn't know, though she was well aware the family were custodians of a sacred trust.

For generations the Dyer family had been trusted servants to an inner order of the abbey. Among the hundreds of monks who lived and worked and prayed in the old order, in the hundreds of years before the abbey was destroyed, there existed a small, secret sect – the most wise and learned of all the monks, who possessed a library of hidden learning. When the abbey was destroyed, the secret library under the hill was kept safe. When Henry VIII sent his men to destroy the abbey, to pull down its walls, stone from stone, to loot the gold and treasure, the secret library was never discovered.

The monks of the inner order were sent away, and now were long dead. But the secret had remained in the possession of members of the Dyer family, who had served as librarians, protecting the store of arcane and dangerous knowledge. Even among the monks, only a handful knew of its existence. And while rumours of the library still existed, only the Dyers knew the truth of the matter. Only Edward and his two elder children could find the path into the secret places beneath the hill.

Charged with such a trust, how could the family change to a new Church of England when they had served the old order so faithfully for generations? It was a sacred promise, a bond between the family and the old faith.

Elizabeth wrangled with her conscience. When her father had shown her the doorway, she had sworn on her life never to tell anyone, except for her own children at the proper time. Now she was preparing to break this vow. Her stomach squeezed, thinking about the gravity of her decision. She had to find a way to save the priest – whose mission was so important Robert had been prepared to risk his life – all of their lives – to save him. And if Thomas Montford could be hidden in the old library, nobody would find him. He would be safe. And a priest of the Roman Catholic Church could surely be trusted with this deepest of secrets. She was sure of him.

But what if anything went wrong? What if she inadvertently led Merrivale to the library? This possibility was too terrible to contemplate. She shuddered, and Merrivale sensed the movement because he half turned his head.

'Are you cold?' he said. 'Shall I take you back to the manor?'

'No,' Elizabeth said shortly. Merrivale laughed and clapped his heels against the horse's sides, so it jumped forward and set off at a brisk canter, obliging Elizabeth to hold on tight.

But she was cold. The icy air nipped her cheeks.

At last they reached the town. The horse clattered over the bridge and up the cobbled hill to the marketplace. Merrivale needed no directing to the Dyers' house. Elizabeth slid off the horse. How long had she been away? No more than a few nights, and already her familiar home looked strange. Cold and dark it looked, dirty and untended, the windows grimy. She took a deep breath, and stepped forwards. Behind her Merrivale dropped lightly to the ground.

Elizabeth tried the door, but it was bolted from the inside. So she hammered with her fist.

'Esther!' she called. 'Mary! It's me, Elizabeth!'

She heard a movement in the house then, eager voices. The bolt was drawn back and there they stood, Esther and Mary. A smile lit Esther's face – until she spotted Merrivale standing behind Elizabeth and the little girl's eyes widened. She opened her mouth as though she were about to cry out, but Mary pulled her out of the doorway, the old woman standing like a barricade between the man and the child. Mary looked from Elizabeth to Merrivale, trying to understand what was happening, why the older daughter was standing on the

147

doorstep with the man who had taken the mistress away.

'Has he come for you too?' Mary said, her voice tremulous. 'Is he taking the little one? What does he want?'

'Mary – no. He hasn't come for Esther. He wouldn't let me see you unless he came too.' Elizabeth glanced back at Merrivale, but he didn't say a word. He stroked the face of the grey horse with his leather-gloved hand.

'I just wanted to find out how you are, both of you.' It was hard to speak, with Merrivale standing guard. Elizabeth had so many questions. Esther pushed past Mary and held out her arms to her big sister and Elizabeth scooped her up. Esther began to sob.

'Where's Mother? I want my mother,' she said. Behind her, Mary began to cluck sympathetically. Elizabeth's heart seemed to melt in her chest but she couldn't surrender to her feelings now. She rallied her strength.

'How have you been?' she said over her sister's shoulder to Mary.

The servant nodded. 'We're bearing up,' she said. 'We're waiting for the mistress to be released. But don't worry about us. I can take care of Esther.' She cast a cold, shrewd glance at Merrivale. Then Mary lifted Esther from her sister's embrace. Elizabeth and the servant exchanged one long, intense look. We are together in this, the look said. I trust you to be strong. We can rely on each other.

Elizabeth backed away. 'I shall go to the old abbey chapel now,' she said to Merrivale. She set off on foot and Merrivale followed, leading the horse.

The broken walls of the old abbey loomed ahead, casting a chilly shadow over the town. Many of the old stones had been pillaged for new buildings, but three old walls remained standing, roofless and broken. Arched windows gave a view of clear sky. White doves and shining black crows nested in nooks among the stonework. Only one chapel remained of the old abbey, left to the town to serve the new Church of England, though the riot of wall paintings was whitewashed and the forest of golden candlesticks were harvested for the King's treasury.

The chapel stood at the meeting point of the three ruined walls. Its doorway was vast, out of proportion with the size of the remaining building. Carved angels on each side of the archway climbed a ladder to heaven.

'Will the parish priest be here?' Merrivale asked.

Elizabeth nodded. In truth she had no idea if the priest would be here, but she improvised.

'I understand he attends the parish church at noon for an hour, to advise his parishioners.'

Merrivale shrugged. He did not look convinced.

'Do you intend to follow me, even into the church?' she said primly.

'Of course,' he said, looping the reins of his horse on the church gate. Elizabeth shrugged, but her heart was thundering. So much could go wrong. They stepped inside. The cold gloom of the chapel swallowed them up. Rows of wooden pews streamed away from them, to the bare stone altar at the front. Merrivale strolled up the aisle, brushing the ends of each pew with his hand.

'There's no-one here,' he said. His voice was very loud, the words bouncing off the walls. Then, even as he spoke, a man in dark robes stepped out of a doorway behind the altar. He nodded to them both, stepped down to the aisle and approached the visitors. Elizabeth trembled. She could hardly breathe. The scene had a terrible unreality. It couldn't be happening. Her mind whirled, but she forced herself to stand up straight. This was no time for her wits to desert her. She took a deep breath, preparing to improvise again, but before she could speak the priest shook Merrivale's hand.

'I am the deacon here. Are you a visitor to the town?'

Merrivale nodded, his eyes like little dark stones. He stared at the deacon.

'I am a servant of the Queen,' he said. 'My name is Kit Merrivale. This is Elizabeth Dyer. Perhaps you know her – a recalcitrant who does not attend your services. The daughter of a Catholic family. Now she thinks she will convert and wants your guidance.'

The deacon turned to Elizabeth, examining her closely. 'Is this true? Is it your wish to turn away from heresy, Elizabeth?'

She looked at the ground and nodded. The deacon seemed momentarily at a loss, not knowing what was expected of him, but Elizabeth piped up.

'Will you tell me about the new prayer book,' she said. 'I need to understand how I can change myself, how I've been mistaken in my old beliefs.'

'Of course,' the deacon nodded. He gestured for the girl and her companion to sit, and he returned to the vestry to fetch the book of common prayer.

Elizabeth sat down, but Merrivale remained standing. She sensed his irritation. He seemed to suspect she was up to something but didn't know what it was, and he certainly didn't want to listen to a priest maundering on about the

150

book of common prayer. The deacon returned, opened the prayer book and began to read.

Merrivale sighed with exasperation. 'I shall wait outside the door,' he said. 'Don't try and nip off – I shall be waiting.' With a scowl, he stomped out of the church. 'You have half an hour,' he called.

The door slammed shut behind him. The deacon stared at Elizabeth, and she stared at him. Then they laughed, both of them, a moment of strange, unsuitable laughter. There was no humour in it, just relief. A release of tension.

Then Elizabeth threw her arms around the priest, held him tight.

'Thomas,' she said. 'I've been so frightened. He might come in again. I'll show you, but we must be quick.'

Elizabeth jumped to her feet and hurried to the east wall. 'My father showed me this place on my tenth birthday,' she whispered. 'I swore I would never reveal this to anyone, God forgive me, even unto death.'

Her fingers searched the rough stone in the fat pillar supporting an arch over the altar. She closed her eyes. Forgive me, Lord, she prayed. And forgive me, Father, wherever you are.

Thomas Montford put his hand on Elizabeth's shoulder. 'I shan't betray your trust,' he said quietly.

Elizabeth's fingertips isolated the swirled nub of rock on each side of the pillar and she pressed them. At first nothing happened. Then she pressed again, harder, willing the door to open. It had been so long, perhaps the mechanism had seized up.

'It's not working,' she said, jabbing again. But something

151

happened. A curious grinding inside the giant pillar, and the smell of dust. The stones moved, pulling back to reveal a narrow space barely wide enough for a man to step through. Dark, chilly, the entrance gave off a breath of earth and ancient incense.

'There is a narrow stairway,' Elizabeth said. 'Go down, and you will find the old library. No-one will ever find you there. There is water – a well. We'll find you food, somehow.'

'Man does not live on bread alone,' the priest nodded grimly. 'Won't you come with me, Elizabeth? I don't want to leave you with Merrivale.'

Elizabeth shook her head. 'If I disappear, what might he do to my mother or even Esther?' she said. 'You go. Now. Hurry.' The priest stepped into the pillar and Elizabeth pushed the nubs in the stone again, so the stones slid back into place.

She ran back to the pew and took up the book again, just as Merrivale stormed back into the church. He glared at her.

'Where is he?' he yelled.

'The deacon? He told me he had to go,' Elizabeth said.

'There is no deacon.' Merrivale spat out the words. The parish priest stepped in behind Merrivale.

'The parish doesn't have a deacon,' the parish priest said. Of course he and Merrivale had met once before, when Isabella was captured.

'Where is he? Where did he go?' Merrivale ran around the church, searching. He peered under the pews and threw open the door to the vestry, disappeared inside for a moment, then returned, his face red and flustered. He strode down the aisle to Elizabeth.

'Where did he go? Was it him? Was that Thomas Montford?' he demanded. He raised a hand, as though to strike, but the parish priest trotted over.

'No,' he said. 'Not in the church!' The priest was nervous of Merrivale too, keeping a distance, blustering his commands. 'There is no other exit from the chapel. If the man you seek has left the church, we would have seen him.'

Merrivale cursed and stamped his foot. 'To think I had him – right under my nose! Where did he go, Elizabeth? I'll have my men come and pull this place to pieces! I'll have them turn the town upside down! And you . . .!' He glared at Elizabeth. 'What shall I do to you, you little bitch!'

The priest clucked again, plump with outrage at Merrivale's ungodly behaviour in the church. Merrivale drew himself up straight, looking as though he would gladly strangle the priest and Elizabeth after him. It was the first time Elizabeth had seen him lose control.

In the depths of her terror she felt a grain of curious triumph. She had beaten him.

Crow Man

He dragged her out of the church. Behind them, the parish priest wrung his hands, protesting feebly. Elizabeth resisted, trying to pull free, struggling and batting at him with her hands, but Merrivale was strong and relentless. He jerked her through the doorway, into the graveyard, and in the bright sunlight he whacked her across the face with the back of his hand. Pain exploded in her head. The force of the blow knocked her to the ground. She felt the inside of her cheek tear on her teeth.

Elizabeth lay on the cold grass, stunned and gasping. Blood dripped from her mouth. She shook her head, trying to clear the white haze of pain fogging her thoughts. Slowly she clambered to her feet again but Merrivale raised a fist and punched the side of her head. This time there was a white flash before her eyes, and suddenly everything seemed very distant – Merrivale with his anger, the broken walls towering above them, the crows flapping on their high perches. Elizabeth lay on the ground, without moving, nearly senseless. But Merrivale pulled her to her feet again. Dimly she wondered if he would strike her a third time, but Merrivale

154

pulled her away from the church, along the path through the graves, to his horse. Then he lifted her onto his shoulder, and threw her over the back of the patient horse.

This time Elizabeth didn't have even the dignity of riding behind him. Instead, she lay across the front of the saddle, on her belly, the blood leaking out of her mouth and over her face. Her ears started to ring, pressure rising in the walls of her skull. Merrivale kicked the horse, turning it around, and they headed out of the town. Elizabeth bumped uncomfortably in front of him. People stopped to stare as they rode past, the horse's hooves skittering on the greasy pebbles, but no-one dared to stop them. They crossed the bridge over the river, and headed along the highway to the west, then turned up the old Roman road.

Vaguely Elizabeth wondered what would happen next. She had made a fool of Merrivale, and he was furious. She was horribly uncomfortable, slung over the front of the horse, and as her mind cleared from the blow, her sense of discomfort grew. Her head began to throb painfully and she felt sick. This was the worst feeling of all, the churning of her stomach, the hot sweat breaking out all over her body as she struggled not to throw up.

She tried to work out where they were going, but it was hard to see what was happening, with her face pressed against the horse's hot shoulder. The hooves seemed frighteningly close, thundering beneath on the ground beneath her.

It was a long ride. Elizabeth lost track of time, because each long, painful minute seemed to last an hour. The blood that leaked from her mouth congealed all over her face. Her head hurt so much, as if her skull were shattered in pieces. And she felt sick.

The journey went on. Finally she lapsed into unconsciousness – whether for a few minutes or longer it was impossible to say – but when she came to, she began to retch. A thin stream of brown, porridgey vomit streamed from her sore mouth, to the muddy ground beneath. Some caught on the horse's leg, and Merrivale cursed her again, kicking at her with his booted foot. But he didn't stop. Elizabeth's body was bruised all over, joints aching, hands and feet numb with cold.

When they stopped at last, the sunlight was fading though the sky was still clear. The sunset broke over a copse of black trees like a yolk. A large stone house was silhouetted in the sunset. Merrivale let her drop in a heap to the ground and shouted out. In a moment, the door opened and a man ran out. Merrivale dismounted, and stamped his feet to warm them up. He barked orders. The man picked up Elizabeth and hurriedly carried her into the house. He called a second man to see to the horse, as Merrivale followed them in. He disappeared into one of the rooms but all Elizabeth could see was the comforting blaze of a fire, before the door was shut.

Elizabeth was carried up the stairs. The man fiddled with a key and unlocked a door. He manoeuvred her inside the room, and then dropped her onto the floor. Without a word, he turned around, went out, and locked the door shut again. For several minutes she lay there, exactly as she had fallen. For her tired, injured body it was a moment of bliss, just to be still, after the long, bumpy, agonising ride. Her face hurt, but the knives of pain in her head drew back a little, if she could be still. If she could just be still. Far away she could hear the voices of men downstairs, but for a moment nothing mattered any more. The priest, Isabella, Lady Catherine, Esther, were all far away. She drifted into a dazed sleep. The darkness swallowed her up.

How long was she asleep? It was still dark, still night-time when the door opened and someone hauled her to her feet.

'Stand up,' the man said. 'You're coming with me.' It wasn't the man who had carried her inside, nor was it Merrivale. This one stank of beer and bad meat. He wasn't careful with her, half dragging her down the stairs to the room with the fire Elizabeth had seen when she entered the house. She was left to stand in front of a table. Merrivale was sitting behind it. There were several other men lurking in the gloom but Elizabeth couldn't tell how many. Merrivale looked sleek and warm, as though he had just enjoyed a hearty meal. He stretched out his legs, relaxed again, perfectly in control.

'Elizabeth,' he said. 'It's time we had a proper talk, you and I. It was a clever trick you pulled off this afternoon. You surprised me. I have no idea how you managed it. You were cunning. I am really quite impressed.

'But it is only a brief setback. I have ordered men to search the church from top to bottom – and then the rest of the town. Your friend will not be safe for long.'

Elizabeth tried to swallow. 'May I have a drink, please?' she whispered.

Merrivale leaned forward, pretending he hadn't heard. 'What did you say?'

'May I have a drink, please?'

But Merrivale ignored her request. 'This place,' he said, gesturing around him at the house, 'has been entrusted to me for the carrying out of my duties for the protection of the state – for priest hunting. I have to say I enjoyed the fine company at Spirit Hill – and it was a much better location for me in the searching out of secrets – for searching out your secrets – but my headquarters' – he gestured around him – 'are so much more private and secluded. No-one can hear us.'

Slowly and ostentatiously he picked up a leather bag from the table and took out from it a bundle of papers. Slowly he picked his way through the folded letters, one by one. Elizabeth's head began to pound again. She wanted to sit down, but she was aware of the other men behind her. What would they do? The house was miles from anywhere. She was alone and at their mercy. They could do what they liked.

She closed her eyes, and prayed. God help me, she pleaded. God help me. Please, Holy Mother of God help me now.

Merrivale picked up a letter with a flourish.

'Ah,' he said. 'What have we here? Yes, a letter intercepted at Oxford warning that the heretic priest, one Thomas Montford, was about to be discovered – suggesting he flee with Robert Dyer, a Catholic sympathiser.' He paused for a moment, waiting for a reaction. Then he continued: 'And I think you know this traitor, Robert Dyer.'

Elizabeth rocked on her feet. The headache filled all the spaces of her mind, leaving her too little space to think. She didn't answer.

'Elizabeth,' Merrivale said sharply. 'This isn't simply a matter of private conscience. The Queen herself has said she does not wish to make a window into men's souls. The priests coming over from Spain and France want to start a Catholic uprising. They want to overthrow the rightful Queen of England. There have been attempts on the Queen's life.'

His voice rose as he spoke, and now he sat forward in his chair, staring into her face. Elizabeth stared back. The fire-light played over Merrivale's face, and the shadows moved, gold and black and gold again.

'Where are they, Elizabeth? I need to find them, Dyer and Montford. And you know where they are.'

A sigh escaped Elizabeth's lips. In the dark forest of her thoughts, a tiny light bloomed. So they hadn't caught Robert. Merrivale didn't know where he was. Robert was safe – somewhere.

'May I have a drink?' Elizabeth whispered again.

'Tell me where they're hiding, Elizabeth. You're just a child. I know you're only caught up in this because of your brother. Why should you carry his burden? Tell me where he and the priest have gone, and I will set you free. And your mother.'

'Where is she?' Elizabeth blurted. 'Is she here too?'

Merrivale considered. 'Yes, she's here,' he said. 'Would you like to see her?'

Elizabeth began to tremble. She wished she hadn't spoken. Was her mother here, or was that another trick, a way to torment her into telling them what they wanted to know? So she didn't answer Merrivale's question. She stared at the ground.

'Do you think I enjoy this, Elizabeth? Stuck in the filthy country where nothing happens. Wouldn't it be good if we could wrap this up, if I could get my hands on the priest and

159

your brother, and then I could let you and your mother go?

'That was Thomas Montford, Elizabeth, in the abbey this morning, wasn't it? Where did he go?'

Elizabeth shook her head. 'I don't know,' she said. 'He returned to the vestry. I don't know where he went.' Her voice croaked, her mouth still tasting rotten from the dried blood. She ached for a drink. Merrivale yawned, lounged in his chair again, letting her see how comfortable he was.

'Would you like to see the Spanish ruling England, Elizabeth?' he mused. 'When the security of the state and the well-being of the monarch are at stake, I have the authority to do whatever I think is necessary to protect us all. Was that Thomas Montford in the church, Elizabeth? Where did he go?'

The questions went on for a long time. She was obliged to stand, and her head ached. Merrivale wouldn't give her a drink. He asked her about her family, about her brother and his friends, about the fines they paid for not attending church. He even asked her about Lady Catherine, how long she had worked for her, what they talked about, what she knew about her husband. He repeated the same questions over and over. Once, when she didn't answer fast enough, he began to shout. Then he was gentle, pouring water into a cup for her to drink, holding the vessel to her lips as the water soaked into her parched mouth.

She told him a great deal – but nothing – nothing – about Robert or Thomas Montford. In the end, Merrivale ordered one of his men to take her back to the room. There was plenty of time, he said. She would tell him what he wanted in the end.

The man who smelled of bad meat hauled her up the stairs and locked her up again. It was so cold. A raw draught blew through the bare floorboards. The shutters in the window were nailed shut. Elizabeth curled up, hugging her legs, trying to pray, but her thoughts were in disarray. Her head spun, Merrivale's voice echoing in her head. It was hard to remember what she had told him. She collapsed into sleep for a while, but even in her dreams, Merrivale persisted with his questioning.

When she woke, the door was opening, and Elizabeth was flooded with dread. Had they come for her already? First light was creeping through chinks in the shutters. Her body was stiff with cold and she was desperate to pee. But they hadn't come to fetch her. Instead a woman was shoved through the door.

Elizabeth's sense of discomfort melted. She sat up straight. Her mouth dropped open.

'Mother?' she said. 'Is that you?'

The woman stood up straight. She raised her hand to her mouth, eyes wide. 'Elizabeth? Elizabeth? Is that you? What are you doing here?' she said. 'Why are you here?'

Slowly Elizabeth stood up. She was shaking all over. They stared at each other, mother and daughter, the pleasure at the reunion overshadowed by a dread of the circumstances in which they found themselves. Elizabeth stepped towards her mother. How tired Jane looked. How gaunt and old. She searched her mother's face, and her heart ached, seeing how weary she was, how beaten down.

'Mum – did they hurt you? Are you all right?'

'I'm all right. They didn't hurt me. They just locked me

up. How many days has it been? I've lost count, Elizabeth. I was so afraid for you – for Robert.'

Quickly Elizabeth raised her finger to her lips. They didn't know who was listening – certainly someone would be eavesdropping.

Jane Dyer nodded, understanding Elizabeth's caution. Tears welled in her eyes. Her skin was greasy, and dusty. She dabbed her face with her sleeve.

'They hurt you,' Jane whispered in her daughter's ear, gently touching the bruise on Elizabeth's face. 'What are we going to do? I could endure anything to protect Robert. But if they threaten to hurt you? What will I do?'

'I think that's why they brought me,' Elizabeth whispered. She rested her forehead on her mother's shoulder. They sat down together in the cold, bare room, arms around each other. Fingers of light poked through the shutters. Outside, the birds began to sing and the wind stirred in the trees around the house.

'What's happening now?' Elizabeth pricked her ears. She could hear voices outside – and the staccato of hooves. Peering out through the chinks in the covered windows, she saw Merrivale riding away. Was this a good sign? Where was he going?

They were left alone the rest of the day. A leather bucket was provided for a toilet. In the middle of the day a plate of boiled barley, grey and congealed, was shoved through the door but neither Elizabeth nor her mother had the appetite to eat. The time stretched out, empty hours in which to brood about the prospect of Merrivale's return and another interrogation. They tried to keep their spirits up, whispering together, reciting the rosary, singing little songs. Elizabeth told her mother about the happenings at Spirit Hill, about Isabella scrubbed and trimmed by Lady Catherine, and the painting of Merrivale's portrait. But she did not say one word about the hiding of the priest.

Merrivale returned just before sunset, accompanied by the servant he had taken to the manor at Spirit Hill. Elizabeth and Jane spied out through the locked shutters. Both men were filthy from the ride, and Merrivale was angry too, doling out curses on the men for their incompetence. The row continued downstairs. They could hear loud voices, the sound of a struggle of some kind, perhaps Merrivale kicking out at his servants. Elizabeth and her mother regarded each other in horror. Merrivale's rage didn't bode well. If he would lash out at his men, what would he do to them? They waited, nerves taut, for the door to be unlocked and the inevitable interrogation. But, unexpectedly, the uproar died down and the perfume of cooking drifted through the house instead. Merrivale was settling down to eat.

An hour or so crept past, and the waiting was a torment in itself. Fear gnawed, never letting go. He would call for them to be brought down sooner or later and there was no telling what might happen then. Judging from his temper, his patience had worn very thin.

A thin, yellow light leaked into the upper room. Elizabeth pressed her face to the rough shutter, to see a huge, fiery moon rising over the trees. It was remarkable. Beautiful – glittering like a jewel. For a moment the spectacle distracted her. The trees pointed up with their black, stringy hands, perfectly still, beneath a moon that *burned*.

She turned back to the room, and blinked.

'What is it?' Jane said.

Elizabeth shook her head. 'Listen,' she said. They both lifted their faces, trying to sense – what? Something had happened. What was it?

The light in the room shifted, throwing shadows awry. Particles of dust began to spin in coils, shining in the moonlight. The house creaked suddenly, seemed to move, like an old woman shifting her aching joints.

Elizabeth and her mother waited, senses acute, trying to work out what was going on. The house groaned. The walls seemed to swell and bulge. The stones glistened. Jane crossed herself, and began to pray aloud. Holy Mother preserve us. Father in heaven protect us. Downstairs, someone cried out.

'What is it? What do you think it is?' Elizabeth ran to the door and rattled the latch. What was happening downstairs? She pressed her ear to the door. It sounded as though someone were tipping over the furniture. There were shouts, a clash, perhaps of a blade against stone.

'Elizabeth,' Jane said. 'Sit beside me. Come now.' Her voice was low, very serious. Elizabeth turned and dropped beside her mother. A shadow passed in front of the shutter. A ribbon of scent tickled her nose, a weaving of church stone, incense, dying roses, cold earth.

Jane started, and gripped Elizabeth's hand tight.

'There's something in the room,' Jane whispered. Her fingers clenched, bruising Elizabeth's skin. 'I saw it – in the shadows.'

*

164

Isabella spent the morning after her trip to the woods scrubbing her clothes. Lady Catherine was furious when she woke up to find her newly scrubbed charge plastered in filth.

'Where did you go? After all the time we spent cleaning you yesterday! Look at your gown! How ungrateful! After all we have done for you.'

Isabella stared at Lady Catherine's feet, and tried to let the words wash over her. But she wasn't entirely impervious. Lady Catherine's anger was fierce as a whip. A tear leaked.

'I'm sorry,' she whispered. 'I'm very sorry.'

Lady Catherine pulled up, hearing the apology. Perhaps she was glad Isabella had come back at all, after her mysterious night jaunt. She might have simply run away for good.

'I'm not used to living like this,' Isabella said. Her gesture seemed to encompass everything – the house, the people, her clothes. Lady Catherine sighed, and nodded.

'I do understand. But don't go out again,' she said. 'You are not to live like an animal any longer, Isabella. You are a Christian, and you must stay with us.'

As a punishment, Isabella had to heat a vat of water and clean her dirty clothes. The cook told her what to do. Isabella was nervous of the cook, the dour woman with the florid face who gave her instructions and inspected her work.

Mud from the wood had badly stained Isabella's white shift, her warm gown and overskirt. The washing seemed to take forever. She was sitting in the kitchen, up to her elbows in warm water, when she heard a horse at the front of the house. She stood up, to look out of the window.

'It's the Catholic girl,' the cook said. 'Going off with the young man. Perhaps he's going to lock her up.' The cook sniffed and wiped her nose. 'High time,' she added, disapproving.

Isabella stared, at a loss to understand why Elizabeth was riding behind Kit Merrivale. The spectacle filled her with dismay. Was she under arrest? Had the priest been found out? When they had concocted the plan the previous night, Elizabeth had assumed one of the servants would be ordered to accompany her to the town, under the pretext of the visit to the parish priest. They had not imagined Merrivale would bother himself to take her.

The cook grunted, indicating that Isabella should return to her washing. Isabella dropped to her knees again, mashing and swishing the stained, sodden fabric in the bucket, but her thoughts racing. She had a bad feeling, seeing Elizabeth clutching on to her enemy, riding away with him. Lady Catherine had provided Elizabeth with a degree of protection, but without that, what would Merrivale do?

All sorts of terrible possibilities loomed in her mind. She hurried her task. When the clothes were washed, rinsed, wrung and dangling above the fireplace, she trotted away from the kitchen to the studio, to find Lady Catherine. Outside the door, she took a deep breath, checked her cap, and stood up straight. She knocked.

'Enter,' a voice called. Isabella opened the door and stepped into the room. The portrait of Kit Merrivale was well advanced now. Lady Catherine had worked fast. The face was painted, though the rich fabrics of the sitter's clothes and the background were yet to be finished. Still Isabella was stunned. She had never seen anything like it – the quality of the likeness, the luminous skin, the very soul of Kit Merrivale

166

staring from his portrait. Handsome and sly, the face in the picture. Ambitious and intelligent, clever and cruel. Yes, even his cruelty was depicted, in the lines of his mouth, in the cold eyes and their careful consideration of the viewer. Isabella shivered.

'What is it?' Lady Catherine said, a trace of annoyance in her voice, at the interruption.

'I wondered, if you would tell me, where Elizabeth is going,' Isabella said.

Lady Catherine lifted her brush from the canvas and looked at Isabella thoughtfully.

'She's gone to the town,' she said. 'Kit's taken her. Are you friends now, you two?'

'Yes,' Isabella nodded.

Lady Catherine turned back to her painting. 'Don't worry, she'll be back later,' she said. 'She wanted to see her sister, you see. Poor girl, she's missing her family.'

Isabella spent the rest of the day worrying, staring out of the window, desperate to see her friend return. The afternoon crawled past. She was called upon to help the little maid, Deb, setting the fires and spreading fresh rushes on the floor. Deb chattered on, but Isabella felt painfully shy, even with Deb, and her thoughts were bound up with Elizabeth, wherever she was.

At the end of the afternoon, as the light began to fade, Lady Catherine began to worry too. They should have been back by now. Where were they? The sun descended. The men of the house gathered in the long hall, waiting for their evening meal. Eventually, Lady Catherine, irritable with the waiting, gave up and ordered the meal to be served. She insisted Isabella sit beside her, though neither of them had the appetite to eat much. They sat up late, by the fire, still waiting, till after ten at night.

Lady Catherine was pale with worry. When she sent Isabella to bed, she patted her on the head.

'Try not to fret. I'm sure there's a perfectly good reason why they haven't returned,' she said, trying to reassure. Isabella nodded, managing a little smile. But she wasn't reassured. She was certain something terrible had happened.

Isabella lay awake, on her mattress in the corridor, as the rest of the household settled down to sleep. Elizabeth was in danger, she was sure of it. There was no other explanation. What should she do? All the long hours of darkness, she lay awake, her eyes fixed on the ceiling, struggling for an answer.

Late the next morning, Merrivale returned alone. He looked tired, and his face was dark. Lady Catherine ran out of the house when he arrived, ran right up to him, dodging the hooves of his horse.

'Where have you been?' she shouted. 'Where's Elizabeth? What have you done with her?'

The servants all looked out, hearing the voice of their mistress, craning to see what was going on.

'Making a fool of herself over that young man,' the cook muttered, loud enough for everyone to hear. 'Making a fuss over the Catholic girl. Good riddance, I say.'

Outside, Merrivale tugged savagely at the reins, so his horse jumped back abruptly, throwing its head in the air. Merrivale swung his leg over the horse's withers and slid to the ground. He threw the reins to the groom, who had come running from the stables.

'Kit,' Lady Catherine pleaded, laying her hand on his arm. 'What happened? Where's Elizabeth? Please?'

Merrivale didn't answer. He jerked his arm away and marched into the house. Lady Catherine trotted after him.

'Kit! Kit!' she called. But he didn't make any response.

Inside the house he threw his whip onto the floor with a clatter, dropped his sodden cloak to the floor, pulled up a chair by the fire and bawled for a servant to take off his boots. Isabella hurried in, with a cup of warm beer and a bowl of porridge left over from breakfast.

'Kit,' Lady Catherine persisted, hovering around him, pleading for his attention. 'You must tell me, what's happened? Where's Elizabeth?'

He picked up the cup and took a long drink. Then he stared at Lady Catherine.

'The filthy Catholic bitch,' he said.

Lady Catherine recoiled, stunned by the venom in his voice.

'What?' she said faintly.

'He was there, right under my nose, and I let him get away. I didn't recognise him! And she was so cool, God's blood. How did she do it? How did she organise it? That's what I don't understand. She hasn't sent any letters out? And where did he go? He just vanished.'

Lady Catherine shook her head. 'I don't understand. What are you talking about?' she said.

'Elizabeth, your dear girl. She's a traitor and a heretic, and you've sheltered her in your house while she plots against the Queen.'

'What?' Lady Catherine said again, flapping her hands in

front of her face, in a curious frightened gesture. She was deadly pale. Neither she nor Merrivale paid any attention to Isabella, waiting with the porridge bowl. But Isabella's hands were shaking. Something terrible had happened. The priest had escaped, by the sounds of it, but where was Elizabeth? She struggled to remain calm.

'She's under arrest,' Merrivale said. 'I need all your men to search the town. The priest is still here. I'll tear the whole place down if I have to.'

'Of course, if you must.' Lady Catherine was distracted, wringing her hands. Her eyes were full of tears.

'Please – please tell me what happened,' she said. But Merrivale was still fuming.

'One of your servants is helping her,' he said. 'Somebody here. How else would she have organised the meeting? So cunning. She fooled me.'

'No.' Lady Catherine shook her head. 'The other servants keep their distance. She isn't popular, because of her faith.'

'And yet she managed to draw you in, Catherine. You made her a friend. Why was that? In your own household! Shall I have you arrested too?'

Lady Catherine was amazed, and horrified. She stretched out her hand to Merrivale, grasped his white, curled hand.

'You couldn't!' she said. 'I thought – I thought we were friends, Kit. Why are you doing this? You know I'm not a traitor!'

Merrivale clenched his fist and pulled it away. His face was full of pent-up rage and frustration. He looked like a little child caught up in a fit of anger – a dangerous child with recourse to boots and fists, and the power to order arrest, imprisonment, torture.

Isabella wanted to run away, to leave the house far behind and crawl back to the crow people, and the safety of the other world. Her heart was thundering and he would hear it, surely. What about Lady Catherine? Would she remember Isabella had gone out the night before? Would she put two and two together?

As if he divined her thoughts, Kit turned to Isabella.

'Come here,' he said. Isabella let out a small frightened sound, but Merrivale simply seized the bowl of porridge. He took a large spoonful, and grimaced.

'Filthy stuff,' he said. Lady Catherine just stared at him, tearful and shocked. She didn't know what to do.

'I thought – I thought I meant something to you, Kit. We had such good times together. We talked.' She looked old and shrunken, her pride sucked out.

But Merrivale was oblivious. Despite his earlier complaint, he ate noisily.

'Leave me,' he said. 'I have the Queen's authority, Catherine. Her protection is my first priority. Nothing else matters. Do you understand?'

Lady Catherine backed away, gathering her dignity. She dropped Merrivale a cold curtsey, and stalked out of the room. But once through the door, she picked up her skirts and ran up the stairs. Isabella hurried after, but Lady Catherine's door was locked. Isabella could hear her sobbing inside.

A gloom settled over the branches of bare trees, the dusky hedgerows and fields. Here and there, the last few golden leaves. The early evening was eerie and melancholy. Isabella walked away from the house, across a field, to a solitary hawthorn tree in a hedgerow of ash and elm. She didn't hesitate now. She didn't look over her shoulder. There was no going back. The situation had reached crisis point and she had to act once and for all. Elizabeth was in peril and Isabella, perhaps, could save her.

She took a deep breath, and threw off her white woollen cap. The cold air prickled her scalp, teasing her cropped hair. Half a dozen crows perched on the branches of an ash tree, before her.

Isabella had wanted to leave the crow people behind, to find her brother and bring him with her to live in the mundane world. Now she was turning to them for help again – as her mother had so many years ago. What choice had her mother had then? What choice did she have? None. None at all.

A haze of red berries still adorned the hawthorn tree, though its branches were bare and black. Isabella shivered, sensing invisible shadows falling about her. She circled the tree, once, twice. Across the field, beyond her, she could see the manor at Spirit Hill. It was far away now. She was leaving it behind.

The crows cawed and flapped in the branches of the ash. Isabella walked around the hawthorn tree for a third time.

The gloom intensified, but features in the landscape seemed to gain intensity. The last rays of sunlight shone upon the trees. Stones underfoot gleamed like gems.

Isabella called out a name in a loud, fierce voice. The crows cawed again, angry now, then flew away in a clatter. Darkness gathered, like skirts, around Isabella and the bent, red-veiled tree. Something stirred in the mass of branches, a movement like an old woman turning over in her sleep.

There was a puff of cold, sweet air – the sound of voices far away. Isabella called out again, a long, complex name that echoed across the fields.

Underfoot, the stones began to move, perhaps remembering the name. Stones have long memories and the summoning disturbed them.

The hawthorn, the tree beloved by faeries, began to shimmer, for the land of faery is the shadow of the ordinary world and the hawthorn sends roots into both, the mundane world and the shadow land.

A dark shape crossed the sky, blotting out the light. A hoarse call broke the air above Isabella's head. She looked up, raised her arms, emotions in a storm – fear, excitement and triumph all at once, swallowing her up. She laughed aloud. The beating of huge black wings sounded like thunder. Two fierce claws, daggered with grey talons, landed lightly on the ground.

The faery was mostly bird now, a huge crow with glossy feathers. Its face was beaked, the eyes bright gold. It looked at Isabella, turning its head to one side. Isabella stepped closer, and carefully climbed on the faery's back. The feathers were cold as ice, and smooth as silk. She pressed her body beneath them, so only her head was visible against the body of the crow man.

'Can you find her?' she said. The faery dipped its head. Isabella didn't have to explain. There was a bond of a sort

173

between them still, the child and the faery. Isabella held on tight as the bird spread its great wings and lifted into the air.

Stone Stairway

Thomas Montford stood in the dark. The stone door had closed behind him, cutting off all light and sound from the church. It was utterly black. The curious perfume of dead flowers filled his lungs. He could taste dust on his tongue, could feel it settling on his face. He hardly dared to move, but he lifted his arms, and encountered the narrow curved walls of the stone pillar. It was like a tomb.

Thomas gasped for air. He had to move – had to find the stairway. The darkness seemed so heavy, he felt it would crush him. He sensed the weight of stone over his head, the pillar bearing the weight of the great stone church.

He shut his eyes, and tried to breathe evenly. Dear God, he prayed, guide me now. Help me, God, help me find a way. In his mind he recited the Hail Mary, trying to calm himself. What was happening outside? What was Elizabeth doing? There was nothing he could do for her now.

Thomas shifted a foot, blindly feeling his way to the edge of the step. There – there it was, the stone giving way to empty space. Slowly, cautiously, he lowered his foot to the next step, keeping one arm against the wall. Down he went again, feeling his way, step by step, on the steep, spiral staircase.

It was a long descent. The stairs went on and on. After a while, Thomas began to feel dizzy. Once, he clutched the wall with both hands, leaning his back against it, afraid he would fall. The wall itself seemed to reel away. It was hard to tell if he were upright or lying down – standing or falling into space. Despite the cold, Thomas broke out in a hot sweat. Dust tickled his nose, and when he sneezed, the sound echoed over and over, bouncing against the stone coil of the spiral staircase.

He rested a moment, clinging to the wall, and tried to pray, but this time the words wouldn't come. Maybe God himself recoiled from this dark, miserable pipe into the Earth. Thomas prised a hand from the wall to cross himself. It was a blasphemous thought. God was everywhere, and no man was beyond his reach, even here, folded away in the dark.

At last Thomas stood up straight and took a deep breath. He had to move on. Down he went, down into the bowels of the hill, beneath the church, under soil and rock, the buried flints of the ancients, the forgotten coins of the Romans, and into the empty spaces beneath the town.

The staircase ended abruptly, at a wooden door that Thomas walked into with a bump. It was a relief, and a shock. He spread his hands and ran his fingers over its surface till he found a simple iron latch, which he lifted.

As Thomas stepped into the room, a warm, white light flared from a stone vessel on a table. Thomas drew a breath – staring in wonder. What manner of light was this? Slowly, dazzled by the brightness, he moved towards it. The room was revealed by the uncanny light – circular and empty, except for the table. The light was a pearly ball hovering above a bowl. The ball seemed to spin, casting out light as it moved. Thomas stretched out his hand to it, but he felt neither heat nor cold. When he reached out his fingers to clasp the light, it dropped out of his reach, only to rise up again when he drew his hand away. Thomas was fascinated. What science had created such a thing? It crossed his mind the device might be magical – and possibly heretical. But he pushed this consideration aside. After all, he was in the heart of the old abbey, where the Roman Catholic Church, in its prime and power, had set up an inner circle of its most accomplished and devoted servants. He had heard of it, oh yes. At the seminary, the priest school, there were whispers of the powers of the most gifted monks in the ancient abbeys. There were rumours that Maumesbury Abbey had such a closed circle – but Thomas hadn't credited it. Never had he thought to see for himself what could be achieved. These great men had created the light.

Magic might be allowed in such circumstances. After all, the three wise men who visited the Christ child were magicians, who had foreseen the future and read the stars. But only the very few, the most wise and learned, could meddle with such matters. The rest of humanity, the ordinary, ignorant rabble, had to be kept safe from such dangers and temptations.

Thomas stretched out his hand again, pleased by the white light, and the graceful way it danced away from him. He was buoyed up with excitement now, the fear of the staircase had passed away. What further marvels might he find? He looked round the room, to a second door in the wall, opposite the first. The second door wasn't locked, and when he pulled it open, the ball of light followed him into the next chamber, floating just an arm's length away.

The light glittered on gold – a hoard of gold.

This second chamber was huge, wider than Thomas was able to see in his pool of magic light. And heaped on the floor, just in front of him, was a marvellous, haphazard pile of the old church's treasure. He saw fat candlesticks, chalices spotted with bright jewels, statues of the saints and the Virgin Mary inlaid with blue lapis lazuli and silver mother-of-pearl. There were giant books bound with fine leather and encrusted with precious stones, tapestries of fine silk, woven with threads of gold. Staring at the careless pile, Thomas was stunned. Never – never had he seen anything like this. He stepped closer, crunching underfoot a rosary strung with beads of topaz and beryl. When the order for closure came – when King Henry had demanded Maumesbury Abbey be destroyed – the secret order must have hidden away their most priceless treasures, in a place that would never be found. He imagined the scene, the men on horses carrying the paper with the King's seal riding across the country, while the monks feverishly gathered as much as they could, grabbing the church candles, tearing down the tapestries. And then the few who knew the hiding place would have locked up the church and carried the treasures down the precipitous stairway, dumping them in a heap on the cold ground. And here it had lain, all these decades, buried in darkness. Were the King's men angry, when the prize could not be found, and the King had to make do with the second-best gold to fatten his treasury? Thomas smiled to himself as he bent down to pick up a cup of gold, still fresh and yellow as butter after all this time. Simple it was, without any engraving or jewelled ornament, but good and smooth and heavy in his hand. Then he put the cup down, and turned the cover of a gem-studded book. The light hovered over his shoulder, showing the fine illumination of the pages, the intricate painted decoration of flowers and birds around the Latin text. So much was destroyed – centuries of books, manuscripts, works of art, learning – but here a glowing, golden pocket had survived.

Thomas stood up and began to explore the rest of the room. Circular, like the first, it was a library. Wooden shelves covered the walls and books burdened the shelves. Few were as gaudy as those on the floor. These works, from all over Europe, the Far East and North Africa, were plain and work-manlike. Maths, science, geography, language, architecture and medicine – from time to time Thomas drew a volume from a shelf and glanced at the pages inside. His heart quick-ened in his chest – how good it was, how marvellous, that such a wealth of books had endured.

But there was more to see. He left the books behind and proceeded to a smaller room beyond the library. Here he found a spring bubbling up into a basin carved in the stony floor. This must be the well Elizabeth had mentioned. He stooped to take a drink, clearing the taste of dust from his mouth. The water was achingly cold. He moved on again, and the path grew more complex. He passed through long corridors, peered into tiny rooms, like caves, some of which had simple beds inside. The passageways twisted and turned, sometimes surprising him, looping back to the place with the spring, or else terminating in a sudden dead end. Always the magic light hovered around him, casting long shadows in the cold, dark tunnels. And it was very cold. The longer he walked, the colder he became, as though the rock walls sucked out the heat from his body. Thomas pulled his cloak closer around him. Perhaps, like the ancient labyrinth devised by Dedalus in Crete, the passageways were designed to trick and trap him. Thomas decided it might be wise to return to the relative safety of the library.

He headed back the way he had come, taking long strides, the ball of light easily keeping up. The corridor veered to right and left. Then, ahead of him, he saw a large door, in a Gothic arch, ornately decorated with wrought iron. Thomas pulled up short, surprised. He hadn't seen this before. The priest hesitated for a moment. He had decided not to be lured by the maze, to return to the library, but the grandeur of the doorway appealed to him. What lay beyond it? The handle was a large black ring, and Thomas could not resist it. He turned the ring, which lifted the latch on the other side of the door with a clunk. Then he pushed the door open and stepped into a chapel.

A stone altar stood at the far end, beyond half a dozen rows of carved wooden pews. A white cloth, embroidered with stalks of ripe wheat and red poppies, still lay upon the altar. Twelve candles burned brightly with white, magic light on a high stone shelf behind the altar, where stood a monstrance – a sunburst of beaten gold on a stand embedded with rubies. The vessel was intended to display the sacred communion bread, and indeed, it contained the holy sacrament – the body of Christ.

Overwhelmed, Thomas dropped to his knees and crossed himself. He could hardly breathe, overcome by the spectacle. Like the holy knights of old, like Galahad seeking the Grail, Thomas Montford had navigated the dark path to the secret chapel, in the heart of the hill.

A stream of grateful words tumbled in his head, prayers of thanks to God. His eyes were blurred with tears when he raised his head, to see the paintings covering the walls.

Across the land, when the altars were stripped in the Reformation, so many fine church pictures had been covered in whitewash. People were tired of the gaudy church decorations of ancient times. They wanted simplicity now. But that hadn't happened here. The wall paintings in the secret chapel had survived, hidden away beneath the town. The pale, gentle face of the Virgin Mary smiled down on him. Her head was haloed with gold, and in her lap, a chubby Christ child raised his infant hand in a blessing. Beside her stood St Joseph, the shepherds and the three wise men. Thomas turned to see more. Yes – there they were, on the facing wall, the archangels – St Michael clad in armour with a sword in his hand and the dragon, Lucifer, at his feet. Then St Gabriel, with a white lily, St Raphael bearing a pilgrim's staff and the fourth, St Uriel, cradling an open book. The archangels were beautiful, with their folded wings and gentle, luminous faces, and all about them another host of angels gathered.

But these other angels did not look gentle. They were tall and slender, and sprouting from their backs were wings covered in black feathers. Their faces were fierce and angular, with bright golden eyes. Long ebony hair spilled from their

181

heads, and they wore a multitude of dull golden bands – bracelets, rings, collars, crowns. Beautiful, yes, as a barren desert is beautiful, or a wild moor in the winter covered in perfect white snow. Not a beauty to comfort, Thomas thought, because it was cold and old and distant. The painting pricked something inside him. The thought, and the contrasting spectacle of the dark angels, filled him with a strange mixture of sadness and elation. Who had painted these creatures? How had he been inspired to create them on a chapel wall?

Thomas rose to his feet and stepped closer to the wall, to see if any signature remained. The angel pictures towered above him, as he searched around their long, white feet for a name or a symbol that might tell him the name of the artist. He peered among them, looking for a clue, until, with a shock, in the veil of paint, he came face to face with someone he recognised.

Thomas stepped back, in fright. His heart beat so loud it seemed to echo in the silent chapel. The magic candles guttered. A pair of eyes peered from the painting into his own. Uncanny the picture, how accurately the artist had captured the face, the bright eyes, the gentle expression and the small, strong body. Thomas stared. He could hardly believe it. How? How could this be?

Standing amongst the dark angels, half their height, peeping out from the forest of their limbs and wings, was a green girl. There she was, mischievous, staring boldly, but still possessing the quiet strength he had recognised on their previous encounters.

But it couldn't be her. It couldn't. The temple beneath

the hill had been locked up decades before that girl was born. And why would she be painted among a host of angels? Thomas shivered and tears pricked his eyes again. His emotions were unsettled, and he tried to master them, to stay in control. It couldn't be Isabella. It was impossible. The painting was a fantastic coincidence, and no more.

The priest tore himself away and continued his inspection of the wall painting. It ended strangely, with an empty, tall golden archway. Beneath, the name of the artist was simply recorded: Jerome.

Thomas shivered. So the painting of Isabella (except that it couldn't be Isabella) wasn't decades old. It was centuries old.

His thoughts in turmoil, Thomas made his way back to the library, with his magic light. Thomas knew something of Jerome, the Maumesbury saint. Robert had told him the stories. St Jerome had lived in the fourteenth century and a hundred years after his death he had been made a saint by the Roman Catholic Church, for his religious poetry and writings. Jerome had lived alone in the cell by the spring in the forest for most of his life, connected to the abbey but not a part of it. Clearly he had been a member of the secret inner order, and he had decorated the chapel with his vision of angels. And with a green girl too – a girl who looked just like Isabella Leland, who had taken Thomas, by coincidence, to hide in Jerome's old hermitage. The thought was nagging, and wouldn't go away. Why was Isabella in the picture?

This time he found the library without any trouble. He wondered if the labyrinth had contrived to take him to the chapel, with its untrustworthy twists and turns. And how was Elizabeth? He had been so caught up with his discoveries beneath the hill, Thomas had forgotten all about Elizabeth. She would be in trouble now, with the priest hunter. There was no telling what he might do to her, and Elizabeth's suffering was due to helping him. But there was nothing he could do now, except to pray. His helplessness was infuriating. He depended on others so much, and so many had suffered to keep him safe. Thomas had brought troubles to the Dyers' door, but God would reward them for it. And the work had to be done, for the sake of the immortal souls of all the English people. He had to go on.

In the library, Thomas put aside the burden of his worries, and focused on the riddle of the green girl in the picture. He scoured the shelves for the writings of St Jerome and found them at last — a study of religious philosophy, an examination of the teachings of Jesus, a collection of poetry, and a plain, battered leather book containing the collected religious writings of the hermit who lived in the woods and saw visions of angels.

Thomas opened the book, and brushed the surface of the fragile pages with his fingertips. Then he began to read.

Isabella flew across a landscape of fields, forests and huddles of dwellings. They travelled fast, and now and then traversed the boundaries of the shadow land, where the snow lay deep and bright fires burned in circles of stone. She glimpsed, at the foot of a grey tower, a creature with a man's face and a stag's horns playing a black violin, and three stray, shrill notes reached her ears. Then the shadow land passed away again, and the steady pastures of Elizabethan England returned, the bare, black trees, the byres where cows huddled against the cold.

The crow faery screeched, as it circled over a house at the edge of a spinney.

'Is she here? Is this the place?' Isabella called. She could hardly speak, her lips were so cold. The faery dipped a wing, and Isabella clung on tight as they plummeted down. The ground rose up so fast she was afraid and squeezed her eyes shut. But the faery landed lightly, and shivered her off its back. Then it took off again and alighted on the stone-tiled roof. Isabella hopped from one foot to another, waiting for the faery to make its move. Was Elizabeth truly inside the house? The shutters were closed, but certainly there were people in the downstairs rooms. Chinks of light escaped from the windows, and smoke was rising from the chimney.

The faery hopped into the air. Its body broke up into a host of tiny pieces – each of which took on a life of its own and scampered across the roof tiles.

The little creatures – maybe three dozen of them – moved very quickly and each found a way into the house. Some jumped down the chimney. Others lifted the tiles and hopped inside. Several scurried down the walls of the house and pushed through the shuttered windows. Dark, curiously shaped, the faery creatures squeaked and gibbered to each other, perhaps still sensing they were parts of one being. Then they were gone, all of them, inside the house.

For a few moments everything was still and silent. Isabella held her breath, waiting to see what would happen.

*

Elizabeth held her mother tight, huddled up close in the grim little room.

'There is something,' Jane whispered. 'It ran from the door.'

Elizabeth swallowed, straining to see. 'Was it a rat?' she said.

'No. No! Not a rat.' Downstairs the chaos continued, shouts among the men and the sound of a struggle. Doors banged.

'What is it?' Jane said. She was shaking, Elizabeth could feel it. They pressed against each other.

Elizabeth tried to pray, but the words wouldn't come. Panic had locked her mind. She had never been so frightened – even with Merrivale. The atmosphere of the house was uncanny. Something terrible was happening, a nightmare, and she didn't know what it was. That was the worst thing of all.

'There it is,' Jane said. She stretched out one trembling hand, and pointed at a shadow in the corner of the room.

Among the shadows, one darker shadow moved and became distinct. Two round, yellow eyes gleamed. It stepped towards them. Jane and Elizabeth stared.

The creature stepped forward, into a pool of moonlight. It was about knee high with a large, pointed head and a skinny body. Its face was squashed, with heavy brows, a long, bent nose and a tiny mouth over which two uneven teeth protruded. The expression in its round, yellow eyes was hard to fathom.

'It's a goblin. A boggart,' Jane hissed. 'Horrible – evil. The

186

Devil's work!' She made the sign of the cross, but the goblin stayed where it was.

Elizabeth shook her head but her mother's words set her thoughts ticking. An idea dawned.

Jane rose unsteadily to her feet, still staring at the creature. 'Stay where you are, Elizabeth. I'll see it off. I'll kick it – stamp on it.' Jane rallied her courage, menacing the goblin, and she drew back a foot – but Elizabeth reached out to her.

'No!' she said. 'Leave it. Don't hurt it. I think – I think it might help us.'

'Help us?' Jane said, dismayed. 'That . . . little devil? Why would it help us?'

The goblin turned its gnarled face to Elizabeth. It blinked. Slowly, it raised its left hand.

'It is going to help us,' Elizabeth whispered. 'Look.'

She stretched out her own, shaking, hand to the goblin and took its dry, clawed hand in her own. The goblin nodded and led her towards the door. It passed its fingers over the latch, and they heard the bolt on the other side drop with a thud to the floor. The door swung open.

Isabella ran up to the front of the house and peered in through the window. She heard a bang, and the men shouting. Then a clatter, as furniture was knocked over. It was hard to see through the chinks in the shutters into the dim room but she strained to make out what was going on. A door banged shut and she saw the glimmer of steel as a sword was drawn and smashed uselessly against a wall. She couldn't quite work out what was happening but the faery

187

was certainly causing chaos. The men were frightened, calling out to each other, crashing about and trying to maim or trample the horde of goblins rampaging through the house.

The shutters flew open, and whacked Isabella in the face. She was knocked from her feet, and fell onto her bottom on the cold grass. Blood dripped from her nose, but she hardly felt the pain. A particularly hideous goblin leered at her through the open window, jumping up and down on the sill, until a large brown jug was hurled through the air, skimming the goblin's head, out of the window, to smash on the ground just an arm's length from Isabella. Despite everything, Isabella erupted with laughter, and the goblin laughed too, its crooked grin almost cutting its face in half. Mossy green and brown, the goblin, skin gnarled and knotted like an old branch, with twiggy fingers. It winked a yellow eye, turned on its heels, and dived back into the room.

Isabella climbed back to her feet, dabbing her nose on her sleeve. The front door flew open, making her jump, and a man ran out of the house. His clothes were torn and he was screaming. Isabella drew back, hoping he wouldn't see her, but there was nothing to worry about. The man was intent on escaping and he didn't look back. His legs flailed about in the mud and he stumbled, all in a panic, desperate to get away from the house and the sackful of imps. Isabella laughed again, right to the depths of her belly. It made her feel good, to laugh, though she wondered if it were a little wicked to laugh at a man's terror. Then again – presumably this was one of Merrivale's men – and what sort of man would follow him? The thought was sobering, and it flashed into Isabella's mind that Elizabeth was somewhere in the house and she might not find the goblins as funny as Isabella did.

She crept to the open door and looked inside. It was hard to see much, as the candles were all snuffed out and smoking. Most of the noise came from a room to the left, the one Isabella had spied on through the shutters. She stepped through the doorway. A staircase rose in front of her. Isabella hesitated, wondering where Elizabeth might be. She wouldn't want to run into Merrivale. Slowly she moved forward, trying to breathe evenly, wishing her heart wouldn't race.

Then Isabella heard a movement on the stair – and she froze. Who was it? Should she run? Had they seen her? The moment stretched. She heard a whisper, and a hiss.

'Elizabeth?' she whispered. 'Is that you?' Two bright yellow eyes shone from the stairway, and a goblin stepped forward leading Elizabeth by the hand. The mother, Jane, followed close behind, clinging on to Elizabeth's arm.

The two girls stared at one another. Isabella could hardly believe her eyes. They had only been apart a day and a night – but how long those hours had been.

'Isabella,' Elizabeth said. 'I knew it. I knew it was you.' She pushed forwards, and threw her arms around Isabella's neck. 'Thank you,' she said. 'I am so glad to see you.'

The goblin stood beside them, looking from one to another, but Jane stepped forward. She stared at Isabella.

'You're the green girl,' she said. 'The one who came to my house.' Her face was suspicious and afraid.

Isabella untangled herself from Elizabeth's arms. 'We have to leave now,' she said. 'We have to hurry.'

Too late – the other door flew open and a man stumbled out. Hard on his heels came Merrivale, shouting and

189

swearing. The first man fell against Jane, and Merrivale stopped short. He was sweating, and wild-eyed. He stared at the fugitives, as though he couldn't believe his eyes.

'God's wounds,' he cried. 'Grab them, man. Don't let them escape.' The first man lurched towards Isabella, and he grabbed her arm. Merrivale seized Elizabeth by the hair. He was breathing heavily, and he stared down into Elizabeth's face. Then he turned to Isabella.

'Damn you both,' he said more quietly. 'So here's your little accomplice. How did you find your way here?'

But Merrivale didn't get the chance to interrogate them any further. He was jerked back into the room, and Elizabeth's goblin sank its fangs into the flesh of the other man's leg. The man screeched and backed away, following Merrivale, but he kept his grip on Isabella and dragged her with him.

'Go! Run!' Isabella shouted. She wasn't in danger. The faery would come to her aid. She wanted Elizabeth and her mother to escape while they had the chance.

The room was full of movement. Many of the goblins were in here, climbing over the walls, prancing on the edge of the overturned table. Papers had fallen all over the floor. Two of the creatures were jumping up and down among the flames in the fireplace. Four more had pinned one of Merrivale's men to the ground, while another danced on top of him. Another man was sitting on Merrivale's chair, under a glamour, apparently believing a particularly evil-looking, one-eyed goblin was his long-lost sweetheart. The man was weeping, as he clutched the simpering goblin's hand to his brow.

Isabella laughed again. She couldn't help it. She wasn't afraid. How ridiculous these men truly were – even Merrivale. But hearing her, Merrivale turned with a howl of rage. He drew a short, slim dagger from his sleeve – and threw it straight at her heart.

'Run, Elizabeth. Now. You heard what she said,' Jane had urged, when Isabella was pulled through the door into the room with Merrivale. 'We have to leave now.' She tried to pull her daughter away but Elizabeth dug in her heels.

'I'm not leaving Isabella! We have to get her out!' The air was dense with noise and smoke, and the peculiar earth and incense perfume of the goblins. Elizabeth edged towards the door, trying to break free from her mother.

'We can't leave her,' she said. She stepped into the doorway in time to see a thin sliver of silver light fly from Merrivale's hand towards Isabella. Elizabeth opened her mouth in horror.

The dagger nosed through the air, swift and deadly. In an instant the blade would be wedged between Isabella's ribs.

But the instant stretched.

What was happening? Elizabeth stared, as the dagger flew the mere handful of yards from Merrivale, to embed itself in Isabella's heart – and stopped in mid-air just inches from her chest. Isabella gasped with shock. She was staring at the dagger, poised in front of her, pointing at her heart like a sharp, silver finger. At last she simply stepped away from it – but the dagger still hovered where it was.

'Isabella!' Elizabeth hissed. 'What happened?'

Isabella raised her hands in disbelief. It seemed she had no idea either. Elizabeth noticed how silent the house had

191

become. Nothing was moving at all. She glanced around the room. Merrivale was frozen, his hand still outstretched, as though he had just released the dagger. Even the goblins were motionless, caught in a host of curious postures all over the room – laughing, jumping, snatching. One had thrown a clay cup in the air and the cup hung there still, just beneath the ceiling. In the fireplace the flames were still, and the smoke was poised in clouds and billows all around the room. Elizabeth whipped round.

'Mother!' she cried. But Jane was frozen too, her arms outstretched to grasp her daughter, her lips apart to summon Elizabeth from the room.

Elizabeth turned wildly. 'What's happened to her? What've you done?' she demanded.

Before Isabella could answer, the tribe of goblins began to evaporate. Their dark, barky bodies dissolved like so much ice turning into water. Swiftly the fluid matter streamed together into one pool in the middle of the room, and before Elizabeth's eyes, the pool rose up, and up, into the form of a tall, white man with long, long black hair and fierce golden eyes. His hands and feet were clawed, and he wore a cloak of inky black feathers. Bands of dark gold clasped his wrists and neck, and great golden rings glinted on his fingers.

Elizabeth stared. She held her breath and her mind emptied. For a moment, the rest of the world disappeared – worries about her family, imprisonment, Merrivale, Isabella – even the course of her own life. Everything fell away – shadowed, faded out by the bright light shining from the creature.

The faery turned, and his eyes fixed on her, and he opened

his mouth to speak. His lips were the dark red of blood dropped on snow. She couldn't make sense of the words he said. Something welled up inside her, an ache – a longing. And she felt as though she were lifted from the narrow bounds of her own life, to see from a great height all the long ages of the earth, the birth of stones, the ending of nations, the rising up and falling away of gods, idols, dynasties and kingdoms. And beyond the realm of her own world she sensed the doors blow open to another realm, an older, darker world that lay alongside her own.

And this feeling – the longing – she recognised it. She had felt it before. Sometimes, in the evening twilight when the land was muted and uncanny, or in the wood at the shrine when the light shifted among the swaying branches, or even in church when she truly cleared her mind and opened a window in her soul to God, and glimpsed, darkly and only for a moment, a huge and endless vista.

Nothing about her own small life mattered. Nothing.

'Elizabeth. Elizabeth!' Isabella was shaking her arm but her friend seemed very far away.

'Elizabeth! Look at me!' Isabella shook her again, becoming more agitated. She clapped her hands in front of Elizabeth's face and finally something snapped shut inside her. Elizabeth stumbled forwards and drew a great gasp of air, filling her lungs. The vision flashed away. The ordinary world closed in.

'Come now,' Isabella said. 'I'll take you to a safe place.'

'What about my mother?' Elizabeth said. 'I can't leave her.'

'We can help her,' Isabella said. 'We'll only be gone for a moment. Come with me now.'

But Elizabeth wouldn't be parted from her mother another time. She turned away and reached out to the frozen figure. Before Elizabeth could touch her mother, the faery stretched out his hand and scooped her up.

Isabella held Elizabeth tight. They were flying again, faster than before, clinging to the feathers of the crow on the journey back to the hawthorn tree where she had created a pathway into the shadow land.

When Merrivale threw his dagger, the faery had snatched Isabella and Elizabeth from ordinary time into a pocket of his own, changeable faery time. He hadn't stopped time – instead he had taken them out of it. For time in the ordinary world was like a constant flowing stream, but in the shadow land time could be shaped and created, bound up, hastened or slowed. In the faery world time could be a raging torrent, or a stagnant pond. The crow people were not carried along by time as humans were. Instead it was a toy for them to play with.

Elizabeth was holding her tight, eyes closed, hardly aware of what was going on. Isabella remembered all too well how she had felt, when she first beheld one of the crow people, by the spring so many years ago. She squeezed Elizabeth's hand. The shadow land was near now, but they still had a long way to go.

The crow faery circled and cawed over the hawthorn tree. Before them, suspended over the topmost branches, a long sliver of light had appeared, like a long tear in a piece of parchment. The faery cried out, and dived through the split, carrying with him the two mortal beings into the shadow land.

Shadow Land

A cold wind billowed, and the crow faery trimmed its wings, looking for balance. Isabella sank deeper into the bird's silken feathers. Elizabeth had fainted away, curled up on the bird back. Her eyes were closed but her lips were moving, as though she were talking to someone Isabella couldn't see. Her hands were held tight to the dense under-feathers.

Isabella sighed. She felt a mixture of emotions, returning to the shadow land. In many ways it was more a home to her than the ordinary world. She had lived here for so long, and its contrary, confusing ways were familiar. But she had never truly belonged, as her brother John had come to belong, among the crow people. She was a changeling, always a foreigner. A guest and not a member of the family. The trouble was, she didn't belong in the mundane world either. She had no earthly family, nowhere to be at home. And how she longed to be at home. She had seen so many marvels in the faery land – the battles of princes, the beauty of the immortal Faery Queen, jewelled forests, palaces of pearl and ice. But she would willingly exchange them all for a mother to cuddle, and a father to pick her up and make her laugh. For a home with a fire to sit by at night in the cold weather, for meals together with her own people, the ones who loved her. The ancient and eternal were altogether too much for one small girl. She wanted ordinary intimacy instead. And yet . . . and yet as the magnificent vistas of faery land opened all around her, Isabella couldn't help the excitement rising.

1241

The men came to arrest her mother at the heel of the autumn, the last dark days of November. They arrived at the cottage early in the morning, a man on a horse and his two constables on foot. Ruth was sitting in her chair, nursing John, and Isabella was crouched by the fire, stirring barley porridge for their breakfast. The men kicked open the door without preamble, and marched into the low cottage. The first man unrolled a piece of parchment and read out in a loud voice a series of charges, accusing Ruth of practising witchcraft, laying on curses, taking part in a witch's Sabbath, consorting with demons and causing the deaths of numerous babies and children. The men seemed to fill the little cottage, and they were careless of it, kicking a stool aside, knocking over the cauldron of porridge so the contents spilled, steaming, all over the floor. Their voices were hard and angry.

Isabella had never been so afraid. They were so helpless – the little woman and her two children – against three strong men.

She was horrified by the men's angry manner, the sense of pent-up violence, and the way they swaggered when they knocked Ruth's pots of herbs from the shelves. This was a show of bravado – and for Ruth and her children, it was a dangerous show. Perhaps the men were afraid of Ruth, believing she was a powerful witch. Perhaps they had talked themselves into believing this, to cover up any unease they felt at making the arrest. After all, they were part of a small community and Ruth had treated one of the constables when his wrist was broken in a fight, and the other had a wife who would have died if Ruth had not supervised the difficult birth of his twin sons. Now neither of the two men would look Mistress Leland in the eye. Instead, they were fired up, and set about wrecking the interior of the cottage.

Ruth was surprisingly calm. She stood up, kissed her son on the top of his head, and handed him to Isabella. Then she kissed Isabella too.

'Don't be afraid,' she said. 'All will be well.'

One of the constables tied Ruth's wrists with a piece of rope and they led her out of the cottage.

Isabella was sick with dread. She knew too well what happened to women accused of witchcraft. There was no way out.

For a day Isabella stayed with John in the cottage. When night fell, John cried and cried for his mother, and Isabella cried too. What was happening to Ruth? How could she help her? She didn't tidy the cottage, she just sat and waited, sick to death, consumed by fear, expecting the worst.

On the second day, unable to wait any longer, she tied John to her back in a shawl and headed into town. The day was bitterly cold, the sky laden with heavy clouds that intermittently wet her with veils of freezing rain. Isabella, who had been unable to eat since her mother was taken, felt cold and dead inside. Her heart weighed heavy as a rock. John wailed and struggled, but she didn't have the energy to comfort him. Instead, head down, she trudged on through the mud and evil weather to the town crouched on the hill.

The people in the streets turned away from her, murmuring to each other. They crossed themselves, or else made the sign against the Evil Eye. Isabella moved amongst them like a leper. People they had helped moved from her path. Isabella tried not to see them, not to hear what they said, but every sideways glance, every word, seemed to scald her.

She went to the courthouse, and hammered on the door, demanding to see her mother. The rain hammered on her bare head, the icy water trickled through her clothes, and on her back John howled and shivered.

A man opened the door. He stared at her, all limp and bedraggled, and took a quick breath as though he were about to chase her off. But something changed his mind. Perhaps he took pity on her, because he stepped back from the door and let her in. He led her to a small cell.

'You can see her for a few minutes,' he said gruffly. 'Don't be long.'

The cell door was unlocked — and there was Ruth, sitting upon the floor on a low wooden pallet with a mattress of straw. The cell smelled, all closed up and musty.

Ruth looked up. Her face was drawn and tired, but her smile seemed to illuminate the miserable cell.

'Thank you, for letting her see me,' she said to the guard. Isabella stepped inside, and the door was locked behind her. For a moment, Isabella just stood and stared at her mother. Ruth stood up, squeezed her hand and patted her daughter's cheek. Then she untied the shawl on Isabella's back so John could stand on the ground.

'How wet you are. How cold!' Ruth said. She picked up John, put her arm around Isabella and kissed her icy cheek. But Isabella didn't know what to say — couldn't speak — and she

198

began to cry, huge, broken sobs, and the hot tears fell. She was entirely overcome with fear and grief, and the day and night of waiting alone in the cottage. They sank down onto the pallet, the three of them, without speaking, and Isabella cried herself into a daze. The cell was dark and gloomy, and the guard banged on the door, saying they only had a few minutes left.

Ruth sat up straight, stroked the tears from her daughter's face. 'You must not be afraid,' she said. 'Listen to me. I've known what would happen, and I've prepared for it. There is no way out now. They will have what they want. And when I am gone, you won't be safe either. They will come after you too, Isabella, and John.

'You must go to the shrine at the spring and open the doorway, as you have seen me do. When the faery comes, tell him it's time for you to be taken. The crow people will offer you sanctuary. You will be safe with them.'

Isabella stared at her mother. Wan as she was, her hair all straggled, never had she looked so beautiful. Her eyes were bright with life.

Isabella swallowed. Inside, her heart seemed to collapse and fall apart, like a drift of leaves. 'Don't leave me,' she said. 'Don't ask me to leave you.'

'The faeries will take care of you. I have a bond with them – I secured a promise they won't break.'

'Then why won't they save you? Why don't you hide in the shadow land too?' Isabella pleaded. 'Why have you given up?'

Ruth didn't take her eyes from her daughter's face. 'Look at me, Isabella,' she said. 'Listen to me. The faery who visits the shrine in the woods – do you remember him? He is John's father, Isabella. John is his son. Do you understand?

'He wants his child. He has longed for him since he was born, but I've kept him for myself. Now I will let him take John, and in exchange, he will care for you too. He will offer sanctuary and protection to one mortal, in order to have his son.

'I've enjoyed a good life. I had my husband, and I've watched you grow and cared for you, and I've had my son too. Now it's your turn to live. I'm not afraid of death, Isabella. It is only the end of one kind of life. But you haven't had a chance to enjoy what this life has to offer, so the gift goes to you. Go to the shadow land until it's safe for you to return.'

Isabella couldn't tear her eyes from her mother's face. John was sitting on his mother's lap, pressed against her, between Isabella and Ruth. John – whose father was a faery.

'I don't want to leave you,' Isabella said stubbornly. *'I can't leave you. I don't want to be alone.'*

'You won't be alone. You'll have John. And I will be with you. I'll be with you always.'

But Isabella wouldn't have it, this surrendering. *'You won't be with me. Not in the way I want you to be. You won't care for me. You won't see me grow up. I won't be able to touch you or talk to you. Why don't you fight it? Why? You are afraid. I know you are.'*

'The world is difficult and cruel,' Ruth said, squeezing her daughter's hand. *'But it's here the sun shines. Of course I'm afraid. I'm frightened of what they'll do to me. But that will be over soon and I'm not afraid of what comes after.'*

But Isabella took no comfort from her mother's words. She just wanted them to be safe, for the family to be together again at the cottage.

'Be brave, Isabella,' Ruth said. *'How can I fight them?'* For a

moment her show of courage faltered. Her lip trembled. 'They've made up their minds,' she said. 'You come from a long line of wise women who've guarded the shrine. I've taught you everything I know, and you are the best daughter a mother could ever ask for. Take care of John, and try to be strong.'

There were voices outside the door, the man who had allowed Isabella in to see her mother was arguing with someone. Then the cell door was unlocked and the guard told Isabella to leave at once. But she flung her arms around her mother's neck and the guard had to tear her off. Then Isabella screeched and kicked and flailed about with her fists as they carried her out.

'Mother! Mother! Mother!' she screamed, blind with grief, almost senseless, except that her voice went on and on, calling for her mother, while the men cursed and swore, struggling to drag her away. Then they dumped her in the street and John was unceremoniously set down on his bottom in the mud to wail, like so much unwanted garbage. Isabella sat on the step, her head in her hands, and John leaned against her. The rain poured all over them, and the people scurrying past into shelter all averted their eyes.

Isabella didn't ever see her mother again. For a long time she remained where she was, on the road outside the courthouse. She was oblivious to the cold and rain, insensible to the people who wandered past and ignored her. It felt like the whole world was falling away. How could she go on? The future was a black wall she hadn't the strength to climb. Why hadn't her mother tried to escape? If the faeries would take Isabella, why wouldn't they take Ruth too? John alternately grizzled or cuddled against her. He was very pale now, and his eyes were swollen with tears. He sucked his hand hungrily, poked her face and tugged her hair.

In the end his strength began to ebb and he curled up, half on her lap and half on the road. Dimly, from a great distance, Isabella saw how cold he was, and realised his life was in her hands.

Darkness was falling when she picked him up and carried him the two miles back to the cottage. To the west, the clouds burned red and gold and the moon rose, large and brilliant, like a jewel, casting silver-grey light over the fields. But Isabella turned her eyes away from the sky, to the ground, and trudged back to the broken cottage.

All night, while John slept on their mother's bed, Isabella sat up and gazed into space. Ruth had sacrificed herself in order that Isabella and John might escape, but this did not fill Isabella with any sense of gratitude. Instead she was eaten up with guilt. If it wasn't for Isabella, Ruth could have been the one mortal the crow people would taken with them, to be with her lover and their child. It was Isabella who was to blame. How was it possible to live with that?

She didn't feel any sense of surprise, learning John's father was one of the crow people. Perhaps there was no space in her heart for surprise. Maybe she had known all along, as the people in the town had speculated. To Isabella's knowledge, Ruth hadn't consorted with any other man since Isabella's father died. On some level Isabella had always suspected. John's black hair, the strange gold flecks in his eyes, all pointed to his faery origin. Then again, he was so delightfully mortal too, his fragrant, perfect blossom skin, his appetites, his cries and smiles.

Isabella felt an iron claw of anger stir in her chest, for the faery who had yearned for his son and cared so little for the mother he would allow her to be executed. Why wouldn't the faery bend the rules to save his lover? Why wouldn't he take them all and

202

keep them safe? Isabella ground her teeth, tears welling. It was no use. The crow people didn't live by the same rules as mortal people, that much she understood. They had no sense of morality or obligation. Their promises were like reflections on the surface of water, impossible to grasp. Yet somehow, her mother had wrested some kind of bond from them – if they would hold to it – bartering the faery's desire for his son in exchange for protection for her daughter. How had she done it? What powers had it taken to make such a bargain?

All the long night Isabella ran over and over the same thoughts, trying in vain to make sense of things, to unravel the tight knot of pain. Her memories were sharp knives. Even the cottage in which she had spent so many happy years seemed hostile, the table thrown over, the precious chair broken, the floor awash with spilled herbs and broken crockery.

Slowly the moon passed over the cottage, and Isabella seemed to sense it, the great white face shining down upon the rooftop.

By dawn, her grief had washed out, leaving behind it an icy, empty space. She blotted out the last painful memory of her mother's face, unable to bear the prospect of the humiliating trial and the cruel, inevitable execution.

Only John existed for her now, and she had to keep going for his sake. So when her brother woke up – her half-brother – she left the cottage and took him to the shrine in the forest.

Elizabeth dreamed she was falling. She was warm and comfortable, wrapped in silk sheets, and the feeling of falling was familiar. She had dreamed it before, and she was close enough to waking to be drowsily confident she wouldn't hit the ground. She was safe from harm, feeling the heat of her

203

sister's body beside her. Their mother and father lay together in the other bedroom, her brother would return from Oxford soon and they would all be together, her loved ones, where she could be most herself. She had nothing to worry about any more.

The ground rose up like a huge, soft hand and cradled her fall. A mound of blankets covered her over. She turned on her side, ready to yield to deep, delicious sleep. All was well. She wanted nothing to disturb her now.

'Elizabeth! Elizabeth!' Like an irritant wasp, a voice broke into her dreaming. She tried to ignore it.

'Elizabeth!' the voice persisted. Shaking too. Someone was shaking her. It had to be Esther, annoying little sister.

'Go away,' she said. 'Leave me alone.' She tried to wriggle away.

'Wake up. You must wake up.' The voice wouldn't let her go, needling into her ears and mind. Reluctantly Elizabeth opened her eyes. Bright light dazzled. This wasn't her bedroom. Disorientated, Elizabeth tried to sit up. Where was she? All she could see was brilliant white, except in front of her, a green girl was squatting and staring at her anxiously.

'Are you awake now? Are you all right?' the green girl said. She moved from side to side, still squatting, as though she were trying to peer right through Elizabeth's eyes and into her head.

Elizabeth squinted, trying to make sense of her surroundings. She wasn't covered in blankets. She was lying in a deep bed of snow, though strangely she wasn't at all cold. She realised she must still be dreaming – you don't feel cold in dreams. The landscape was obliterated with snow, a vast

204

spreading plain under a vivid blue sky. Very far away, mountains rose, blue with distance. She focused on the green girl who was hopping up and down now, very like a little frog. The green girl still seemed very anxious and Elizabeth wanted to reassure her. Everything is fine, she thought. No need to worry. It's just a dream.

'Elizabeth, it isn't a dream,' the green girl said, in a very loud and startling voice, as though she had heard Elizabeth's thoughts.

'You've got to wake up properly,' the green girl shouted. 'Believe it – you're here. And we haven't got long. We have to move.'

The green girl moved closer and clasped Elizabeth's face in her hands. She leaned towards her and whispered in her ear. Her breath was very cold.

'Kit Merrivale,' she hissed. Elizabeth shook her head. A storm of thoughts and impressions blew up in her mind. Merrivale. The name resounded like a gong and everything fell into place – imprisonment, her mother, the goblins crawling over the house, Isabella and the faery with eyes of gold – and the knife flying towards Isabella – the knife!

She gulped for breath, the shock of remembering like a splash of cold water.

'Isabella!' she cried, her voice choked. 'You – you're – I saw the knife – I thought you would be killed!'

Isabella stepped back, and Elizabeth stared at her.

'Is this – is this the shadow land?' Elizabeth gestured to the plains of snow.

Isabella nodded.

'You look different, Isabella.' Elizabeth was trembling. She had no real idea where she was, what would happen. Maybe she hadn't truly believed in the shadow land, until the faery assembled himself from his goblin parts and reared up before her. It was one thing to hear stories of elves and faeries and monsters – to imagine them in secret places, in the shadows. It was another to find the real, predictable world tugged out from under her feet. There was no safety in the ordinary world – but at least the dangers were known. Here she felt she was walking on thin ice that might break at any moment. She had no idea what would happen – what to expect.

Without thinking, she began to pray, the words of the Lord's Prayer unrolling in her mind. The priests had always warned them that magic was the Devil's work – so was the shadow land the Devil's work? It certainly didn't look like hell, which was a place of heat and fire, eternal torment and punishment, so the priests said. Worst of all it was a place of no hope – where the souls of the damned must endure agonies for eternity knowing God had turned his face away from them. No, this wasn't the Devil's country. She didn't feel despair. Although the priests apparently didn't know of it, Elizabeth felt the shadow land had to be a holy place. She could sense it, in the vivid colours, the clarity of the air. Perhaps, like Moses when he saw the burning bush that wasn't consumed, she should remove her shoes as a sign of respect.

Even Isabella was different. Elizabeth stared at her friend. She had always appeared outlandish – with her stained green skin, her claw nails and hair like a bear's pelt. But here, in the shadow land, the realm of the crow people, Isabella seemed inexplicably larger and brighter. Under the supervision of Lady Catherine, some of the moss colouring had been scrubbed from her skin and her hair was cropped. Here in the shadow land, Isabella glowed as bright and green as an emerald. Her face was beautiful and luminous, her eyes shone, her hair hung to her waist again, a silky forest green, and the sunlight glinted on jewels in a band around her head – except there were no jewels, in reality. The jewelled band flickered in and out of sight.

'You look . . . I can't explain it, but you look different,' Elizabeth repeated. She tried to understand it, to pinpoint the difference. It was as though she was seeing Isabella's vital, essential self – her immortal soul – all the ordinariness blasted from her, all the muddy mortal clutter of doubt and meanness and worry that might shrink and cloud someone's unique and remarkable self, all that was peeled away. It was as though she had only ever seen her friend at a distance before, through a clouded glass. Now she could see Isabella truly, and her heart warmed. How could you not love someone when you'd seen how beautiful and precious and unique they really were? She mustn't forget this, not ever.

'You also,' Isabella said quietly. 'You're different too. It's this place.'

Elizabeth stood up. She wondered what she looked like. Was she beautiful and remarkable too? She breathed deeply, drawing in the keen air. And she laughed, her fears receding. Her mood had turned over, and the newness of the shadow land seemed exhilarating instead of terrifying. She turned to Isabella.

'I'm ready,' she said. 'I'm here now. What happens now?

What's next?' She surveyed the snowy plains. They were miles and miles from anywhere. How far would they have to walk? Isabella took her hand.

'It's not so far,' she said. 'Everything is different here.'

They set off towards the distant mountains. The snow was soft, a powder of glittering crystals. They broke the smooth, endless snow surface with their feet but looking behind them, Elizabeth saw the snow scurried over the marks they left, and their footprints vanished.

'How long will it take us? Where are we going?' Elizabeth asked. She was excited now, wanting to see more.

'Soon,' Isabella said. 'At the right time.'

'Where did the faery go? The one who brought us here? And what about my mum? She's still in the house, isn't she? With Kit Merrivale.' Worry rose up again, thinking about her mother. Just like her feeling of exhilaration a moment before, the feeling was overwhelming, and threatened to swallow her up. And the feeling was reflected in the landscape. The mountains, the plains of snow, even the vanishing footprints began to seem ominous and hostile. What had she been thinking? They were helpless and alone. They would die out here, with no-one to hear them calling for help. Elizabeth stopped walking, paralysed by panic. She couldn't breathe and she shut her eyes, desperate to escape, her fear closing in tight.

'It's all right. Don't be afraid. Open your eyes.' Isabella was squeezing her hand. 'Try not to worry,' she said. 'What you're feeling changes everything. Let your fear go. Let it go. Or we won't get anywhere.' Her voice was very clear and calm. Elizabeth opened her eyes.

'Keep walking,' Isabella added. 'Come on. I'll talk while we go. We haven't got much time, you see.' She sounded like an adult talking to a child, gently cajoling and encouraging, trying to inspire confidence. She's lived here for centuries, Elizabeth reminded herself. She belongs here. Trust her. Elizabeth nodded, still holding her friend's hand, and began to walk again.

'The faery who brought us here, he's my brother's father,' Isabella said. 'My brother John is the son of the crow prince. Faery royalty.' She gave a small smile. 'He loved my mother. As much as any faery can love a woman from the shadow land. That's what they call our world, you see. We think the shadow land is a reflection of our own real world, and of course they think our world is a reflection of theirs. And because we live and fail and die and they live for ever, our world seems a very pitiful place – crudely formed, a lower world. Except that it seems to attract them too. They can't leave us alone. Despite their disdain, they keep coming back.

'I've learned a great deal about the crow people, but I don't entirely understand what it is about us they need and desire. But there's something. Some connection between us.'

Elizabeth nodded. 'So what happened to your brother?'

'My mother was accused of witchcraft and executed,' Isabella said in a small, tight voice. 'She managed to save us. She made some kind of pact with the Crow Queen – the prince's mother.'

'John's grandmother,' Elizabeth added.

'She agreed to take care of me, if she could have him. And she wanted him so much. Passionately. It's hard to understand quite how they think, but maybe she didn't like my mother – at least, she didn't like her son loving a woman made of dirt. That's what they think of us, you see. That we're made of dirt.'

Elizabeth frowned. 'We are made of dirt,' she said. 'That's what it says in the Bible. For dust you are, and unto dust you shall return.'

Isabella looked away, at the distant mountains, and controlling a quiver in her voice, she went on. 'So I stayed here a long time. In some ways it doesn't seem so long – in another way, it feels like forever. It is always like that in the shadow land. Not days and nights lined up, one after another. A few times I went back. I made friends with a hermit at the cell one time. Jerome. He was my friend. We learned a lot from each other. He knew who I was. But I never felt very safe in your world and I didn't want to be apart from my brother, so I came back again. The faeries allowed me to stay, but they have never cared for me very much. The crow prince has helped me, for my mother's sake. Sometimes I've called on him. But I'm not one of them. Not like my brother. He is one of them. This is all he can remember and he has faery blood. Royal blood. He is more faery than human now. He's a warrior and a mage. He's a prince and a hero. John can't remember the ordinary world. But he's all I have. He was all I had – until I met you. And there was something about you – I can't quite explain it – I knew you were special. I could see it. I knew you'd be my friend and you'd help me find a place in the world again.'

Elizabeth looked at Isabella and nodded. Her friend's trust and faith weighed heavily, but it was precious too.

'I will do everything I can,' she said, putting her hand to

her heart. 'But it seems I've just caused you more trouble. You got caught up in the same situation all over again – except that this time it's my mother in danger.'

'I wonder if that's why you seemed special to me,' Isabella said. 'I couldn't help my mother. I didn't help her. She made a choice – but I've always felt guilty. I didn't want her to sacrifice herself for me. How could I live with that? If I can help you save your mother, maybe some of the debt I made for myself will be paid off.'

'What's happening to my mother and Merrivale and the men in the house? What's happening now?'

'Nothing,' Isabella said. 'They're still there. We're still there – in a way. The faery pulled us away from that one moment. You saw that everything just stopped? Except it hasn't really stopped. When we go back, we'll return to that same moment.'

Elizabeth frowned. 'I don't understand,' she said.

'Why do you think I am still a girl after three hundred years?' Isabella explained patiently. 'Time isn't the same in the shadow land. I haven't spent long enough in the ordinary world to grow up or grow old. The shadow land has its own weird time. It's not the same. Maybe it doesn't have time, or maybe it has all of time in one place.

'Imagine time is a long, long piece of string. When the faery took us away from Merrivale and the house, imagine he tied a knot in that piece of string so he made a big loop that lies alongside it. We're in that loop. We've got this piece of extra space out of time. But it's not a very big piece and when we go back, it will be to the knot where we started out. Do you see?'

211

'I think so,' Elizabeth said slowly. Did she really understand? On some level what Isabella was telling her made sense. On another, she revolted against the idea. So much nonsense! How could time be tied in knots? Then again, how could she be here? She would just have to accept it. She must trust that Jane was safe, for the time being. There was nothing else she could do.

'I think there is a way I can save your mother, Elizabeth,' Isabella said. Her voice was low and serious. Her long, grassy green hair lifted and snaked around her head, even though the air was still. The sunlight glinted on the coronet of jewels that appeared and disappeared again from her head.

'I understand things much better now, than when I lost my mother. I know so much more. Even more than she knew, because she never crossed over to this side, even though she called up the faeries and they visited her. She was clever and wily, in dealing with them, but I can be too. I will find the Crow Queen and we shall make a deal.'

For a moment Isabella did not look like a twelve-year-old girl any longer – even a twelve-year-old magical green girl. Elizabeth was a little afraid of her friend because when she spoke of cunning and wiles, Isabella's eyes were old. All the three hundred years of her long life were there, the weight of her mother's horrible fate, the fear of persecution, the centuries living in the shadow of her faery brother, trying to make a space for herself among the terrible, beautiful crow people. Yes, she did look her age. Older than the trees in the forest, older than the rocks at the root of the earth.

But the moment passed. Isabella smiled, the weight of her centuries passed away and once again she was Elizabeth's friend – shy and vulnerable, generous and kind, with an inner strength that soothed and comforted.

'So we're looking for the Crow Queen,' Elizabeth said. 'Where does she live? How will we find her?'

'How many miles to Babylon?' Isabella answered, with a grin. 'East of the sun and west of the moon. Under a shadow, between the stars. Turn right at midnight and walk until dawn. What I'm saying is, there isn't a known way. Perhaps she's everywhere. But don't worry. We'll find her.' Isabella raised her arms. 'Look,' she said. 'We're on our way.'

Elizabeth raised her face. Without her even noticing, they had reached the once distant mountains. She shaded her eyes to see better, and just as Isabella's coronet of jewels flashed in and out of existence, so, superimposed upon the bleak, perilous mountain ranges, she saw a mighty city with palaces of grey stone, slender towers, terraces in the clouds, bridges with countless arches poised over tumbling rivers, steep roads and onion domes glittering like pearl.

Despite its magnificence the city looked as cold and perilous as the mountains, and faced with it, Elizabeth shuddered. Isabella said there wasn't a known way, but the unknown path had brought her here, and she was afraid to go any further.

Faery Queen

After two long days underground, the silence weighed heavy. The floating orb gave light enough, and he had water to drink from the spring. By the end of the second day the first pangs of hunger had died away and strangely it was the silence that troubled the priest most. From time to time, simply to create a noise, he rattled the string of topaz rosary beads inside the golden chalice, to please himself with the sound of it.

It was hard to gauge time accurately, but his body seemed to know when to sleep and wake, and this had happened twice. On waking, he found the chapel with the wall paintings, and kneeled and prayed before the shining monstrance. Then he drank and washed at the spring before returning to the library to read.

It was the opportunity of a lifetime, to browse in the abbey's secret library, a collection beyond value – a window on the accomplishments of the most learned monks, in what had been one of the most powerful monasteries in Europe. There were books of poetry, history and law, the lives of saints, obscure philosophy, ancient maps rolled up and sealed with wax.

Thomas was a clever and educated man, the second son of a loyally Catholic nobleman from the north of England. He had spent his youth pursuing the interests of rich young men – chiefly hunting and fighting. But his family were proudly Catholic, and the practice and traditions of the Catholic faith were a part of family life. And as Thomas grew older, the appeal of hunting and fighting waned. His father died, and his elder brother married and became head of the vast estate. What was there for Thomas to do? He was restless and frustrated, full of thwarted energy and ambition. Somewhere a path waited for him – a destiny – but the way was clouded and dark. For a while he thrashed about helplessly – drinking too much, chasing women – but his heart wasn't in it. These were empty distractions. He struggled for direction but just couldn't see what it was he had to do.

Then it was spring, an early Easter. The lambs were playing in the fields, the primroses were pale and pure along a muddy lane where Thomas rode on his horse. His heart was glad, for the warm weather and the young animals. The gospel of the resurrection was fresh in his thoughts. He remembered the church altar, stripped bare for the crucifixion on Good Friday, and now adorned with the purest white linen and wreaths of wild flowers for Easter Sunday.

And then he knew what he had to do. His mind was full of light, as the idea dawned. He would devote his energy and passion to the cause, and bring people back to the true faith. That same day he told his elderly mother he would join the priesthood and serve the Catholic Church.

Thomas sighed, as he looked up from the book on the table before him. He was privileged to be here, reading the works of greater men. A less courageous part of his mind worried how he would ever get out. Only the girl Elizabeth knew exactly where he was and how to open the door. If she had been captured or arrested, or was simply unable to get back to the church, might he starve to death? He struggled to put these fears behind him. God had protected him so far. He must trust in the Lord to preserve him now. He was afraid, yes, but he must stay focused on the task at hand.

Thomas was fascinated by the books of science and magic, though most of them exceeded his understanding. He longed to know how the light orb was fashioned. Why, Queen Elizabeth herself employed the services on one John Dee, who studied magic. How John Dee would relish an opportunity to see this treasury of books. Most often, however, he returned to the writings of St Jerome, the hermit of the woods from the fourteenth century who was blessed with visions of angels, and painted them upon the chapel wall. Thomas wanted to know why Jerome had painted a green girl among them.

At the end of the second day, he found what he was looking for. In a long, ecstatic piece of writing, Jerome described how a column of angels with wings of black feathers descended upon the forest at the Virgin Mary's shrine in the woods. He wrote how beautiful they were, how he fell to his knees in worship. And they left behind a little girl for him to care for – a green girl whose name was Isabella Leland.

She was a child, Jerome wrote, of quiet strength and great wisdom, who taught him the properties of healing herbs and explained to him much about the nature of angels. She also told him her mother had been executed for practising witchcraft.

Thomas faltered in his reading. Witchcraft? How had this come about? Surely the woman must have been innocent if she could call on angels to take care of her daughter.

He read on, burning with curiosity.

They were friends, the hermit and the angels' child, for several months. The girl lived wild in the forest but she still lived in terror of persecution and the witch hunters. Then one day an angel returned to claim her and Isabella disappeared. Jerome returned to the abbey for a time and confided his visions to his fellow members of the secret inner order. The visitations were considered too strange and dangerous for even the ordinary abbey monks to know about, but Jerome was invited to recreate his angels on the walls of the underground chapel.

Jerome also examined the court records for the previous century and found the notes taken during the trial of one Ruth Leland.

'She was tried by the civil authorities, not the church, after a wealthy and powerful local family brought a charge against her because a baby had died,' Jerome had written.

'In fact it appears that the church authorities tried to protect her because the brothers of our esteemed secret order respected her learning and knew she had spoken with angels at the Virgin's shrine, as I have done. The malice of the bereaved family knew no bounds, however. Our own servant,

Matthias Dyer, spoke in her defence at the trial and poured scorn on the superstitions of the ignorant but the accused woman would not reveal the name of the father of her second child, a son called John. Her adamant refusal went against her, and despite the testimony provided by the abbey the judge found her guilty. She sentenced to be hanged by the neck until she was dead.'

The priest was stunned. His first feeling was an over-whelming pity for Isabella and her mother. It was tempting to think that England had been a better place, three hundred years ago when the Catholic Church was at its most power-ful. Even then, he realised, there was injustice and cruel superstition.

He looked back over Jerome's notes on the trial. The name of Dyer jumped out of the page. How much did Elizabeth know of this story? A connection had been made between the two families a long time ago. One of Elizabeth's forefathers had tried to defend Ruth Leland and on behalf of the secret order had spoken at the trial. It was an extraordinary tale.

Jerome wrote little more about his green visitor. He only saw Isabella one more time. This was many years later, when he was an elderly man and life in the cold cell at the shrine was becoming an increasing struggle. Isabella returned to him alone and she had not grown older – she was still the child he remembered, despite the years that had passed. She had in her arms a bundle of dry old bones which she begged him to keep secret and safe, though she would not explain who the bones belonged to or why they should be treasured. But Jerome kept his promise. He carried the bones to the abbey and secured them for safe keeping in the chapel under the town.

Thomas closed the book. In the silence of the library, he could hear the beating of his heart and a curious singing in his ears. Isabella lived with the angels. It was hard to believe. He had seen her – spoken to her. Smelled her even, her perfume of the cold woods, leaves and dirt. She had seemed so flesh-and-blood to him then. But she had helped him, hadn't she? And more than once. Probably he owed her his life. Maybe God had sent her to make safe his path. It couldn't be coincidence she had returned at this time, first warning him about Merrivale's arrival at the Dyers' house, later helping Elizabeth guide him to the hidden place beneath the hill. Thomas crossed himself and offered prayers of thanks. His fever of excitement burned up again. He had placed his fate in the hands of God, and God had sent the child to protect him.

Of course Jerome's visions of angels became widely known about despite the efforts of the abbey to suppress them. During his lifetime, he was popular with the local people, who went to the shrine in the woods to pray or seek a blessing. After his death, he became a saint to the people long before he was officially beatified in Rome by the Pope. Now though, in the England of Queen Elizabeth, saints were not so popular any more. St Jerome was mostly forgotten. Thomas stroked the cover of the book, lost in thought. Where was Isabella now? Where was Elizabeth? What would happen next?

Isabella shaded her eyes and stared at the great stone city. She knew how hard this was on Elizabeth, how afraid and disorientated she must feel. At least Elizabeth had a guide to help her – Isabella hadn't had such a friendly human hand to show her the way when first she came to the shadow land. The Faery Queen had taken John from her and Isabella was left to fend for herself in the Queen's palace.

The two girls stood before the huge silver gates leading into the city. Elizabeth blinked and rubbed her eyes.

'What do you see?' Isabella asked.

'It changes. Mountains – and here, a grove of birch trees. And then it shifts, and I see a huge city and a shining silver gate. Which is true, Isabella?'

'They're both true. The shadow land has many layers. They shift and you have to fix your sight on the one you're looking for.'

Elizabeth pursed her lips. How lovely she looked, covered in the glamour of faery land. Her pale hair hung long and loose to her elbows, glittering with threads of gold. Her blue eyes shone bright in the triangle of her perfect white face. Sometimes she looked like a tiny child, a little girl lost. Then again, when she lifted her head, how proud and regal she was, like a princess, full of power and authority. Isabella smiled.

'It is the city we want,' she said. 'At the heart of it we'll find the Queen's palace. But the city will be difficult. It is wishing that will take us the right way – but the Queen needs to wish it too. Or at least, she must not wish us not to find her.'

Elizabeth frowned. 'I don't understand,' she said. Her gaze went vacant for a moment, as if she were looking at something far away, that Isabella couldn't see. Then she came back again, and focused on her friend. 'I'll follow you,' she said. 'I trust you. How do we open the gates?'

'Easy. We walk through the birch trees. It is sneaky,

the way we can do that. The faeries can't, you see. They get caught up in one particular story and then they have to follow it to the end. We can wriggle in between them all.'

Elizabeth looked at her sideways. 'You've learned all this, living here,' she said. 'It must have been hard.'

'Like being a mouse,' Isabella whispered. 'You can't feed from the table with the men, so you learn how to scuttle under the floorboards and steal the crumbs. You find little secret ways around the house that the men are too big to use. That's what we are – sneaky mice. Can you do it? Look for the birch trees, and fix on them.'

'Hold my hand,' Elizabeth said. 'So we can pass through together. I don't want to be on the other side of the gates to you.'

They stared at the silver gates, and Isabella summoned up in her mind the image of the great mountains that lay beneath the spectacle of the faery city. The towers and mansions and roads receded – the gate began to melt, and its bars became the slender trunks of the birch trees. Isabella took her friend's hand and they stepped through.

A great noise rose up behind them, and Elizabeth whipped around.

'What is it?' she said. The silver gate had reappeared and they were standing inside the stone city. The snow had vanished and a clamour rose from the plains – the rattle of swords, and fierce cries of warriors, the screams of the wounded. The scent of smoke and blood drifted from the scene of a great battle. Long banners of scarlet and gold floated above the ranks of two great armies as they fought together, throwing up a cloud of dust.

221

'Why are they fighting? What's happening?' Elizabeth clutched Isabella's arm. Isabella shook her head.

'Don't be afraid,' she said. 'The battle goes on and on. It doesn't matter. Look away. Come with me.' She pulled Elizabeth away from the gates but her friend kept looking back, torn by the spectacle of the battle.

The city loomed all around them. Tall houses flanked the stone road. Occasionally the road opened into a square with a fountain and flowers. The architecture was beautiful and strange – even nonsensical. Doors were not necessarily on the ground – many were set on the first or second floor so that anyone stepping out would tumble to the road. Some of the buildings had no windows at all, while others had windows that didn't reveal the interior of a house, but views of magical landscapes, forests and deserts, or vistas of other cities. Towers sprouted, but defying the normal logic of gravity they leaned or floated above the ground. The sky continuously changed, as though days and nights were racing above their heads. Sweeps of darkness followed daylight. Clouds hurtled and boiled, followed by intervals of burning sunshine. The city was a cauldron of images.

Most strange of all, the girls couldn't see anyone. The place was deserted.

'It frightens me,' Elizabeth said. She was still holding Isabella's hand tight. 'I don't like it here. Where are they?'

'They're here,' Isabella said. 'We just aren't seeing them at the moment. Don't be afraid. They won't hurt us.' But Isabella was nervous too. With the notable exception of her brother John, she had never brought anyone to the shadow

222

land before. Although the crow people wouldn't hurt the girls, they might certainly play some very cruel tricks.

'What did you mean about the faeries and stories?' Elizabeth said. 'Tell me more about them. What are they like?'

They plodded on, through the never-ending maze of streets. Isabella sighed. How could she explain? For so long she had lived around the crow people, mostly in the shadows of the Queen's palace to be close to her brother John. It had been very hard, to see how swiftly he embraced his faery side and became one of them. She had skulked around the faery court, snatching every moment she could to be in his company.

John was tended by a faery nurse, who for her role in this tale of the changeling son, took on the appearance of a bent old crow woman with a pelt of grey feathers and an ugly, beaked face. The boy had slept in a golden cradle, his clothes were adorned with pearls, and every day he was taken to the Faery Queen to be cuddled and doted on. He became one of the crow people. He didn't stay a child as Isabella did, the girl made of dirt. John became a prince of the shadow land. In the end, he all but forgot about his sister. He had a new name – in the language of the crow people he was called Beloved of the Queen. But Isabella never forgot about him. She still loved him, the only remaining family she had. She travelled the realm of the faeries but she had always returned, to hide in her mouse holes, to catch a glimpse of her brother.

'Isabella?' Elizabeth said sharply. 'What is it?'

'It's hard to understand what they are like,' she said. 'The crow people don't live like us, in straight lines with every day being new and unknown. Their lives are long, long stories that happen again and again. They re-enact the same tales – they're caught up in them. My mother told me some of the stories. Others I've seen for myself. There is the story of a princess who is cursed and locked up in a palace in a sleep of a hundred years until a warrior prince breaks through the enchantment and restores her to life. There's another story about a girl who wanders through a forest of snow where she's torn apart by wolves – but one of the she-wolves gives birth to her again and the girl becomes the queen of the wolves, except that she has long, red hair like a cloak all around her.

'There are so many – more than I will ever know. The stories aren't exactly the same each time and over the centuries they alter bit by bit and find a new shape.

'Of course the faeries speak and argue and play and feast – and sometimes cross over to our world – but it is the stories that make the shape of a faery's immortal life. I don't know if the faeries create the stories or the stories dream up the faeries. I think that's why the Faery Queen loves John so much. He is a fresh beginning. John is a new story – and he makes the old stories new as well.'

Elizabeth gazed at the stone road. She was frowning, probably trying to make sense of Isabella's words.

'We've been walking for hours,' she said. 'Everything still looks the same and I'm getting tired. How much longer is it?'

Isabella sighed. 'I don't know. Be patient. Think about the palace. Think about being there.'

Elizabeth stopped short. 'Why did you say that?' Her voice was short. 'How can you say such a thing?'

Isabella also halted. 'What?' she said.

'No. No!' Elizabeth jammed her hands to her head, blocking her ears. 'Don't say that!' She looked at Isabella, her eyes widened as she backed away – then she made the sign of the cross and shook her head.

'What is it?' Isabella demanded. 'What are you seeing? It's me! Your friend Isabella!'

Elizabeth seemed to hear other words entirely because she moaned and crossed herself again. She wouldn't look at Isabella's face. Isabella stepped closer, holding out her hands, but Elizabeth stepped back and back. Isabella's thoughts raced. What was happening? What trickery was this? How could she make Elizabeth see the truth?

Elizabeth clutched her hands together and surveyed the faery city. The illusions were falling away. The walls faded, and inside the houses she could see ghostly figures. They acted out their daily tasks – setting a fire, grinding wheat, baking, sewing – but sensing Elizabeth, they looked up and stared with empty eyes from hollow faces. Their hands were worn to the bone and their clothes were rags. The voices of the spirits echoed in Elizabeth's mind. Beware, they said. Do not trust her. Elizabeth glanced at Isabella and her heart seemed to freeze.

Don't follow her, the voices said, or you will be trapped, as we are. Turn back. Leave before it is too late.

'No,' Elizabeth moaned. 'No, it can't be. It can't be.'

So many eyes fixed upon her. The voices spoke of their suffering and despair. Was this a circle of hell after all? The place of no hope. The current of pain and grief swirled around her, summoning images of long nights all alone in the cold, and a hunger that would never be satisfied, and grief beyond the reach of comfort. How bitter it was, to be alone. She saw her father in Venice, his face in his hands, and her sister Esther weeping in the house in Maumesbury, the housekeeper long gone. And there was Robert, tormented to reveal his secrets, and her mother, locked up for years, till her hair turned white and she lost her wits. There was nothing to be done. Elizabeth had failed them all.

'So you see the truth,' Isabella said. The beautiful green girl had disappeared. Now Elizabeth saw a hideous goblin lady. She was still only child height, but worn and decayed like a corpse. The skin stretched over her face was dry as paper, her lips pulled back over black and broken teeth. Her hands were torn, the skin in rags, though great, glittering rings shone from her fingers. Pieces of stained silk and velvet were wrapped around her body but they didn't disguise the bare ribs, the bony feet.

How can anyone live for three hundred years? the voices whispered. This is what she truly looks like. Clear your eyes. Don't follow her any further, Elizabeth.

Isabella laughed. 'Now I have you,' she said. 'Your immortal soul belongs to me. There is no purpose in calling on God here, because he won't hear you. There is nothing you can do.'

Elizabeth didn't feel frightened any more. She hadn't the energy for it. Instead, despair was swallowing her, like a great, cold bog. It seeped through the alleyways of her mind, and filled the bright spaces of her thoughts and memories. Slowly she turned from Isabella and wandered back through the city.

This way the road was easier, leading her downhill. Her feet carried her slowly but surely. Left behind, the Isabella demon jumped up and down, cursing and uttering blasphemies, but Elizabeth didn't care any more. All she had treasured was lost. All the joy had been sucked from her life. She was like a pile of dead leaves blown about by a chilly wind. The future was an abyss of inevitable loneliness, suffering and decline. Nothing mattered any more.

One of the sombre ghosts stepped out into the road and beckoned her to follow it into a house. Elizabeth passed across the threshold into a dim little room. The ghost nodded, and gestured to a low stone couch by the wall. Elizabeth laid herself down, curled up her knees to her chest, and closed her eyes. The marble couch was hard and cold as ice as she slipped away into a peaceful, dreamless sleep.

Isabella tried to work out what Elizabeth was seeing. The crow people were all around them. What were they saying to Elizabeth? She seemed to think Isabella was evil, and whenever Isabella spoke, Elizabeth apparently heard something entirely different. Elizabeth's courage and spirit seemed to ebb away. Her eyes glazed over and her shoulders sagged. Broken, defeated, she turned away from Isabella and trudged down the stone road.

'Elizabeth!' Isabella called out. 'Please! Listen to me. They're playing with you. Believe in me! Please!' But Elizabeth paid no attention. She stepped off the stone road, into one of the grand houses, and disappeared from view.

Isabella didn't know what to do. It was a cruel trick, to split them up. Should she leave Elizabeth to fend for herself and set off in pursuit of the Faery Queen alone? Should she follow Elizabeth? She hopped from one foot to another, unable to decide. The faeries were powerful. If they really wanted to keep Elizabeth, what could Isabella do about it? On the other hand, how afraid her friend must be, lost and alone, trapped in a very bad dream. She had to help her.

Isabella ran to the house but the walls had sealed against her. The window provided a view of a dim, snowy forest. Isabella slammed her fist against the wall in frustration.

'Let me in!' she shouted. 'Let me in!' Her voice echoed in the stone city. The silence seemed to mock. Then, far away, she heard music and laughter. The sound rippled along the road like a ribbon. Elizabeth's house shifted on its foundations, like a woman adjusting her skirts, the walls folding and creasing. Then the house shrank, in a heartbeat, until it was a tiny box small enough for Isabella to hold in her hand.

'No!' she shouted. 'No, that's not fair!' The ribbon of laughter drifted past her again, through the empty city, and disappeared. Isabella choked back tears. It was too hard. How could she fight them when they shaped reality?

'I hate you,' she whispered. 'For what you did and what you didn't do. I hate you.' She bent down and picked up the house. The whole city was shifting now. The towers, mansions and market squares became insubstantial. The colours faded to a succession of greys, and then the city entirely disappeared. Isabella was left in a rocky wilderness, a plain of broken granite interspersed with a few bare and stunted trees.

The wind howled. She opened her fingers. The tiny house was now a simple piece of rough stone.

The wasteland stretched around her, as far as the eye could see. Despite the long years in the shadow land, Isabella had never felt so utterly alone. There was no-one in the mundane world or the shadow land she could call on for help. She was nothing.

Isabella crouched down, pressed her back to the wind, and clutching the stone to her chest, she began to cry.

She spent many years in the wasteland, growing ragged and mad. She had no-one to talk to, except the friend she imagined lived in a piece of stone that she always carried around. She eked out an existence eating raw roots and leaves. The sky was always grey with cloud and sometimes the rain poured down. She huddled against the rocks in narrow ravines to protect herself from the weather. From time to time she would see a flock of birds flying overhead, and once, far away on the horizon, she saw a knight ride past on a black horse. She called out to him, but the knight was caught up in his own quest and didn't respond. Finally words deserted her. Isabella lived like an animal, without a voice in her head. She forgot her own name.

Bleak days and nights, empty years, storms and rain.

'Isabella. Isabella.' The voice was delicious. Isabella stirred in her sleep. The voice sent thrills down her spine, and seemed to touch the deepest places in her mind.

'Isabella, wake up now. Wake up.' Isabella turned over. It was hard to wake up. She'd been asleep a long, long time. Her memories were jumbled.

'Sleepyhead,' the voice admonished gently. 'There's plenty to do. Come along.'

Isabella's eyes flicked open and she gasped. Swags of

blossom nodded overhead. The air was sweet with the scent of apple and apricot. She was lying in an orchard on soft and lush grass, embroidered with spring flowers. And beside Isabella, stroking her hair, was her mother Ruth.

For a moment, Isabella couldn't breathe. She was overcome. Memories tumbled over themselves in her mind – the long years in the wasteland, Elizabeth, Merrivale, Thomas Montford, Jerome, John.

'I said I would be with you,' Ruth said. 'You didn't believe me then.'

She was pretty again, as she had been before their troubles began. Her face was fresh and bright.

Isabella struggled to speak. 'Is this another trick? Is it really you?' It was agony to doubt her mother, but it would be worse to believe it and then find out Ruth's face was another mask for the Faery Queen.

'It is,' Ruth said gravely. 'I've come to help you, but I haven't much time.'

'Where are we?' Isabella said.

'We're on the borders of the shadow land,' Ruth answered. 'There are many worlds beyond the ones you know. The mundane world and the shadow land are like the two sides of one coin, they're inseparable. However large they are, however much they seem like the beginning and end, the two worlds are like one single pebble on the beach of creation. Your journey has only just begun. I'm only one step ahead of you, that's all.'

A breeze passed through the trees, stirring the blossom, and Ruth looked over her shoulder.

'The Queen senses my presence,' Ruth said. 'I have to

go soon. This is what you need to help you see a clear way.'

In her hand she held a piece of glass, silver and shining like a pool of water in her palm.

'A mirror,' Isabella said. 'Don't go. Please don't leave me alone again.' She reached out for her mother, and embraced her, holding her tight.

'We'll be together again one day,' Ruth whispered. 'Don't forget what I said. I'm just one step ahead of you.'

Ruth got up and began to walk out of the meadow. The breeze picked up, scattering petals from the trees. Very quickly, she became distant and insubstantial, blurring into the pale sky. Isabella strained her eyes to see, to make her out, but Ruth had disappeared.

On the grass the mirror lay, reflecting the blossom. For a moment, Ruth's face seemed to pass across the surface of the mirror. Slowly Isabella picked it up. In her hand she still held the stone from the city. She sensed her mother's presence, which was comforting and gave her a feeling of strength and determination. The games were over, the battle had begun. So much time had been wasted.

'The stone city,' she called. 'The stone city!'

Elizabeth stared at her own face. It was disconcerting. How could she be looking at herself?

'Elizabeth? It's me – Isabella. Can you hear what I'm saying?'

'Of course I can hear you.' Elizabeth sat up. She had been lying on a very hard and uncomfortable couch. She rubbed her eyes. Isabella was holding a small mirror in front of her face.

231

'Look in the mirror,' Isabella urged. 'Can you see what is real?'

'Where am I?' she said. They appeared to be in a cold living room, with a bare hearth and a distinct lack of any adornments.

'Look at me,' Isabella demanded.

Elizabeth was puzzled. 'I am looking at you.'

'And you can see me – as I am?'

'Of course – what do you mean?' Elizabeth felt a little irritable, as though she had woken too quickly. 'I had a strange dream,' she said, struggling to remember. 'It's very annoying. I can't think what it was about.'

'We have to go now. The Queen's palace is very close. We can find her,' Isabella said. Elizabeth got up and smiled. Everything seemed to make perfect sense to her now. She had succumbed to her own doubts, but now her fears had evaporated.

'Of course we do,' she said. 'Show me where to go.'

It was night-time, the city was bright with moonlight. At the top of the stone road, clearly visible, stood the palace of the Faery Queen. The colour of pearl, the palace glimmered in the silvery light. It was a forest of archways, towers and domes with tall windows full of stained glass. Elizabeth ran after Isabella through the open gates, across the white-paved courtyard to the huge, arched doors that opened to admit them.

They ran along corridors of marble inlaid with precious stones, which seemed to burn and provide the palace with magical illumination. Unerring, Isabella led them up a great stairway to a pair of tall, golden doors carved with leaves and grapes.

'This is the great hall – the Queen's throne room,' Isabella whispered.

Elizabeth felt nervous again. 'Why hasn't anyone stopped us? Does she know we're here?'

'Of course she does,' Isabella said. 'Now we have to ask her to help us.'

The golden doors opened, and the two girls stood together on the threshold of the room. It was vast. The walls receded into the distance, lined with tall, arched windows. Tiles of white and silver paved the floor. Isabella took Elizabeth's hand and they stepped in together.

At the end of the long, long room the Faery Queen was sitting upon a throne, on a dais. The court was gathered all around her, tall men and women with long black or golden hair and cloaks of inky feathers. Their bodies were adorned with bands of gold, heavy bracelets and belts and necklaces. They wore rings in their ears and upon their long, white fingers. Elizabeth trembled to see them. So many beautiful, fierce faces were focused on the two little girls who had dared to step into the Queen's courtroom. Perhaps she would have faltered, if Isabella hadn't held her hand so tight. It seemed to take forever, to cross the tiled floor. Step by step, closer and closer to the source of the Queen's fiery gaze.

A tall man was seated at the Queen's right hand. He looked like the others, lean and pale with the marvellous ebony hair to his waist and decorations of gold, but his soft, brown eyes were not like the cold, yellow eyes of the faery people. This must be John, Elizabeth thought. This is Isabella's brother.

In front of the dais, Isabella dropped to her knees and pulled Elizabeth down beside her. A murmur rose among the assembly, like the wind, and died away to a perfect silence. Elizabeth lifted her face and regarded the Queen.

Of all the crow people she was the most fair. Her skin was white as snow and her slanted eyes shone an antique gold. Two locks of her hair were plaited with beads of pearl and amber. The rest was loose and fell in thick coils to her feet. She wore a crown the colour of iron in which a single white gem shone like the moon outside the window.

It was hard to gaze upon the Queen's face for long – like trying to look at the sun.

'You want to take my grandson from me,' the Queen said. Her voice was old and cold. The crow people began to murmur again and a man stood forwards, reaching out for Isabella. It was the Queen's son, John's father – the faery who had taken them into the shadow land. But the Queen raised her hand and he stepped back, into the gathering.

'I am the first and the eldest of the crow people,' the Queen said. 'What you call the shadow land has sprung from me. These are all my children and grandchildren.' She raised her hand and gestured to the court. 'But you, little dirt girl, wish to claim the one who of all of them is most dear to me.'

Elizabeth shivered. The Queen was as ancient and chilly as the deepest, darkest days of winter. How could they oppose her? But brave Isabella rose to her feet.

'I wish to make a contract between us, like the contract that was made with my mother,' Isabella said.

The courtiers began to stir uneasily, but Isabella was dauntless.

'I have a claim on John because he is my brother – my flesh and blood. But I understand he has pledged his allegiance to the crow people and I am prepared to relinquish my claim on him provided you will help me.'

Elizabeth shook her head in puzzlement. What did Isabella mean? Was she prepared to give up her brother? She glanced up at the Faery Queen, who had her eyes fixed on Isabella.

The faintest tremor of emotion passed across the Queen's face. She leaned forward.

'The crow people do not love, Isabella,' she whispered. 'We have fierce loyalties and burning desires. But these don't amount to love in the way that you know it. Love is a quality unique to the people made of dirt. But I do love John. He is one of you, as well as one of us, and this has woken something inside of me.' The Queen pressed her fist to her chest, her face compressed in pain.

'I loved him from the moment he was born but your mother denied him to me for two long years. Can you understand what agony those years were to me? Time for us isn't as it is for you. Two years was an eternity. That is why I wouldn't protect her when she came to me for help. I was angry. I took you but I wouldn't raise a hand to protect your mother.'

Elizabeth squeezed the hem of Isabella's dress in her fingers, hoping to comfort, but Isabella didn't falter. She didn't take her eyes from the Queen's face.

'Tell me what you want,' the Queen said.

'This is my friend, Elizabeth.' Isabella pulled her up to

standing. 'It's a small thing I want – but precious to her. Her family is in danger and I want you to help them. Keep them safe – and I will burn the bones and John will be free to stay here for ever.'

The Queen turned to John. 'Is this what you wish?' she said.

John got up from his chair and approached his sister. He dropped to his knees and took her in his arms.

'Isabella,' he said. 'My sister. I don't even remember you.' His eyes, with their strange flecks of gold, searched her face.

'But you have a part of me. You're my flesh and blood. But this is what I want. These are my people, Isabella. This is my home.'

Elizabeth saw her friend's eyes fill with tears. Isabella threw her arms around her brother and held him tight. How long did the embrace last? Many days and nights and weeks and years. It lasted for ever – except, of course, that time is different in the shadow land.

Then she loosed her grip and stepped away. The faery prince, once her brother John, stepped back to his grand-mother.

On her throne, the Queen nodded. 'The contract is drawn up and agreed,' she said. Beloved of the Queen sat down and she placed her jewelled hand over his.

The Hunt

The priest bent his head to pray. His head was light and clear from fasting. The candles in the chapel burned bright, and the gold leaf glittered on the wall painting. In the shifting light, the angels seemed to move on the wall, as if they were talking among themselves. Thomas crossed himself and his eyes filled with tears. He had seen so much and his heart was full of gratitude and the love of God. How unworthy he was, and yet how blessed. Soon he would have to leave the hidden rooms (when Elizabeth rescued him, for surely she wouldn't leave him to starve for much longer – she would find a way?) but he would carry with him for ever the knowledge of the secret library, which had survived the ravages of the heretic King Henry and his daughter Queen Elizabeth.

Thomas held the jewelled rosary beads between his fingers and tried to pray. He found it hard to concentrate. His thoughts were drifting away, perhaps because of hunger. Although he tried to steer his mind towards prayer, he wondered instead what had happened to Elizabeth and her family, and he mulled over the remarkable story of Isabella

237

and her guardian angels. She had endured so much – losing her mother, living apart from ordinary mortals for hundreds of years. And now it was a brutal time, with heretics revolting against the authority of the Roman Catholic Church – an authority set up by Christ himself. Perhaps these were the last days, prophesied by the Bible – the turmoil before the end of the world. So many had suffered and died for their faith, and he risked the same ghastly end. His thoughts spiralled away, and with a sigh he reined them in again, moving his finger to the next bead for another Ave Maria.

Perhaps Thomas drifted into sleep as he prayed. When he came to, with a start, the unfailing candles had dimmed. The flames were shrinking back, and shadows filled the chapel. He rubbed his face and rose from his knees to sit on the wooden bench behind him. The walls of the underground room seemed to close in. Thomas was uncomfortably aware of the weight of earth and rock above his head, and he remembered with a shudder the horror of his descent into the dark, on the long stairway. Despite the shadows, the angels on the wall seemed to glow. The eyes of the archangels glittered, and blinked. They dipped their faces to one another and their lips moved. Thomas pressed his hands against his eyes. The air smelled sweet, of frankincense and rose petals, above the older, earthier smell of cold stone.

'Father in Heaven, what is happening?' he whispered. He took his palms from his eyes and looked again.

The archway painted on the chapel wall shone out. A noise, like the rending of stone, filled the chapel. A sword of light slashed through the wall. The line stretched. Light beamed through the gap, too bright to bear. Thomas shaded his face, and a dark figure moved towards him. It stepped from the light, through the tear in the wall.

Thomas rose to his feet. His mind was full of clamour, fear and excitement falling over each other. He crossed himself.

'Isabella, is it you?' he whispered. The green girl nodded.

'Thomas,' the girl whispered. She placed her small, green hand on his shoulder. 'I need you to help me,' she said. 'Be quick. Don't be afraid. Then we can take you away from here to a place where you'll be safe.'

Thomas shook his head. His hands were shaking. He was accustomed to being strong and brave – he relied on it. Now he felt unmanned – like a child.

'Help you?' he said. 'How can I help you?' He looked into Isabella's face and remembered everything he had read. Two hundred years ago this girl had visited and befriended St Jerome. A hundred years before that, her mother had been executed for witchcraft. But Isabella, smiling at him, still possessed the air of strength and quiet confidence he had noticed before. He held out his hand to her.

'Isabella,' he whispered. 'I will do whatever I can. To the very ends of my life I will help you.'

She gestured to the wall, to her picture.

'Do you know who I am?' she asked. 'Do you understand?'

Thomas nodded, keeping his eyes on her face. 'I read about you,' he said. 'In Jerome's writings he speaks of you, Isabella. He found the notes of your mother's trial.'

Isabella looked away and nodded. 'I wasn't brave enough to go to the trial,' she said bitterly. 'I ran away. I couldn't bear it. I left her alone.'

Thomas placed his hand on her shoulder.

'You did what you could,' he said. 'You were only a child.'

'And still a child,' Isabella said.

'Do you know where Elizabeth is? Is she safe?'

'She will be safe. But there's something I have to do first. Then we'll be returned and all will be well.' She hesitated then, as if she were uneasy about telling him the nature of her undertaking. Thomas felt a tremor of doubt. Would this be some kind of test?

'Tell me,' he said. 'What must we do?'

Isabella sat upon one of the chapel benches and Thomas dropped down beside her. She took a deep breath. 'My brother's bones are hidden in the chapel, and I have to burn them,' she said.

Isabella waited for the priest to respond. Thomas had read the account written by Jerome, and now, like him, believed the crow people were angels. And perhaps they were angels – God's messengers. Perhaps all of the angels seen in biblical times and since were truly the citizens of the shadow land, and like a mirror, they reflected what the people made of dirt wished to see. Of course at other times, poisoned by their own fears, mortals had seen the crow people as evil demons, imps, goblins – and any human who had dealings with them had been cruelly punished. It was important the priest continued to believe they were angels – but she realised this might not match up with the ritual burning of bones. Why should an angel ask them to do such a thing?

'Will you help me?' she said.

The priest narrowed his eyes. 'Why do we have to burn bones?' he said.

Isabella sighed. 'I can't explain,' she said. 'But it's necessary. Will you trust me? Will you have faith? You said – you said you would help me to the ends of your life.'

The priest sat up straight. 'I did,' he admitted. 'To the end of my life – but not to the peril of my soul. The burning of remains – it smacks of—' He pulled up short.

'Of witchcraft?' Isabella finished, in a low voice.

'I'm sorry,' Thomas said. 'Can't you tell me why it's necessary?'

Isabella slowly shook her head. If she began to explain about the shadow land and the destiny of her brother, Thomas might begin to doubt the divine origin of the angel. So much depended on this. She needed his help.

The priest had paled and a sweat broke out on his forehead. He crossed himself and crossed himself again.

'I do have faith in you,' he whispered. 'Forgive me my doubt. Where are they? Where are the bones?'

Inside, Isabella rejoiced.

'Jerome promised me my brother's bones would be sealed into a reliquary, and preserved here for ever – in the chapel of the archangels,' she said.

'A reliquary? There are none here. None I've seen.'

Isabella's heart sank. 'There must be,' she said. 'Who would have moved it?' She rose to her feet and circled the tiny chapel.

'It's here, I know it,' she said.

'If you're right, there's only one place it can be.' Thomas stood up too and walked towards her. They stared at the golden monstrance.

'Beneath the altar?' Isabella said. 'Is that what you think?'

The priest didn't answer. He made the sign of the cross in front of the monstrance, lifted it from the altar and placed it on a bench. Then he folded back the altar cloth. The altar was a large stone box, covered in weathered carvings, with a huge limestone slab for a lid.

'It'll be heavy,' he warned, as Isabella came to stand beside him. She ran her fingers over the cold, pale surface. 'Are you sure this is what must be done?'

'Yes,' Isabella said. 'See if you can push it aside.' She wondered if the priest were strong enough. He was a big man, well built, but even so – the slab was enormous. Thomas walked from one end of the altar to the other, sizing it up, trying to calculate out the best way to push.

'Stand back,' he said. Isabella moved away from the altar and watched. Be strong enough, she urged silently. Be strong enough, Thomas Montford.

The priest leaned forward, pressed his hands to the side of the slab, and brought his weight to bear upon it. His face reddened with the strain. His body contracted and heaved – but the lid didn't move.

'Try again,' she said.

Thomas shook his head

'I am weak from lack of food,' he warned, but he did as he was told. He moved to the other side of the altar and began to push again. Beads of sweat popped from his forehead. He let out a roar that filled the tiny chapel – and at last, the heavy lid shifted. The noise was terrible, the agonised grating of stone against rough stone. When Thomas's strength gave out, the lid was still upon the altar, but it was skewed to one side. A cloud of ancient dust rose from the opening he had created. Isabella ran forwards.

'Is it there? I can't see,' she said. The priest lifted one of the perpetual candles and lowered it to the black mouth, shining the light into the hollow body of the altar.

'What's that?' he said. Isabella strained to see. The candle-light glinted on some reflective surface inside. Thomas stood up again, handed her the candle, then tipped himself over to reach in.

'What is it? Can you get it?' Isabella was impatient now. This had to be it. She wanted the priest to get out of the way, so she could see for herself.

'I have it,' he said. Carefully Thomas rose up from inside the altar. In his hands he held a dusty wooden box with a lid of thick glass. He manoeuvred it past the lid and placed it on the ground. Using his sleeve, he wiped the dust from the glass top. The box was finely carved and inlaid with gold.

'It's inscribed,' Thomas said.

'What does it say?'

'It's a name, Isabella. It says John Leland.'

Isabella almost snatched the box away from him. She peered through the occluded, dusty surface into the reliquary. Normally a saint's bones would be stored in a box such as this, so the faithful might receive a blessing from visiting the holy one's remains. Jerome had kept his promise and locked away John's earthly marker in a place that would never be discovered, in the altar in the secret chapel, underneath the hill. She cradled the box, and closed her eyes, wondering if she might sense something of her brother in the bundle

243

of dry bones. While these relics existed, Beloved of the Queen was not entirely a member of the race of the crow people. For as long as she held the bones, the faery prince was also her brother John, he was also a child made of dirt and Isabella – his sister – still had a claim on him. She embraced the box and shut her eyes, remembering the baby boy she had loved and cared for so very long ago. Could she let him go now? Apart from her mother, there was no-one she had loved more. John was the last member of the Leland family – her only relative.

Isabella sighed. The little boy she had cuddled and fed and adored was long gone. The man he had become was someone very different. He had his own family and his own new world. She had longed to bring him out of the shadow land to be her brother again but she knew too well how little he would want to leave his life with the crow people.

The bones were the last bond John had with the mortal world. When Isabella destroyed them, he would be entirely one of the crow people.

'I love you, John,' she whispered to the bones in the box. 'I know you're someone different now, but I still love you. Even when you're one of the crow people I'll still love you.'

She felt a searing pain in her heart, to give him up. But John had been lost to her since the moment the Faery Queen had lifted the child from her arms and taken him away.

Isabella opened her eyes. The priest was staring at her. His expression was concerned but kindly.

'Are you certain this is the right thing to do?' he said. Isabella nodded.

They carried the box to an empty chamber and built up

a pyre using broken pieces of furniture and old robes. The priest had a flint but he was doubtful this unlikely pile of kindling would light at all. Isabella smashed the reliquary glass and tipped out five long bones. She laid them on top of the wood.

'Go ahead,' she said. 'Light the fire now.'

The priest looked at her and nodded. 'I'll try.'

He crouched beside the pyre and sent a spark spinning into it. The spark hissed, and a small finger of smoke rose up. Within a minute, the entire heap was ablaze. Flames ate into the bones. The fire gave off a bright golden light but little smoke. The priest stepped back.

'It isn't an ordinary fire, to burn so bright and fast,' he observed.

Isabella watched, hypnotised, as the bones ignited and strange green flames danced over them. It felt as though a long thread tightly ravelled around her heart was slowly coming undone.

Within minutes the fire was utterly burned out. Everything was consumed – cloth, wood and bones. Only a very fine ash remained.

Isabella sighed. She felt tired and washed out.

'Are we done now?' the priest said quietly. They walked away from the pyre, the light orb floating before them.

When Thomas watched the flames, his misgivings melted away. There was a rightness to the deed, even though he didn't understand what they were doing or why. Probably he was picking up this feeling from Isabella, as she stared into the fire with her calm, gentle face. What was she thinking about? He could see emotions flickering across her face – grief and loss and also release. She would tell him if she needed to. He trusted her. Together they walked back to the chapel.

'When you and Elizabeth are together again, when her father is home, ask them to examine the records of your mother's trial,' he said. 'I think you will be surprised. She was not alone and friendless, as you seem to think.'

Isabella turned to him quickly. 'What do you mean?' she said.

Thomas smiled but he didn't have time to tell her any more. He could see something moving in the chapel – a dark figure. 'What is it?' he whispered.

'Don't be afraid,' Isabella answered. 'It's an angel. They've come for us now.'

It was as if one of the paintings had stepped from the wall. The angel was tall and pale, with great black wings like a cloak, and hair inky and soft like a crow's feathers. It was beautiful and seemed to blaze with an unearthly glory. Thomas dropped to his knees, and a sound like a sob left his lips. The priest's eyes filled with tears. He was overwhelmed with gratitude for the vision.

'My cup runs over,' he whispered. He raised his eyes to the angel, and beheld a white hand held out to him. Unable to master his emotions, but unwilling to refuse the hand, Thomas rose to his feet and offered his own flawed, mortal hand in return.

Isabella ran across the chapel and jumped through the rent in the chapel wall, disappearing into the light. The angel didn't speak. Its hand was smooth and cool, like a piece of

246

marble. They moved towards the archway. Thomas put his fear behind him and placed his trust in God's messenger, to protect him.

They stepped through the wall and the world fell away behind them – chapel, library, town, earth, faith, life. For a moment, Thomas was wiped clean – everything gone. He soared up to the heavens, to the palaces of God's light, and his mind was full of music.

Elizabeth blinked. The knife was still hanging in the air, moving slowly, slowly, towards Isabella's chest. The days and years of time she had passed in the shadow land seemed to swirl off, shrinking and diminishing. How long had she been away? A fraction of a moment, judging by the progress of the knife towards her friend. The faery prince, John's father, had brought them back to the house in the winking of an eye. The tableau was just as they had left it – Jane at the doorway, Merrivale with his hand outstretched, releasing the deadly knife. Elizabeth was frozen to the spot, but she watched as the faery picked up the letters strewn over the floor – the letters linking Thomas Montford and Robert Dyer in a conspiracy to get the priest out of Oxford. The faery ran his fingers over the writing, and the letters swarmed all over the page like ants. Then, for a moment, the faery stared at Merrivale with an evil smile. Its face shifted, with the smile. A cruel beak emerged, the eyes became round, the yellow iris slotted with black. Talons stretched from the faery's fingers and the feathered cloak shaped itself into two vast wings. Perhaps Merrivale could see what was happening too, because his eyes widened with horror as the faery knocked the dagger

247

away, seized him by the ankle and dragged him out of the window.

Merrivale screamed. The knife dived into the floorboards, with a clatter. The clay cup fell to the ground and smashed. Smoke billowed into the room from the fireplace and all of a sudden the room was full of noise and commotion. Jane ran in and grabbed her daughter.

'Are you all right? I thought Isabella would be killed.'

Merrivale's men were at a loss now. They looked around the room in bewilderment. The goblins had disappeared – and so had Merrivale. In a moment, the situation had utterly changed. Jane hugged both girls to her. The men stared at them, not knowing what to do.

'What happened?' Jane whispered to them. 'Where has Merrivale gone?'

'I don't know,' Elizabeth said. 'But I think we should be safe now. I don't think he'll come back.' How strange it was. When she had visited the shadow land the ordinary world had seemed so distant and insignificant. Now, after just a few moments, her memories of the shadow land seemed to be fading and losing their colour, like a dream. Perhaps that didn't matter. For now, she had to focus on their perilous situation. They had to get away.

Isabella, Elizabeth and Jane looked at one another. Jane nodded. She stood up straight, pushed the hair from her face and became, as once she had been, the proud wife of a prosperous Maumesbury merchant, and part of an ancient and distinguished Maumesbury family.

She stepped forward and looked at Merrivale's three remaining men.

248

'Where is your master?' she demanded. 'I wish to speak to my accuser.'

The men were uneasy. 'I heard him scream,' one said.

'Where did the creatures go? The goblins?' said another. The third made the sign against the Evil Eye. They looked at Jane suspiciously, as though they suspected she was the cause of the unnatural visitation.

'I don't see any goblins,' Jane said coldly. 'Why have you dragged my daughter out here? I demand to be released.'

Elizabeth was thrilled. Jane was so strong. The months of fading and weeping and self-pity had fallen away, at this time of need. Jane had risen to the challenge.

The men were at a loss, disorientated by the fight with the goblins and uncertain how to proceed without Merrivale. But one of the three took on the mantle of leadership. A young man, stout and greasy, he cursed Jane under his breath.

'Catholic witch,' he said. 'You're here to face charges of treason.'

The other men rallied, inspired by the resolve of their friend.

Elizabeth shivered. Would Jane stand firm?

'Where is your evidence?' she demanded. The stout man gave a cruel smile. He was regaining confidence now. After all, they were three men facing a woman and two young girls. They had the position of authority. He nodded to one of his fellows, who picked up the letters strewn on the floor. Elizabeth stepped forward.

'What do the letters say?' she asked.

Without looking at the letters, Merrivale's new deputy said: 'You know too well what they say, Miss Dyer. They tell how your brother Robert Dyer was helping a Catholic priest – a traitor and a heretic.'

'Read them to me,' Elizabeth demanded. 'Read me the evidence.'

The man snorted. He grabbed the letters from his fellow and unfolded the first page. But his derisive grin soon faded. He dropped the letter and began to read the next. Quickly he flicked through the others, before throwing them to the floor.

'Where are the other letters?' he hissed at the other men. 'These are the wrong ones.'

Jane looked at Elizabeth, unable to understand what was going on. Elizabeth gave her a quick, sly smile. She touched her mother's arm, trying to reassure.

The men shouted at each other. The leader was rifling through the letters trying to find what he needed. They were scattered all over the floor now and Elizabeth picked one up. She began to read – and clapped her hand over her face to stifle a laugh. The pages held fragments of a long story – a folk tale about a faery prince and a changeling. It was nonsense. Jane took the paper from her daughter and glanced at it.

'You have no evidence!' she shouted, above the argument of the men. 'You have no reason to hold us! My husband will hear of this! You are acting above the law. The Queen herself will hear of this vile persecution of a woman and two helpless children. You must take us back to the town at once!'

The men were at a loss, arguing amongst themselves. They couldn't understand where Merrivale had gone and they were also afraid of the goblins. Perhaps they did think

Jane had summoned them – but if Merrivale returned, what trouble would they face, if they let the prisoners go? Two of them said they wanted to run away as fast as possible, leaving the haunted house behind. The third was more afraid of Merrivale and what he would say when he returned from whatever place he had disappeared to.

Elizabeth kept hold of her mother, and also clasped Isabella's hand. She was certain the men would let them go.

And so it proved. The two outvoted the one. There were four horses in the stables, including Merrivale's fine grey. The men hurriedly saddled them. Fear was getting the better of them now. They mounted and galloped off, shouting and cursing each other – and cursing Merrivale most of all. That left Merrivale's grey for Jane and the girls.

It was a long journey home and took many hours. They had only a vague idea where they were, and Isabella guided them from her memories of the flight on the back of the crow. They took it in turns to ride. Despite the distance and their weariness, it was a joyous time for Elizabeth. The weight of fear was lifted. The threat had been taken away, and they were together.

Elizabeth held on to her mother and talked excitedly of how happy they would be now, at home together with Esther, her father and Robert. She said Isabella would live with them too and all would be well again. Although the memories of the shadow land had receded, she felt as though her senses had been sharpened. How beautiful and splendid the world was – how vivid and green the meadows, under a sky of the brightest blue. The last scarlet hawthorn berries blazed on the bare, brown bushes. The air was fresh and sweet with the scent of the rain the day before. Everything was perfect and marvellous and miraculous.

Isabella told them the priest would be taken to the north of England, where he had said he would find shelter and protection. Jane did not question this any further – and neither did she ask about the goblins. Perhaps she didn't remember clearly. Certainly she wouldn't wish to.

Elizabeth chattered on, but she was sensitive to Isabella's loss. Her friend had given up her brother in order to save Elizabeth and her family. This happy reunion would never have happened without Isabella's courage, wit and sacrifice. When Jane rode the horse, Elizabeth took her friend's hand. Of all the marvels Elizabeth had seen in the shadow land, the one that still burned in her mind was the image of Isabella's faery self, the beautiful, shining creature she had seen in the plain of snow. That was who Isabella truly was. While ordinary life might wear her down, occlude her brilliance with worries, age, boredom or disappointment, Elizabeth had seen her friend's true likeness.

'I shall never forget who you are,' she whispered. 'I know you've lost your brother. I understand it must hurt. But let me be your sister.'

Isabella nodded. She turned away from Elizabeth and wiped her eyes, but she squeezed her friend's hand tight.

Darkness was gathering when the threesome reached the town on the hill. Tired and filthy from the journey, they trudged up the cobbled roads to Silver Street. A single candle burned in the window, and a small face stared through the glass. Seeing them, the face disappeared, and a moment later the front door opened.

'Mum!' Esther cried out. 'Mum!'

Jane ran forward and swept up her daughter in her arms. 'Esther,' she said. 'Oh Esther. I thought I'd never see you again.'

Mary the housekeeper scuttled to the door. 'Merciful Father in Heaven!' she whispered. 'Mistress, I was so afraid! And they said Miss Elizabeth was taken as well. I didn't know what to do!' She didn't know whom to hug first.

Jane led the grey horse to the stable at the back of the house and Mary ran inside to build up the fire and find something for the family to eat.

Merrivale screamed till his throat was raw and his voice gave out. He was flying through a freezing darkness, dangling upside down, beneath a giant crow. From time to time the monstrous bird cawed, or shifted the grip of its lethal claws on his ankle. The bird wasn't careful with him – Merrivale swung to and fro like a rag doll. They travelled through light and darkness, but always it was cold, till his flesh seemed to freeze on his body.

The crow cawed one more time, a triumphant, guttural cry, and let its clawed feet unfurl. Merrivale slipped free and plummeted down, down through miles of sky. His fall was so far and so spectacular he had the time to consider the eerie black forests sprawling beneath him, and the veil of snow on the ground. He saw three ordinary crows flap away in alarm – then with terrifying speed the earth rose up to smash him to pieces. Merrivale closed his eyes . . .

. . . and when he opened them he was lying in the snow beneath the trees. Merrivale sat up, gasping. He was unhurt.

How could this be? No time to think – he heard a movement among the trees. He peered through the dark trunks. A grey shadow stirred. It was a wolf.

Merrivale's heart seemed to rise to his throat. Instinctively he reached for his knife – but of course the knife was gone. He looked around for a branch – anything to defend himself – but the shadow moved again, and Merrivale realised the trees were alive with wolves. Six, a dozen, maybe more. They edged closer, staring with cold, yellow eyes. How calm they looked, how sure of themselves, how certain of their meal. But it was Merrivale who growled, his mettle up now, infuriated by the wolves' self-satisfaction. Did they think he would lie down for them to eat? No, he would put up a fight – using his boots and fists and teeth if he had to.

The wolves took another step closer. Their wise faces gazed up at him. Merrivale crouched, ready to fend off the attack, but suddenly something distracted the wolves. A long, melancholy note sounded through the snowy forest, from far away. The wolves turned from Merrivale, considering the sound of the horn. The note came again, sad and resonant, weaving through the dense winter forest. Merrivale didn't wait to find out who the hunter might be. He seized the moment of the wolves' inattention to break through the circle and flee.

Merrivale ran through the snow. Branches slapped his face. Roots seemed to reach up from the frozen soil to trip his feet. The horn was closer now, and Merrivale wondered if the hunters might save him. But he heard the wolves howl and there was something about the sound of the horn that made him doubt he would be helped. In fact, the prospect of the hunter frightened him more than the circle of wolves. He didn't know why – hadn't the time to think about it. The eerie note snaking through the trees filled him with an unspeakable fear. Despite the cold, a burning sweat broke out all over his body. A primeval terror rose up like a fire in the pit of his stomach – from the oldest, darkest part of his mind.

Puffing, struggling through the snow, Merrivale began to run faster. He could hear the patter of the wolves' feet in the snow, and the thunder of hooves. How could horsemen ride so fast through trees? Closer they came, and closer. Once he stopped to look back, struggling for breath, and glimpsed the hunters riding towards him. The horses were black with red eyes, and mounted on their backs were horned men, devils with long dark hair and pointed white teeth. In their hands were spears decorated with feathers. The devils howled when they saw their prey, and the sound of their blood lust was more terrible than the howling of the wolves. Merrivale turned and ran again.

Soon they would have him, soon. He was exhausted, his muscles giving out, his heart thundering. Soon he would be pulled down by the wolves and the hunters would pierce his vulnerable, precious body with their wicked spears. No way out now. He could hear the panting of the wolves, could smell their hot, meaty breath. Just one more step, just one more.

A wolf jumped at his back and the weight of it knocked him to the ground. He screamed and rolled over, batting the beast away with his fists – but they were all around him. Their wolf faces loomed over him, armed with teeth.

In the moment before death, panic ebbed away. It was all over now. Nothing he could do.

The scenes of his life rose up in his mind but Merrivale saw them only distantly, without a connection.

The wolves plunged their teeth into his throat and the spears of the hunters pierced his body over and over again. The sky coloured over with crimson, and all about the body of the man, the snow was red too, with his blood, like a great cloak.

I am dead, he thought, leaving the pains of his body behind. I am dead.

The priest had been walking a long, long time. His boots were worn through and his clothing was soiled and ragged. His face was dirty. He didn't know how far he had walked, or where he had come from. Dimly he recalled his name, and the purpose of his journey. It was like waking from deep sleep, or making a path through the thickest fog. Only now were his thoughts – like the landscape – coming into focus. He had dreamed . . . what had he dreamed? The priest stopped, trying to remember. He had dreamed of angels. A smile played across his face. He began to murmur his prayers.

Up ahead a man was coppicing a hazel tree, cutting back the branches to a stout stump on the ground. The man looked up when he heard the priest approaching. The track was muddy underfoot, littered with fallen leaves.

'Where will the path take me?' the priest said, gesturing ahead of him.

The man put his axe down and eyed the traveller. 'My

village is a mile ahead of you. And York is another ten miles beyond that,' the man said. His accent thrilled the priest. It was the familiar sound of his childhood.

The man looked the priest up and down, perhaps noting his damaged clothes.

'You've been a long time on the road,' he said. 'What's your name?'

The priest hesitated. His family name was well known in this part of the world. His brother owned half the county. He said: 'Montford.'

The man's eyes widened. He put his hand to his hat in a belated gesture of respect. Then he said: 'Are you the brother that went to France?'

'I am.'

The man nodded. He crossed himself, and his eyes watered. He dropped to his knees. 'Bless me, Father,' he said. Thomas smiled and raised his hand in a benediction above the man's head.

The man asked nervously: 'Will you come to the village, then, and baptise my daughter in the true faith?'

Thomas smiled and laid his hand on the man's shoulder. 'You take a risk, inviting me to your home.'

'You have friends here,' the man said. 'There are places for you to stay and much work to be done.'

Elizabeth sat on a stool in a garden full of flowers stitching a hem on a fine piece of linen. She could hear Isabella and Esther laughing in the kitchen, as they helped the servant knead dough for bread and buns. From the doorway a perfume of fresh bread and flour drifted, pleasingly combining with the scent of lavender and honeysuckle from the garden.

How utterly delightful it was to be warm, she thought, allowing her needle to rest for a moment, as she closed her eyes and turned her face to the sun. Swifts wheeled above the rooftops, and swooped over the garden. A large cat the colour of marmalade jumped onto the garden wall, complementing perfectly the mellow colour of the bricks. How lovely everything was. How perfect – if you had the eyes to see it. Ever since the voyage to the shadow land, the ordinary world had glowed with a particular brightness, as though Elizabeth were seeing it for the first time. She longed to hold on to it – the feeling of new sight.

Her mother came out of the kitchen, carrying a fresh bun flavoured with cinnamon.

'This is for you,' she said. 'Are you hungry?' The bun steamed slightly. Elizabeth smiled, folded the piece of linen and carefully stowed it in her workbox. Jane touched her daughter lightly on the head and passed her the hot bun. Elizabeth cradled it in her hand, enjoying the warmth.

'It smells delicious,' she said. It was hard to say precisely why Jane looked different now – but she did. The grey worry had faded. Of course they were still as hard up as before, but since their terrible adventure the straitened circumstances didn't seem to matter so much. The family was still held apart by the people in the town because of their faith, but they at least were a comfort to each other.

They hadn't seen Robert but a letter had come from Spain where he was studying to join the Catholic priesthood. Jane was sad not to see him, but achingly proud of his decision. And because they had so nearly lost everything, they were all very glad of each other – appreciative and gentle and eager to be happy. Besides, it was early summer and the weather was fine. The light stretched deep into the evenings and they had plenty of time to talk, play cards, sing and pray together.

Jane returned to the house and Elizabeth stared at the golden bun in her hand. How perfect it looked. Almost a shame to bite it. The swifts circled over the house again in a tight, black knot. The cat stretched lazily and stretched out on the top of the wall.

Distantly she heard a knock on the front door and wondered vaguely who it might be. Isabella had a number of callers now. She had an extraordinary knowledge of healing herbs and it hadn't taken long for news of her skills to travel around the town. People who had previously shunned the Dyer household were prepared to overlook their inconvenient faith because they wanted a herbal brew for toothache, or a broken bone to be set. Even though she was a child, Isabella's skills surpassed those of the barber surgeon and the town apothecary in curing the sick. And apart from her understanding of plants, she possessed a manner of such strength and calm, her presence by itself was enough to soothe women in the extremity of childbirth, or children suffering agues and fevers. Isabella was a miracle, and Elizabeth never tired of her company and friendship. And knowing her through and through, Elizabeth was also aware that even now, life was not always so marvellous for Isabella. She had lived on her own for so long, that the constraints of everyday life with a family – however kind – were sometimes too much to bear. Although Isabella's green was wearing off to reveal a more ordinary cream and pink skin colour, she was still a wild girl at heart. Every now and then, overcome with a longing to get away from the town, Isabella took off into the forest and spent days and nights on her own, moving among the trees and animals. Elizabeth suspected Isabella also thought about her brother very often.

She squeezed the bun, and lifted it to her mouth.

'Elizabeth! Elizabeth!' Esther came flying out of the house. 'Elizabeth – it's father! He's come home at last! Quick, come quick!'

Elizabeth jumped to her feet and dropped the bun. She picked up her skirts and ran inside. In the kitchen the particles of flour still hung in the air, puffed up from the table when Mary, Jane and the girls had hurried to the front room.

Elizabeth heard her father before she saw him. His voice, at once so familiar and now so strange.

'Esther – let me see you! How you've grown!'

For a moment Elizabeth hesitated, tears gathering in her eyes. It was too much, to have him home again. They'd struggled on without him for so long now. She swallowed.

'Where's Elizabeth?' he said. Elizabeth stepped forward, into the doorway. There he was, her father Edward. And he did look a little different. Thinner. His hair had grown long and the grey was more evident than she remembered. He looked older.

'Elizabeth,' he said, his voice thick with emotion. Edward had his arm around Jane's waist, but he stepped forward when he saw his elder daughter.

'You've changed,' he said. 'How grown up you've become. Are you still a little chatterbox?'

Elizabeth stepped forward. 'Was your trip a success?' she said, in a small voice.

Edward smiled. 'It was good enough. But it doesn't matter. I'm home again with my family, in the place we belong.'

Elizabeth looked to Isabella, who was standing a little apart from the reunited family. Edward nodded. 'Your mother wrote to me and told me about our new daughter,' he said. 'She is not as green as I imagined from the description – but she is even more beautiful and remarkable.'

Still Elizabeth hesitated. She feared letting go. How could she bear it? It was too good to be true. Edward smiled again, more gently now.

'Haven't you a hug for your father?' he said quietly, holding out his arms. Elizabeth blinked and a tear spilled over. Then she ran forward, and pressed herself against him.

Scarlet poppies floated above the ripe wheat. The sun was fierce and glorious on the high summer morning. Isabella strode along the dry, white lane, kicking up dust. Soon the harvest would begin.

She carried a basket and was heading for the manor at Spirit Hill, to meet Elizabeth. Twice a week Elizabeth still visited Lady Catherine to keep her company, and often Isabella went too. Lady Catherine had been happy enough for Isabella to stay with the Dyer family – though she sought assurances from Edward they would not press the Catholic religion upon her.

Isabella and Elizabeth had given Edward a careful account of their adventures. They told him about the trial of Isabella's mother's three centuries before, how angels took her from her own time and became her guardians. Isabella explained how she had befriended St Jerome at the shrine.

'And now the angels have returned her to us, so we might care for her,' Elizabeth said, and Isabella smiled.

Once, late at night, Edward made his way to the secret library and read the saint's account and saw proof of their tale, the painting of Isabella with the angels on the wall of the chapel.

'My forefather defended your mother,' he told her afterwards. 'The monks of the abbey didn't wish to see her persecuted by the civil courts. There is a lasting bond between our families. The histories of the Lelands and the Dyers are woven together.'

The manor at Spirit Hill loomed in the distance. They were good companions, the two girls and the lady of the manor. Lady Catherine was teaching them how to paint.

Isabella sighed happily. She was content to live with the Dyers. They had become a cheerful, kindly family and took great care to make her welcome. She was growing fond of them all. From time to time, sadness would sweep her up and she would be lost in the recollection of everything she had lost. Sometimes she yearned for the mysteries of the shadow land and longed to see her brother. Grief, like a black cloud, would fog her mind and mortal life would seem small and petty, lacking in beauty and colour. But these times passed. Her skin was hardly green at all any more. Looking in Lady Catherine's glass mirror, Isabella was always taken aback to see how much she had come to resemble her mother.

She was a Leland still. One day, in the future, she would

go back to the shadow land. She was a priestess and sensed the presence of the crow people in quiet places. Sometimes, in the corner of her eye, she would glimpse a flash of black feathers, the glint of ancient gold.

The chamberlain admitted Isabella to the manor and escorted her to the studio, where Elizabeth was grinding pigments in the stone bowl. Lady Catherine stood before a fresh canvas.

'Isabella!' Lady Catherine said. 'How was your walk from the town? Did you find the herbs you needed? The cook has terrible pains in her stomach. She has been moaning and groaning for two days. Will you talk with her?'

Isabella nodded. Lady Catherine was cheerful today. Her husband was expected home within a week and she had told them he had promised to take her back to court at the end of August. She had ordered a lavish new dress of embroidered silk for the occasion.

The studio smelled of linseed oil, but the windows were open and the fragrant summer air drifted in. Far away, Isabella could hear the voices of the men working in the fields. In the corner of the studio a curious portrait was displayed on an easel. Perhaps it was strange Lady Catherine should still have a painting of Kit Merrivale – but he had never returned to claim it. In any case, the picture was remarkable and neither Lady Catherine nor the girls wanted to sell it or lock it away. As Elizabeth pounded the pigments, and Lady Catherine told them again about her marvellous new dress, Isabella stared at the picture.

Kit Merrivale was a good-looking man, it was true, though Lady Catherine had captured so accurately the cruelty hidden behind the pleasing proportions of the face. Now, however, the picture had changed. In fact, Kit's entire demeanour had altered. He looked like a man in fear for his life. Day by day the picture altered subtly. Sometimes the sitter looked terrified. Sometimes he looked sad and haunted – or crazed, or tortured with grief. And the background changed too. Most often Merrivale was sitting before a landscape of snowy forests but from time to time this became a great stone city, or a range of barren mountains. Oddly, Lady Catherine did not notice these changes as clearly as the girls. She was blind to the degree of the alterations. She marvelled at the way the painting seemed to change moods but attributed this to her own skill – indeed she reckoned it her greatest work and talked of taking it to court. Except that Merrivale's inexplicable disappearance had not made him popular at court. Most people speculated that he had been murdered by a rival faction in Queen Elizabeth's network of spies and informers.

When Isabella had brewed a purging tea for the cook's bad stomach, she left the manor and headed for the shrine in the forest. She and Elizabeth often tended the holy place. Elizabeth prayed to the Virgin Mary and St Jerome, while Isabella remembered her mother and the crow people. It was a significant place for them both, because it was also at the shrine the girls had first met.

The glade was full of sunshine and fresh green grass. Isabella sat beside the spring and washed her face and hands in the icy water. A fox trotted through the dappled shadows under the trees and across the glade, to drop its red muzzle to the water for a drink. It didn't fear Isabella. Sometimes the graceful deer would come.

264

In the last few weeks, another forest beast had called at the spring to drink. A less noble creature than the fox and the deer, this beast was filthy and clumsy. Its teeth were broken and black, and its hair unkempt and ragged. Once it had been a man. It still wore ragged clothes and a single pearl earring. Would it come today? Isabella was determined to win its trust. She had the power to heal the creature, to bring it to its senses again. In her basket she had rolls of fresh bread, plums and cheese.

She waited patiently until the evening but the creature didn't come. Perhaps it was wrestling with its own devils, or speeding through the forest away from imaginary pursuers no-one else could see. Isabella sighed. She pitied the beast for its suffering and delusions. Its eyes were full of fear. One day, with her help, it would find a way out of the terrifying mazes of its mind.

She left the food inside the remains of Jerome's cell and walked away from the shrine. Perhaps the creature, which had once been a man, would find the gift and enjoy the food. Anyway, she would return soon with more.